Praise for

***The Refusal* and *The Outcast* have, b [illegible] shortlisted for FIFTY-FIVE romance book awards and are winners of TWENTY-ONE book awards:**

Both were gold medalists in the Global Book Award, also winning both the Pinnacle Book Award and the NYC Big Book Award. *The Refusal* also won the National Indie Excellence Award and the National Excellence in Romance Fiction Award for best first book. *The Outcast* was a finalist in the Foreword INDIES Book of the Year and has also won a silver IPPY award

—

Praise for *The Refusal*:

"From start to finish I couldn't put it down. Any required adulting went out the window and instead I lived and breathed Janus and Jo's world." – **Geraldine Brookhorn, Romance Writer**

"The Refusal *is guaranteed to be your next bingeable romance."* – **Indies Today, Book Awards**

"The thrill of the chase was intoxicating, and I didn't want it to end. The Refusal *by Eve Riley is an exhilarating read, and I recommend it to those who love a good steamy romance."*
– **Literary Titan, Book Awards**

"Inhaled this book! Smart. Fresh. Nerdy and hilarious rolled into one! This isn't your typical romance – It's smart, edgy, with well-written suspense that also happens to be romantic! Loved every page of this book! Can't wait for more!" – **CK, Amazon Review**

"The Refusal *is overall one of the best romance novels I have read in a long time. I can't wait to read the next in the series."* – **T.S. Simons, Author**

Praise for *The Outcast:*

"I couldn't put it down and it kept me guessing till the very end. The Outcast *was a joy to read!"*
– **BookishThespian, Book Blogger**

"If you love modern love stories dripping with passion, you don't want to miss out on this. The Outcast *is a standout romance novel with a dark twist. I cannot wait to get my hands on more books by this author!"* – **Readers' Views, Book Awards**

"I don't know where to start! The Outcast *is a spicy, page turner that I couldn't put down! Kate and Fabian are perfect and bring opposites attract to a whole new level."*
– **Chelsea Karney, Amazon Reviewer**

THE SECRET

EVE M. RILEY

THE TECHBOYS *SERIES*

3

EVEMRILEY.COM

Published by Eve M. Riley.

ISBN: 978-1-9163982-6-9

Ordering and Enquiries Information:
Quantity sales. Special discounts are available on quantity purchases by corporations, associations, and others.
For details, contact the author at www.evemriley.com

Cover design and interior formatting:
Mark Thomas / Coverness.com

NOTE TO THE READER

Warning: This book is intended for adults and incorporates sexual scenes.

The book contains references to generational trauma, including parental violence and prior sexual assault.

For Joe, for the jokes and the fun and the amazing son you are.
You make my life better, every day.

PRESENT DAY

CHAPTER 1

Liss

Monday, January 17, 2022

"You asshole!"

Stéphane lifts his head from where he's stirring his coffee and all the color drains from his face. I turn around to see a blonde woman weaving through the tables of the NYU café toward us, and when I look back at Stéphane, he's thrown back his seat and is heading around the corner of the table. What's going on?

"You thought you could have some whore on the side and get away with it, did you?"

What?

The clink of dishes and buzz of conversation die down as everyone cranes their heads to see what's going on. I try and grab Stéphane's hand but he's already beyond my outstretched fingers, making his way toward her. When he reaches her, her hand flashes out and he ducks. Her swipe at him skims across the top of his head like two cartoon characters in a fight and a giggle presses at the back of my throat.

"You thought your wife wouldn't find out, didn't you, you fucker!" she shouts.

His *wife*?

Oh *crap*. My head sinks into my hands.

Then I hear Stéphane's voice, low and urgent. "We can't have this conversation here."

He can't …

I push back my seat to stand, and several eyes on the neighboring tables swing over to me, riveted.

The woman is the polar opposite of me. Dyed blonde hair, long red nails, and thick makeup plastered over her impeccable features. I'm wearing the gear I need for riding my bike in the rain, my pants splattered from the road. No way did I have any time to put on makeup this morning. Then I meet her gaze, now homed in on me as I head toward them, and her lip curls.

She shoots out a hand that waves up and down my body. "This is her? This … witch?"

Witch? *I beg your pardon*. I smooth a hand over my wild curly black hair. *I'm not carrying a wand, lady*. The laughter presses back up. I've never been described that way, but my concentration has moved from her to him and, fucking hell, his face is contorted into the kind of grimace I think you never want to see on the face of someone you're sleeping with.

He picked *me* up, goddammit. There was no wedding ring, no texts or calls he tried to hide. And he was always available at weekends and evenings … I mean I was surprised a guy of forty-five was single, but by God he was persistent. And he knew what he was doing in bed. No insecurities, just a ton of confidence in what he did to me.

Fuck. Him.

"You have a *wife*?" I say loudly, and he winces.

He'd started talking to me about what we might *do together* in the future. I am so bored with guys like this. I like to flirt and I enjoy men. Men like that too, right? So why does it always go wrong? My history is shit. Fair enough, I've done everything you shouldn't do: cheated, gone out with the best friend, flirted with other guys to rile them up. *You're a game player, Liss.* Not in a bitchy way, though perhaps all games are bitchy in the end; more in a test-their-sticking-power kind of way. Every time something like this happens I'm reminded that I need to switch it up, but then along comes another sexy guy and I start imagining what he can do to me in bed, and so I flirt and somehow it all gets out of hand. *Really, this is the last time I'm doing this.* Stéphane seemed like a decent guy. Fuck all men who present one thing but underneath are something else entirely. I tuck that reminder of my past away as sourness settles in my gut.

"Liss ..." he says, raising his hands in a placating gesture as he turns toward me.

"I didn't need to know her name, you fucker," his wife hisses. "And don't even think about coming back home tonight."

He lives with her? Oh God. Well, I guess it's not surprising because she's his wife but ... Her eyes narrow as she opens her mouth, but Stéphane takes hold of her arm as if he's going to manhandle her out of the café ... She wrenches it out of his grip, taking a step back and bumping into the table behind her. As she looks around to apologize, a smile stretches over her red lips, and she leans down and the next second Stéphane has chocolate fudge cake with whipped cream slapped in his face.

I kind of want to applaud. His expression is so comically surprised, and a smile curls over my face as cream slides down his trendily unshaven jaw. *Oh my God.* Maybe metrosexual designer stubble was a warning sign. Yes, Liss, add that to your already too long list of what to avoid in men in the future.

My watch buzzes at me with the forewarning of an impending alarm. Oh, fuck, my lecture! A sigh seeps out as I take one last look at Stéphane and turn on my heel.

"Liss, Liss!" His voice follows me to the door of the café, followed by his wife screeching something else which I don't bother to listen to. Another ignominious end to a rotten relationship. At least I've got the sense to draw a line under them now.

But when I examine my phone after my morning lectures, an email is sitting in my inbox asking me to come to see HR before the close of play and cold fingers trickle down my spine. Is this about Stéphane? As I scroll down the email, it mentions an issue being referred to HR from Alan Cartwright. *Stephane's boss.* Holy shit. This is fast, even for the university … I close my eyes. If Stephane's in trouble, my reputation will be trashed too. My dread turns to horror when I push through the door to the department two hours later and almost crash into Stéphane heading in the opposite direction.

"Liss!" His eyes widen, and he gives me an oily smile. I used to think his smiles were cute. "We need to talk, she …"

"No, we don't."

"We're separated."

"What?"

"Carrie and I, we're separated."

"So why did she come screaming into the café?"

He tosses his long fringe out of his eyes. "Sometimes she still thinks she still has a claim on me, but she doesn't."

Her "don't come back tonight" echoes through my thoughts. I shake my head. What a load of bullshit. I raise my chin.

"What did HR want?"

"They said this"—he gestures between us and my stomach curdles—"is against university policy. Which is ridiculous! They said they need to start an internal misconduct investigation. I denied everything of course, but they're still putting me on probation, which is terrible for me: I came here on an exchange visa as head of department, Liss! I don't have a green card yet, and my kids …"

My eyes bug out. "You have *kids*?" I can't even start on the rest of his lies.

He winces.

"You fucker!"

He presses his fingers to his lips. "Keep your voice down! We don't want this investigation to get any worse. Let's meet later and …"

Oh my God. I swear I am never getting married. "No fucking way, Stéphane. I'm not meeting you later or any other time in fact."

I push past him, but his voice follows me as he tries to catch my arm. "Liss, you need to …"

Shaking him off, I head into the office behind him. He lied to the university about us? That seems really dumb.

The HR lady, Diane, is nice but firm, and somewhat sympathetic when I fill her in. But clearly the process is the process, and when she tells me I'm also being put on probation, I want to cry. I can't afford this, I can't.

I don't have the money. It took me forever to structure my life this way. I volunteer in the poorest parts of Africa, come back, and make enough money to go back out again. I want to change the world, to do good, and this allows me to do it. A long sigh seeps through my teeth. The university tolerates me working in this ad hoc way when I'm back, filling in for classes. If this puts a stop to that, I'll … Why oh why did I risk something so important to me? I should have known better than to get involved with someone so close to my working life. *My working life.* I almost laugh. The university doesn't feel like work at all. I go to Africa, then come back and talk about it.

My parents loathe my life. My dad hates what he sees as my "wasted promise." After I got good grades at school, my dad had a law career and two-point-four kids all mapped out for me, and every time I go home we have a shouting match about what I'm doing. I have to hold on to the fact that the good I'm doing outweighs the vision he had, although what good I'm able to do now …

When I ask Diane about my open-ended contract and intermittent volunteering, she purses her lips at me. "I'm sorry, Liss. Your contract is very unusual, as I'm sure you know. If you leave to volunteer, we won't be able to re-employ you because of the red flag on your record, and until it's resolved we'd be obliged to pass that on to other potential employers, too." She pushes her glasses up her nose.

Jesus Christ. So I'm stuck here until this is all resolved.

CHAPTER 2

Liss

Wednesday, January 19, 2022

Out of the window of my apartment, a cold blue sky scatters fingers of light down between the buildings. It's three years since my two best friends from college met their other halves: Jo met Janus, and then Kate got together with one of his best friends, Fabian, and I'd be lying if I said I didn't feel left out of their cozy circle. I have watched my friends' lives move on with a soul-burning envy I didn't think was in me. And I'm not that person: My fire fixes the world's problems, and I don't waste time looking over my shoulder. *You had it, Liss, and you lost it.* I still don't understand how it slipped away from me.

I don't want children right now—I like my wanderlust life—but there's something about seeing your closest friends' lives move on … Jo's kid is like a combination of Janus and her in miniature: all dark tousled hair and freckles. And I like being Auntie Liss, the babysitter who turns up with furry toy rabbits and coloring books but can step away to the peace and quiet of her own apartment. But I'm also still fighting the same battles for funding, persuading people that volunteering is worth their time. How disillusioned will I be in another three years?

A car's brakes squeal, and the driver leans on the horn and shouts an obscenity out of his window. A different kind of chaos swirls into my head—hot African sun, cheerful morning calls, and children's laughter—and warmth flows through my body like a hot vent, something sharp stabbing through my chest.

I glance at the clock and flinch. Jesus, I have to give a lecture in forty minutes. Throwing my coffee back, I bang on Matt's door with a heavy fist. Matt is the PhD student who took over the lease for the apartment after Kate moved into Fabian's place. I can't pretend I don't miss her, but Matt is a decent guy who amiably manages my absences in Africa by getting people in to cover the rent. He deserves all the credit because I'm a pain in the ass to share with.

"I'm taking a shower, Matt!"

I get a grunting reply and throw myself around the apartment, squashing down my gloomy thoughts, and rain hits my shoulders as I step out onto the street. *Stop wallowing!* I click open the lock on my bike and throw myself on it, pedaling furiously through the freezing rain, making it with moments to spare, my Keds stuck to my feet. The lecture hall is steaming with wet clothes and half full when I arrive, and as I mentally file through the pictures and stories I'm going to tell, my chest eases. *I get to talk about my life for an hour – how cool is that?*

After my class ends, students start to funnel out, the chatter of voices replacing the laughter at the final few photographs of me covered in mud. In my peripheral vision, John Arnold, the head of African Studies, slides in the door and my heart sinks. I hope he's not here because of Stéphane or, heaven forbid, a complaint. He stands to one side while I speak to a couple of students, who are charming and eager, but it's all I can do to tamp down my nerves.

"John. How are things?"

"Good, Liss. I'm glad I've tracked you down. How are the lectures going?"

"Fine, I think. You haven't had a complaint, have you?" *Shut up, Liss.*

He laughs. "Never for your classes, you'll be pleased to hear. Students love all your real-world experience."

The tenseness at the back of my neck eases. "I'm sorry about all the …" I gesture toward the door. I have to say something about the situation with Stéphane. John won't be handling it, but no doubt they've made him aware.

He waves a hand, cutting me off. "I'm not worried about it, Liss. As far as I'm concerned, it's none of my business, or the university's, but they have their process to go through." He makes a face.

"I didn't know he was married!" His sympathetic expression forces the words out before I can stop them. I've only ever had one personal conversation with John before. My face flushes hot.

He grimaces. "From what I've heard this isn't the first time this has happened with Stéphane."

My eyes are like saucers as shock rolls through me. *Seriously? And the university knows that?* And … *that* explains HR pressing on the gas pedal. This is not about me at all, it's about Stéphane. "The two-faced asshole," I mutter. *I need to stop talking.*

John coughs. "Exactly," he says, shifting from one foot to the other. "Actually, I wanted to chat with you because an opportunity has come up that I thought you might be interested in. Some funding has come to the university to do research and development with refugees on the border between the Democratic Republic of the Congo and Rwanda, in particular, in Kiwanja."

I stare at him.

Oh my God. Kiwanja.

He tilts his head at me.

How many years is it since I heard that name? A thrill shoots down my spine, and it really shouldn't. *He's not there now, Liss. You know this.*

"… I knew you'd been to the DRC before, of course, a while ago …"

I swallow, like the timeline isn't etched on my brain. "Three years."

John frowns at me. "You've been volunteering for three years? That's very commendable."

Commendable? More like foolish. *I promised myself I'd never go back there. I put it all behind me.*

"We need someone who can travel all over," John says, oblivious to my discomfort. "The funder wants to assess the damage done to local communities now the rebels have withdrawn. It's not the safest place in the world, and I would totally understand if that was a problem." He swallows. "But since you'd been there before, I made the mistake of telling them about you, and now they're desperate to have you. They've included quite a decent budget, actually."

My ears prick up. "They've offered the university money?"

"Salaries."

"They'd *pay* me? It's not voluntary?"

John laughs, no doubt at the thrill in my voice, as he shakes his head. "Not at all. The plan is to send several researchers out to examine the infrastructure, security, and land mines, among other things. They want you to look at population, social issues, health, and schools. Talk to the local people. You're good at all that. It'd be up to you to define the brief. They have no idea how bad the situation is on the ground, and they want to understand where longer-term investment should go, the numbers of people that are still displaced, and encourage them back to their homes. The constant movement of people across the border has created chaos, but I think you'd love all that. You'd need to visit a few of the refugee camps and go back and forth over the border, too. There's a healthy budget for getting the resources needed and employing local people."

It's like a bright shiny present with a big bow has been dropped into my lap. And *research.* Dan was a researcher once, traveling around and talking to local communities. But if he had got a job like that, I would've been able to find some trace of him, and I found none. It was like his life stopped three years ago. A strange sickening feeling washes through me. *What happened to him?* I can't reconcile the deadening silence with how he was when he came to Manhattan. *Ugh, Liss. Put a sock in it.* John is smiling at me. I might get paid to be out in Africa, escape an East Coast winter, and *decent* pay too. I only just stop myself from clapping my hands. *Practicalities, practicalities.*

"But the semester has just started. I'd be leaving you high and dry."

John's smile just widens. "You've put a lot of hard work into making things happen out there, and it seemed like such an exciting opportunity for you, I couldn't resist letting you know, despite the fact I'm self-sabotaging by being down a lecturer."

Honestly, he's a really nice guy.

"What's the salary?" I wince at him in apology. This might be a deal breaker. I'm carrying debt from my last stint abroad, which I've never done before, so it's proving to be more of a struggle back here in New York than I'd anticipated. *I'm not giving my father more ammunition concerning my career.* Career, hah! But I guess this might be the opportunity to change that.

John names a sum that's almost double what I'm getting paid by the university, and my jaw drops. He laughs at my expression.

"Being honest with you, it's partly danger money, although I've been assured by the local manager of the VSO that the rebels have gone from this area and the government is in control. They're paying three salaries and an allowance on top for whatever needs to be done."

"Who's managing the overall budget?"

"Well, that's still an open question, but I thought I might put you in charge of it."

"Me?" My voice is an incredulous squeak. I can hardly take it in, it's a huge step up. I can't turn this down, can I?

John smiles at my incredulity. "I'm sorry to spring this on you. Of course, given the way government works, they've taken six months to decide and now they're in a tearing hurry because they've awarded the university the contract. They wanted someone on the ground in twenty-four hours. I said we'd let them know in twenty-four hours and send a person out there in forty-eight, so I can only give you a day to think about it."

I nod at him, so grateful I want to hug him. Just as my life was looking unbelievably dreary, this comes along.

"What about my being on probation? Do I need to …"

"This is being classed as a departmental contract and as such doesn't come under the central university administration. I've cleared it with the powers that be, and the rest will be sorted out in your absence. I thought you might like to be out of the way for a while." His eyes twinkle at me.

I swallow down the lump in my throat. God knows what he's done to swing this.

"It sounds amazing. Thank you so much, John. You don't know how grateful I am," I babble.

He nods and smiles. "You've helped us out in a lot of tight spots, Liss. You're an inspiring teacher and a great field person. It's nothing you don't deserve."

The lump in my throat swells—I *am* going to cry. I dip my head and stare at my notes, swallowing. His hand comes out, hovering, and I shake my head, chewing my lip. Do I really need to think about it? No, no I don't.

"I'll go. I don't know how to thank you."

He beams at me. "That's great news." The relief and delight in his voice are palpable.

"I hope I'm up to the task."

He laughs and shakes his head. "You're this bubbly, organized person. You negotiate and sort things out like no one I've ever met. I've been looking for a good opportunity for you for a while."

He has? I press my hand to my chest. "Let me get out there first and see how bad it is."

He laughs. "Just go and kick ass. Go and spread some good. God knows, few enough people care," he says, and I laugh too, lifting my head. His words and the respect in his tone are like a balm after my meeting with HR, and the hard defensive shell I always seem to carry around, the feeling that I need to justify myself because I will always be called into question, softens a bit. Try as I might, I can't seem to throw it off completely.

"I'll send you some documentation. Just charge any costs back through expenses until we get the finance set up. I've done some of my own checking into the security situation out there, but I want you to keep me abreast of it when you're out there, okay?"

"No problem."

I gather up my laptop and purse and walk with him to the lobby and my hands are shaking as I say goodbye and push open the large double doors out into the street.

Am I making this decision because of what happened in the past or because it's a sensible option for me? The memories cascade down in front of my eyes, and I find the nearest bench, collapsing down. I study the splintered wood on the bench, the soft crumpled cotton of my green pants. The sun is filtering through the trees, students happily chatting in groups. It feels like the most normal thing in the world, but it's not heat and dust, shouting and chaos. I need to calm down, to bring myself into a more rational state of mind. *He's not there.* It's just a place and a name. *Three years.* That first day he arrived at the house, the broad shoulders, the tousled blond hair, and dust-ridden clothes, and my God, so tall: a powerful body that went on forever. The heat of his skin under my hands. I snap shut the trapdoor in my brain. Reliving those memories will drive me insane.

I don't know how long I sit there, but when I look at my phone, the file from John is sitting in my inbox, so I head to the café on campus and spend a happy hour reading the documentation about the project and the problems the local population are facing. Hundreds of thousands of people displaced, poor or no sanitation, the risk of serious disease. *I want to get on the ground.* Pulling up a flight app, I hum as I search for flights, pressing the "pay now" button and cradling my coffee to my chest as I gaze at the soaring atrium and all the students, heads bent forward in concentration. A 6 a.m. flight out of La Guardia, but whatever—I can sleep on the plane.

I cycle home through the rain and make lists in my head. I'm always ready to go at short notice, but nonetheless I check my vaccinations and visas, and by 5 p.m. I'm all organized. I text Matt and he sends me a thumbs-up. Honestly, he is so chill. Then I message Kate and Jo. They already know about Stéphane, but they're both thrilled about my escape and horrified that I'm leaving again. And my chest expands: They don't think I'm wasting my life; they have my back no matter how badly I behave, no matter how little time I spend on them. And, goddammit, I need to talk to the people who don't have my back: I should call my parents and let them know too. Cold drips down my spine.

My father has a history of trying to sabotage my plans. During my childhood he often prevented me from doing things he didn't approve of. If he didn't like a friend of mine, he'd make sure we had to go somewhere else when I was supposed to see them at a party or someone's house. So I quickly learned to stop telling him about anything or anyone. I still have this nagging fear he'll prevent something from happening if I tell him too soon.

He put me forward to play on teams or act in plays I didn't want to. The pièce de resistance came when he applied to law schools on my behalf without my knowledge and forged my signature. This resulted in a huge showdown, and we've never recovered from it. I had to take a year out, a blissful year of traveling and working, so I could reapply for the Environmental Science degree I really wanted. When I think of Dad, all I see is his red angry face shouting, inches from mine, fury etched deep in every line. His continuing anger over my life is rooted in the fact he can no longer stop me from doing what I want: I'm a thorn in his side. And my mom tried to keep the peace. Am I angry she didn't step in more? Perhaps, but I can also see that she is not that person.

So when I press the number, I'm steeling myself for a boatload of abuse from my dad.

"Hello, Lauren speaking."

"Hey, sis," I say cautiously.

I'd like to think my relationship with my brother and sister hasn't been affected by Dad's nonsense, but of course it has. He played us off against each other. Because they conformed and I didn't, he's always telling me how superior they are to me.

Lauren is the eldest and a doctor in pediatrics, and I've laughingly told her how many children she could save in the poorest parts of Africa, but her only response is how much it'd piss Dad off if she moved abroad.

Trying to convince my siblings how manipulative Dad can be is an uphill battle. He's controlled their lives and still controls them. But despite all this, Lauren and I have a solid relationship: We both care passionately about our vocations, and if I play it right with her and don't stray onto the subject of Dad, we have a lot in common.

"Liss! How are you doing?"

"I'm great thanks … You?"

"Oh, you know, too much work, too little time."

We always start like this, cautiously circling. My desire to burst out of it into something real is like a pressure at the back of my throat.

"I've been offered an amazing job, and so I'm excited."

"Wow, Liss, that sounds excellent." She laughs. "But will it make Dad happy?"

Why is this her first thought? Is she being sarcastic? But no, that's not my sister's style. Ugh. And who cares? It makes *me* happy. She's partly joking, because I always make him angry, but still. She defines what she does by making him happy, and I hate it. She probably hates the fact that I do the opposite.

"God no. I know you know me well enough to understand that I'd never do anything just to please Dad. It's a project in the Democratic Republic of the Congo, going back to a place I went to three years ago." My voice catches and I swallow down the lump in my throat. "They're funding an initiative to work with the people and communities after all the fighting, and they want me to run it. The pay's a lot better, so you can imagine I'm super excited about that. I'm working on getting to the point where I make such a difference there, Dad will just have to apologize to me." That's bravado talking, but, fuck it all, I don't need anyone putting a damper on my enthusiasm before I'm even out there.

"Don't hold your breath for that. Do you want Mom or Dad?"

Damn, I've made her uncomfortable now: She hates confrontation. How does she survive as a doctor? I would have thought the medical profession was full of it, with a boatload of difficult patients. Perhaps she calms them all down with her niceness.

"Wait, tell me about you before you run off. What's keeping you so busy at work?"

She pauses, and I sense she's on the edge of flight, debating whether the conversation will become more difficult.

"Some delightful and very sick kids."

Another long pause. Then she says, "I'm here with David for a few days."

David is Lauren's super-sweet boyfriend, the kind of guy that would never do for me, who'd run a mile if you flirted with him. He treads a thin line with Dad because Dad thinks he's not aggressive or macho enough, but he's incredible to Lauren and earns serious money because he's an uber-smart computer programmer. So, Dad finds it hard to find fault with him. Lauren picked someone the complete polar opposite of our father, and I want to shout that from the rooftops.

"The lovely David! How is he?"

"Oh, he's wonderful, as always."

Do I detect a sigh in her tone? I hope David proposes to her soon. They're perfect in their sweetness together.

"On our anniversary he took me on this romantic camping trip, candles, champagne, the works. I thought he was going to propose!" Her voice drops to a whisper, and I smile, glad she's relaxed into confiding in me.

"And he didn't?"

"No." It comes out on another soft breath, and I make a mental note to have a word with him and tell him to get off the fence.

"I'm sure he will—he's probably just nervous. He's crazy about you, Lauren."

"Is he? Sometimes I wonder if he's married to his job."

Lauren has never spoken to me about David like this, and I squeeze my eyes shut. *Damn.* I have extensive experience with guys who disappoint. She's talking to me now … and nobody else in the family is going to help … Can I play helpful younger sibling here?

"You two have been together for five years. He runs around doing all sorts of stuff for you, and he's at home with you now, isn't he? He puts up with Dad. If you think he's not fully invested, you're crazy."

She laughs, but I can hear the pleasure in her voice when she says, "I do like chatting with you, Liss. You cheer me up."

"Don't be silly. Put David on, I want to say hi."

Can I do something about this? If I don't chat with him now, it'll never happen.

"Don't say anything to him! I don't want him to think …"

"I won't," I say, crossing my fingers behind my back. I'm the poke-your-nose-in interfering kind of sister: the *best* kind.

"Love you, sis," she says, and I raise my eyebrows as warmth hits my chest.

"David!" She calls as she moves away from the phone. "It's Liss! She wants to say hello!"

My mom's voice starts up in the background followed by David's, seconds before his deep tones fill the line.

"Hey, Liss, Lauren just told me you're heading off to Africa again."

I smile as I walk across the carpet in the lounge to peer out of the window. "Yes! And I'm getting paid this time, so as you can imagine, I'm thrilled."

He laughs as I tell him excitedly about the job, and he gives me none of the familiar judgment I endure from everyone else: He's genuinely pleased for me.

"Anyway, enough about me. How are things with Lauren?"

"What?" There's a pause. "Did she say something to you?"

Wow, okay. That was quite defensive for David. *Something's up.* I hum to myself as I stare out of the window. Would he confide in me? God knows he won't talk to anyone else in this car crash of a family.

"She told me about the incredible camping trip you took her on."

He chuckles. "Yeah, that took a bit of planning."

"It sounded lovely."

"It was," he says, on a long, controlled release of breath. "Why are you asking me about it?"

"She talked about how romantic it was, that's all. You two have been together for five years. I was curious."

There's silence and a shuffling noise and then the sound of a door being closed.

"*Why* are you bringing this up?" His voice drops to a low growl.

I'm not going to betray my sister's confidences. I don't trust guys enough for that, even sweet ones like David.

"I wondered whether you were planning to propose. Are you thinking about it?" I hold my breath. Have I stepped out too far? Don't break the silence, Liss, don't let him off the hook.

He groans. "She mentioned it, didn't she?"

"David …"

"Shit. She did. *Goddammit.*"

"Talk to me."

Another prolonged pause, and he clears his throat. "I don't want to …"

"David."

"Alright. *Alright.* Mrs. Pushy Boots. I've been considering it for a while, okay? We went on this camping trip, and I worked hard to make it special. I got a ring. The whole works. I wanted to do it right. But despite being all geared up, I lost my nerve and I don't know …" He emits a gusty sigh.

"What don't you know?" This is like treading on eggshells.

His breath huffs down the line. *Goddamn it, David.*

"She's this unbelievable person, Liss. Super smart, incredibly kind. Why would she say yes to me? I'm a programmer. What do I have to offer her? She's like this bright, bright star."

I almost burst out laughing. He's exactly the same: super smart, incredibly kind. Doesn't he realize that?

"Yeah, but, David, firstly you're also this amazing, smart, great guy, and secondly that's her decision, not yours. She understands best what will make her happy."

"Your dad doesn't want me for her."

He's caught on to this? Oh. My. God.

I try and bottle down the fizzing inside so I can listen to him, but I've lost my breath, words stuck behind a huge blockage in my throat.

"She likes to please your dad, you know that. She doesn't like conflict."

Fucking hell. "Why do you think my dad doesn't want you for her?"

If I keep asking questions, maybe I can stop myself from punching my fist through a wall.

"He told me. Years ago. He said I wasn't fit to lick her boots, and she could do so much better than me."

I cover the microphone and swear loudly into the quiet of my apartment. If my father was near right now, I'd punch him. The idea of jumping on a plane and screaming at him directly about what a dick he is plays through my head. He'd never say anything nice about *me* to a guy; he views me like something he found on the sole of his shoe. If my sister's love for David overcomes my dad's disapproval, I'll be really impressed. I take a few calming breaths.

"He's the biggest asshole on the planet."

"Yeah, but if I'm lucky enough he also might be my father-in-law." David never bad-mouths my dad; he just smiles while I bitch about him.

"Plus, you'd have an amazing sister-in-law."

He laughs. "I would." He lets out a long groan. "I fucked it up with that camping trip, didn't I?" The desperation in his tone eats into me. "I should never have done it. What was I thinking? Oh my God. She knows I planned it and bottled out. What must she think of me? *Oh, shit.* I'm crazy about her, Liss, but I can't … we have to split up."

What? Where did that come from? "David, Jesus, don't be a numbskull. She doesn't know that at all, and you guys are made for each other. Just ask her. Please. Forget my dad. It's not worth sacrificing your future for some asshole comment from him. He makes comments like this all the time. Don't give idiots power. If she says no because she's trying to keep my dad happy, then she's an idiot."

Silence.

"David?"

"Don't give idiots power, I like that."

A pigeon lands on the windowsill and fixes me with a beady stare, cocking its head.

"She's crazy about you, and it's her decision. If you love her, you have to let her make that choice." I shift and the bird takes off in an angry flap of gray. *He disappeared and gave me no choice.* My blood fizzes with a horrible cocktail of anguish and anger.

David clears his throat in my ear. "I'll think about it, Liss."

God help us. "Not good enough. Promise me you'll ask her soon. If she says no, at least you'll know."

"I don't want to know."

"Fuck that. That's selfish. Will you please? For me? For her?"

Another long silence as I examine the peeling paint on the window frame.

"David?"

"Oh God, okay. Okay. I'll do it. Oh shit, what am I agreeing to?"

"Something you want," I growl. "Now put my mom on."

An hour later I'm off the phone and chopping zucchini for the pasta I'm making for Jo and Kate tonight—our last time together before I leave. The conversation with my mother went better than expected and, to my absolute delight, Dad was out at some golf tournament. So, barring any spontaneous calls from him to give me a hard time—something he used to do regularly when I was at college but seems to have given up on now—I've dodged a bullet and hopefully managed to sort my sister's problem out at the same time.

A lightness washes through me as I sip on my wine. I can't believe I'm escaping all this bullshit. It's astonishing the power of one random conversation to change things, perhaps alter the direction of your life forever.

THREE YEARS EARLIER

CHAPTER 3

Liss

Friday, December 14, 2018

The glass on the bar swims in and out of focus. What happened to the guy who was sitting next to me? Oh God, I feel *great*. Light and floaty. I swing around on my barstool, sliding sideways with the momentum, and without warning I'm looking at the underside of a counter and dirty wooden floorboards. A large hand appears in my peripheral vision, and when I blink up, all I make out is a mop of hair and a huge chest. The right thing to do is clearly to rest on it as he pulls me up.

"Whoops! I went around a bit fast," I say.

"Yeah, sure did," he laughs. "You okay?"

I push my curls out of my eyes and peer at him. *Not bad.*

"Let me buy you a drink," he rumbles.

Even nicer.

The next thing I register when my eyes blink open is a stained ceiling. My hand is curled around yellowing sheets. I take in rough walls with holes in the drywall. A muffled buzzing noise is coming from somewhere. Shit. My phone. I groan and turn my head toward a mountainous body stretched out beside mine. *Story of my life.* He rolls over and I inhale a faceful of stale cigarettes and beer.

"Shut that thing up," he growls, and I lurch out of bed, completely naked, and rummage through piles of clothes, plates, food, and pizza boxes on the floor.

"Bitch, whatdatellya?"

"Okay, okay, keep your pants on," I mutter. He's probably not wearing any. I giggle.

"What the fuck?"

I glance back at him. He's sitting up now and he's a huge bloke, covered in tattoos, and hair, hair everywhere: beard, dark mustache, wild long locks. I vaguely remember getting on the back of a bike. Where the hell am I? *I was in Brooklyn.* He helped me across the street from Duff's Bar. *I couldn't stand. Shit.*

"Bitch. What the fuck are you doing?"

Pulling up jeans and a tangle of T-shirts, I stand on something hard. Fortunately, it doesn't crack under my foot: one of the better pieces of news I seem to be receiving this morning.

I hold it up in my hand and give him a smile, and he collapses back down on the mattress.

"You need to get the fuck out."

I have no idea if we slept together, but given we don't have any clothes on, I'm guessing we must have. But as I comb through the stuff on the floor to find my things and head out, a long arm shoots out and grabs my wrist and he hauls me back onto the bed.

"On second thought, you're going to keep me happy this morning the way you didn't last night."

In seconds I'm on my back and he's on top of me, hard length pressing into my mound.

"I don't think ..." I try and wiggle out from under him, and he laughs.

"Yeah, baby, keep moving like that. You going to suck me off? You promised me that last night before you passed out on me."

He rubs against me, his hand scrabbling between us as he tries to find my entrance. What was I thinking? Something gags at the back of my throat at the scent of stale sweat as he presses his cock farther into me and crushes me into the mattress. I lock my legs and shift my hips out of the way.

"Come on, baby, don't make me force you."

Force me? What the hell?

"I've really gotta go: That was my alarm for work," I say. It sounds pathetic, and he laughs.

"Na, baby. You promised me last night."

He thrusts forward with his hips as I try and twist out from under him, but I make the mistake of moving my thigh and somehow his cock is between my legs. Grabbing my ass, he pushes, shoving all the way inside. His grip is bruising, and the pain makes my eyes water.

"Fuck, you feel amazing," he says, nuzzling my neck.

"I don't want to do this."

"Yeah, you do. Real up for it last night you were. All over me."

I wriggle and push at his shoulders, but he's way bigger than me and he grasps my wrists and pins them to the crumpled sheets on either side of my head. He chuckles, pulling out and thrusting back in hard. The sting tightens my breath.

"You're hurting me. Stop. No." I desperately try and shift my hips away as he jerks back, groaning.

"Yeah, baby, I like that."

"Condom," I say, but he just laughs again.

"No way. You're way too good bare."

Oh fuck, oh fuck. He pumps away at me shuddering and moaning as I stare at the ceiling. My throat constricts. This is my own goddamn fault.

Then he lifts up and stares at my chest, grunting. "Fuck. Fuck, yeah. So fucking good. Look at your tits. Thought they'd be stellar last night. Oh, fuck yeah, baby." His hips stutter and he lets out a moan and jerks over me as he comes.

"Yeah, fuck." He leans down, takes a nipple in his mouth, and pinches it in his teeth. Tears leak out of the corners of my eyes and into the pillow.

"That was perfect, baby. You want to stay to fuck again later, I'd be down for that."

He doesn't look at me as he rolls off and sprawls on his side of the bed. I stare at a brown stain on the ceiling. What just happened? I can't bring myself to think the word. I'm not sure how much time goes by, but a sudden gentle snore rising up from next to me galvanizes me into action.

Jumping up, I scrabble frantically to gather my stuff but he doesn't stir. I find a filthy bathroom down the corridor and shoot inside to pee. The inside of the toilet bowl under the waterline is full of slime. I pee in it nevertheless, and I'm suddenly desperate to wash him off my skin, to scrub and scrub. The tiles are black with mold, the showerhead caked in limescale, but I start the shower. The water is freezing, so I hop around the icy room waiting for the warmth to come through. Minutes tick by. Fucking hell. I dart into the cold stream, scouring across my body with a gritty, foul-smelling deodorant soap. What on earth was I thinking last night?

This is the third time this week I've got hammered. The other two nights I don't remember but at least I woke up in my own bed. What a fucking failure I am, getting forced into sex with some awful guy. I run a hand down my arm then pinch the skin, over and over, watching the bright red spots appear, and warmth spreads through my body as I suck in a shaky breath. I've got some tablets in my purse. Just a little something to help me through today. Have I had many this week? Ugh. Normally I'm more careful than this.

My phone ringing pulls me out of the now warm shower, and I frown down at the picture of the handsome guy on the screen as I drip water onto the floor. *Nick, my somewhat ill-tempered hookup partner.* What on earth?

"Hey, babe, are you here?" The rumble of New York traffic slots in behind his voice.

"Where are you?" I say, crossing my fingers.

"I'm at Juliana's? Breakfast? Are you close?"

"Oh shit, yeah." Oh my God, he's going to be furious. Nick slots his hookups in with miliary precision. And he's an asshole when he's in one of his moods.

"Fuck, babe, where are you?"

"I'm at Jo's," I lie. "We had a few drinks last night and I crashed. I'm just leaving."

"Jesus, Liss! You're so goddamn disorganized! It'll take you at least thirty minutes to get here. You don't keep people waiting like this: It's fucking rude."

"I'm sorry, I'm sorry. I'll catch a cab."

The line goes dead. Jesus, I really don't want him to be angry with me.

Then I'm out on the street, heart racing as I look for a cab. Images of biker guy's hot breath and sweat plunking on my skin keep popping into my head. Why couldn't I wriggle out from beneath him? My hands shake as I tie my dark curls into a makeshift topknot. Who can I talk to? Kate's on a night shift this evening, but could I call Jo?

What would she think of me?

I don't want someone telling me to go to the police, or even worse saying, "You poor thing." My mind skitters around the word *rape*. I said no and he kind of insisted? Why didn't I fight harder? I don't want to be vulnerable, but God, spinning this through my head on an endless loop is going to drive me mad. The wet street and indifferent faces provide no answers. My mind flitters to my two siblings and particularly Lauren with her safe obeying-my-father life and her fantastically steady boyfriend, David. If I told her something like this, she'd freak. Why am I always interested in these men? *Goddammit*. If this is a pattern I'll repeat in the future, I think I'll end up feeling suicidal. I can't cope with this being anything worse than a dreadful mistake right now.

What am I doing here, getting myself into problems like this? I finished my master's six months ago, and by rights I should be looking for a 'proper' job, whatever that means.

I shiver as I keep looking for a yellow light. Despite its pockets of trouble, Africa is the only place I feel safe. A sharp certainty flashes through me. I've got money saved—I've just got to survive through Christmas and then I can get out of here and go back there again.

CHAPTER 4

Dan

Thursday, December 20, 2018

I roll my shoulders as my father paces across the old, tiled floor of the farmhouse kitchen, my stomach sinking. There's so little time before I'm back at college. My father stops abruptly and slams his fist down on the table. "You do your share of work on the farm!"

What? I've been milking since dawn.

"I've got two weeks before I go back to college!"

"A college I'm paying for!"

"And I'm straight into the final part of my thesis when I get back. I have a mountain of work." My jaw tightens.

Sun burns down on the glowing wheatfields and distant hills outside the window. My father places his hands on the rough wood, red face looming over where I'm sitting and his voice drops, low and dangerous. "I could very easily stop paying, then you'd have to come back here and work full time."

"I can work anywhere I like. I don't have to work for you."

His fist flashes out, and my head jerks back as pain blooms across my cheekbones.

"Don't talk back to me, boy. I want you down in the fields with the thresher after you've finished that." He gestures at the pile of lamb and couscous on the plate in front of me, then he turns on his heel and stomps out. The door of his study slams shut.

Jed's standing with his arms folded against the wall, a smirk on his face. Sometimes I hate having an older brother.

"I can't wait to see the last of this place."

Jed shrugs. "You get into trouble because you don't play his game."

"You mean drinking twenty-four-seven and sleeping with any woman who's willing?"

"Yeah, it's a terrible life."

I don't get Jed's willingness to be involved with my father's nonsense. Day after day of grind on the farm whenever my father can be bothered to be here followed by wild nights of drinking, then disappearing off to the city.

"Who are you seeing tonight?"

"Samantha."

Oh God. Samantha's a scheming bitch. He doesn't half pick them. "That still going well?"

He shakes his head at me. "She gives an awesome blowjob. You should try it some time. You know women flock around Dad. I can get any woman I want, anything I want in bed, and I do."

"And Samantha's happy with all these other women?"

He shrugs again. "She knows the score."

My lip curls. "I'm not really interested in some meaningless fuck."

Jed laughs. "Yeah, tell me you think it's meaningless when your cock is in their mouth and you're coming apart."

The idiocy of their life. Burning through it like they're never going to see a reckoning, like there's never going to be a day of trouble. Do they even think about the people they've pissed off and fucked over?

Jed's still chuckling. "My cautious fucking brother, just fucking live a little, okay?"

"Yeah, I don't think I like what your 'living a little' entails. More like screwing everyone over," I growl.

He slams his fist on the table, just like Dad. "We're all getting through this with him the best we can." He hisses. "He's beaten me the same as you."

And God. The images flood into my head. Dad making me stand against the rough wood of the barn as he lay into Jed with the buckled end of a belt. Jed was ten, I was eight. I can still hear the screams, and the shivering quiet that those screams eventually gave way to.

"I don't know why Dad's so interested in what I'm doing. It's not like there aren't plenty of workers on the farm."

"The fucking thing's falling apart. He's not here that often and does nothing when he is here, you know that. He likes to shout and threaten people when he's here. I'm not really around enough to keep it all on track." He blows out a long breath, and now I understand the scowl, see the tightness in his shoulders.

Jed could hardly walk when my Dad had finished with him. I helped him back to the house, iced all his bruises, treated the welts. He couldn't get upstairs so I made him up a bed in the lounge and slept next to him on the sofa, holding his hand as tears drifted silently down his face.

My hackles lower. We looked out for each other, and he stepped in front of me sometimes too. I have a ton of work to do on my thesis, but being located in the DRC for the next few months will help with that, and this, this is way more important.

"When is he going back to solving financial problems in the city?"

"When you go back to college. He's decided he needs to keep an eye on you. Said you had too much freedom. Loafing around on a course." His eyes narrow on me. "You need to play a smarter game, little brother. I worked on him for years persuading him to let us both go to college, how much we could add to the farm with a better education. He's been rumbling on to me about stopping funding your course. Keep in touch with him, play the game a bit, and suck it up."

Trouble is sucking it up with my father usually means he dumps a whole load of shit on you, and woe betide you if you don't deliver—he'll lay into you sooner than blink. I touch my hand to my cheek and hold up my hands.

"Okay, okay."

"Here," Jed says, pulling some ice from the freezer and wrapping a tea towel around it. "Stick that on your face."

"How often is he dragging your ass back here from agricultural college?"

Jed screws his face up. "He was okay at first, but since that poor harvest in my second year it's being going downhill ever since. It unsettled him, I think. He calls me all the time. Usually when he's drunk and has just fucked some woman. He wants me up here several times a week."

Jesus. And fuck. That's a six-hour drive. Jed shrugs. "It's fine. I'll get through it. Just play the game and don't be another problem I have to solve."

I watch his broad back as he disappears through the doorway. Will I ever escape this place? My father? His tentacles stretch right across Africa. What I wouldn't give for a way out. In some ways I do get Jed's hellraising lifestyle—what else is there? My PhD is just my way of prolonging the inevitable: I'll come back here and sweat in a barn for the next God knows how many years of my life. It's depressing as hell.

CHAPTER 5

Dan

Tuesday, January 15, 2019

The grimy window reminds me of the farm, although the view is very different: a mud road through the bush. Hours of being jolted around and my butt and back both ache, my throat is dry and tight. We ran out of provisions ages ago, but I'm still drinking it all in. Four months out here in the middle of nowhere to finish the thesis for my PhD. And I love staying out in the rough of the country, where the asphalt gives way to dirt, away from the heat and mud and flies in sprawling cities and slums. It's a fantastic escape from family responsibilities. I roll my shoulders. *Enjoy this little bit of freedom.* God knows, I may never experience it again.

The sun is coloring the sky orange when we reach our destination: a small African town out in the middle of the bush. And I peer out of the window, fascinated. I'm here to study the dynamics of rural communities firsthand, and hopefully explore from here. All I know is I'm staying with a lady named Gloria whose husband is a linchpin in the aid work here.

John, my driver, jumps out and stops a man in the street, asking for directions. My mouth curls up: Google Maps is so limited out here; you find your way by everyone knowing everyone else. Taking my book out of my pack, I make a note to think about communities that work this way. Soon after, we're pulling up outside several prosperous-looking single-story buildings a few miles out of town. It isn't anything anyone in the West would describe as affluent, but they're made of concrete and have roofs and a yard, all of which says money in rural Congo.

A smiling man appears at the door, and John jumps down shouting something at him in Swahili, and I broadly catch the gist of the insult before they both laugh and hug each other. Climbing slowly out of the car, I straighten my compressed body as they chat away. I pick up every third word: something about "Westerners" and "volunteers." *There's other people here?* Some new conversation after this long and boring drive would be amazing. John turns to me with a smile.

"Dan, this is Adebe. He works with the aid agencies in the region."

"Come, come." Adebe beckons, having watched my painful exit from the vehicle. "We will have a cold beer, yes?"

His eyes widen as I thank him in halting Swahili. He makes a comment to John, who laughs, and I'm sure he's said something about Westerners and local languages.

"I am surprised you speak our tongue," he says, with a delighted grin and in excellent English. And given that French is the official language in the DRC, I'm impressed too.

"Ton anglais est très bon," I say in my less than expert French, and he cracks up, clapping his hands in delight.

I like him. The directness and the sense of humor are all positive signs. Out of nowhere, the idea that no one is aware of who I am swamps me and I'm lightheaded as tension seeps from my body.

"I've lived in Africa a while."

It's all I want to say in explanation. Adebe ducks in through the low doorway into a gloomy interior and I follow him in, out of the heat of the evening. Three people are sitting at a makeshift table, and my eyes are drawn to the dark-haired girl at the end. She has the kind of lively face and laughing eyes that you could lose yourself in, and an unrestrained smile splits her face as I shake hands with the other two people, an older guy named Brian and a blonde-haired blue-eyed woman named Emma. But my eyes keep straying to the muscles that run down the woman at the end's thin arms, and the mass of crazy curly hair that frames her face and highlights her dark-chocolate eyes fringed by thick lashes. She looks like she's spent forever under a hot African sun.

"Liss," she says, holding out her hand.

"Dan," I say, grasping the slim wiry fingers in mine, and warmth moves up my arm to my shoulder. A broad smile curves over my lips in response to hers. The idea that there's more company than I was expecting here—and particularly *her*—races through me. My summer is looking better and better.

"What are you all working on?" I say, pulling a rickety chair out from the table and sitting down at it. A cold beer magically appears in front of me.

Liss lets out a drawn-out groan that goes straight to my groin, and Brian laughs, holding up battered hands for my inspection.

"Building." He rolls his eyes.

"Ah," I nod knowingly. I've done my fair share of that and also have the scars to prove it.

"How long are you all here?" I say, looking at some old armchairs next to the table, one with a book propped open on it.

"As long as they'll have us."

"Or until the funding runs out," Emma interjects.

"Or probably my money before that," Liss mutters as her mouth curves ruefully.

"What are you building?"

"Water supplies, sanitation mostly," Brian says. "Access to clean water is a huge problem."

And yeah, I get that. Water is the cornerstone of the worst diseases right across Africa.

"And what do you all do for fun around here?"

Brian chuckles quietly, and Liss raises an eyebrow. "Sleep?"

"On your own or …" I wink at her, but it feels clunky. Come on, I'm not that rusty. I can still flirt, right? Something about her smiling face makes me feel a little bit reckless.

She scoffs. "I think you need to see the beds and dorms before you start making any suggestions." She winks back at me, and an electric feeling buzzes down my body. Energy radiates off her like a furnace. I examine her soft, thick curls, the pink bow of her lips.

"Hey, hey, no propositioning the ladies," Brian says, waving his hands over the table.

Emma rolls her eyes. "Fat chance of that here."

"Cards," Brian declares firmly. "That's what we do for fun."

I rub my hands together, trying not to keep staring at Liss. "Poker? That's right up my alley."

And they all laugh.

CHAPTER 6

Liss

Wednesday, January 16, 2019

The day after Dan arrives, I wander out into the rising heat with my coffee from the volunteers' accommodation at the back of Gloria and Adebe's house to find our new guest sprawled, fast asleep, in a hammock tied up in the shade outside the building. *He slept out here?*

His body glows in the half-light of an African dawn. The dusty clothes he was in last night are twisted up around his torso, his shirt half unbuttoned. My mouth goes dry at the smattering of blond chest hair, toned abdomen, and the trail disappearing into his shorts. An indecent amount of muscle is hidden under that baggy bush shirt. A rattling noise in the kitchen behind me makes me jump, and I blush even though no one's caught my ogling. I stick my head back through the beaded curtain.

"Coffee's made and in the pot, yeah?"

Emma lurches sleepily across the small catering area, nodding, and I collapse into one of the garden chairs on the veranda beneath the eaves of the building. Dan shifts in the hammock, but it tips precariously then dumps him unceremoniously onto the ground. I snort as he rolls and groans, then sits up and blinks, shaking his head. With a sleepy grin, he glances over at me, and my stomach dips at the tousled hair and the lazy look in his eyes.

"Coffee?" I say, gesturing at my cup to hide the pink climbing up my cheeks.

He croaks out, "Sure," and grins at me like he's worked out just what effect he's having. *Damn.* Where's my normal flirt mechanism? I scuttle through to the kitchen, and by the time I'm back outside, Emma and Dan are cozied up with each other on an old, battered sofa that's beside the plastic chairs. Emma's leaning right into him, and I hand him the coffee as he studies me with raised eyebrows. *I'm scowling. Dammit.* But he pats the empty chair on the other side of him and turns toward me when I sit down.

"I'm sorry your first view at sunrise was me being dumped in the dirt. Monkeys would have been so much more exciting."

Laughing, I examine him over my cup. Is he flirting? He was friendly last night, and maybe he was also checking me out. Whatever, I think he's got a reasonable sense of humor.

"I've seen a lot of monkeys. I don't often come across blond-haired, blue-eyed guys outside my bedroom in the morning," I say, winking and crossing my fingers behind my back.

A hint of pink hits him high in his cheekbones, but his eyes meet mine.

"Can't say I wake up to many beautiful chocolate-eyed women either," he says with a grin.

Oh Lord. He volleyed that one straight back. Emma's eyes widen as a laugh escapes me, all my smart one-liners disappearing down a plughole.

"Seriously, though, did you actually sleep in the hammock overnight?" I stammer out. *Really, Liss?* Is that the best you can come up with?

He rubs the scruff on his chin, eyes still droopy with sleep and his blond curls in a crazy halo around his head. My stomach does a strange loop.

"It was cooler out here." He looks down at his hands and then squints at me, smiling. "I was expecting a different comeback from you than that," he says.

If Emma wasn't here, perhaps I'd have come up with a wittier response.

And as if answering my prayers, she clears her throat.

"Brian will be up soon. I'm going to get dressed," she says as she stands and straightens, frowning down at me. I smile blandly at her and watch as she disappears through the plastic fringes that cover the door.

"I was actually going to say how much I enjoyed the view of some nice abs and a happy trail." A grin spreads across my face as I nod toward where his shirt has covered him up. I blow on my coffee and peek at him over the rim of my cup. "But maybe that's too forward?"

He shakes his head as his mouth twists, and if anything, his cheeks are pinker.

Then he winks. "Anytime you want to see my abs, Liss, just let me know."

Oh dear, oh dear. My smile widens as my shoulders ease. Dan, you are never going to come out ahead in a flirting showdown with me.

I press my hand into my chest. "Now that sounds like an amazing offer." I nod at his chest. "How about now?"

He gapes at me, and I laugh. "Don't challenge me to a flirting duel—I'll win hands down," I say, smiling wider now. His eyes roam over my face and then he raises an eyebrow, and his hands come up to the top button on his shirt, and when he undoes it, I get a tantalizing glimpse of curly blond chest hair.

And now my face is going pink. Goddammit, I am *not* a blusher. How did we go from good morning to him taking off his shirt so fast?

I flap my hand at him. "I didn't mean it, you idiot."

His hands drop down and the cutest bashful grin I think I've ever seen breaks across his face. He sits back in his chair, smiling as I shift in my seat. "I'm afraid I never back down from a challenge," he says, laughing, then he looks off to the side, letting out a groan as he scrubs his hands down his face. "God, I'm sorry. We've only just met and I'm taking off my shirt!"

And oh, this is *fun*. He's a nice guy.

"Don't apologize. I think I asked for it, and a striptease an excellent start to a day, I'd say. It doesn't happen nearly often enough. I was about to offer …"

His hand shoots out to clamp over my face, causing me to jump, and something lights up in his eyes, heat definitely, but …

"No more. I'm going to imagine that I'm the only person that's stripped for you first thing in the morning."

And oh! He's possessive, too? Interesting. *Throw me over your shoulder and do something bad to me.* I lick his hand, and his eyes bug out. Now what am *I* doing? I've never done something like this with anyone, but I'm giddy with how much I'm enjoying it.

"Will kissing you shut you up?" he says, eyes dancing.

"That's actually a question?"

He purses his lips and studies the horizon with a smile then looks back at me. Today has taken a very strange U-turn. And I won't be able to get that curly chest hair out of my head. He stands up abruptly and stretches.

"Well, this little exchange has been fun, but I need to get ready for the day." And he gives me a wink before lifting the beaded curtain and heading indoors.

I stare at where he's disappeared. A bit of banter and then … *nothing*? I wanted it to go somewhere. Although exactly where it might lead at this time of the morning when we live in dorms in a small concrete building makes me scowl at my own stupidity. He's good at the flirting game, and I like him, but I've read too much into things before. He's so gorgeous, I'll bet he crooks his little finger and girls come running.

Sighing, I shove my feet back into my flip-flops and head into the dark interior. Dan's nowhere to be seen, and the makeshift door to the men's dorm is closed. There's no sign of Emma either, but singing is drifting in from the outside toilet: a little hut at the far side of the yard with a rainwater collection system for washing. I shoot into the women's dorm and scan the six camp beds, sucking in a couple of shaky breaths as heat settles around me. *What am I doing?* I strip out of my sleep shorts and T-shirt, I throw on clean underwear, roll on some deodorant and pull on khaki shorts and a long-sleeved shirt. It's not the most flattering, but the dust ruins everything here.

When I head outside, Brian, Dan, and Emma are sitting on the veranda downing coffee as I sink into a chair. Dan's gaze skitters across mine before fixing on Brian.

"What are you guys up to today?" he asks.

"We're working on a toilet block at a village school a few miles away," Emma replies. "Want to come out with us and see it?"

"Sounds great. I've got three case studies to put together for my thesis, so I need to visit as many villages as possible. My professor recommended this area as one that has the full range of socioeconomic and political problems: land disputes, disease, war … you name it." He laughs, and it's all I can do not to stare at his lips, his perfect white teeth, and, holy shit, think about his mouth on other places. How am I going to be remotely sensible working alongside him?

"Yeah, that's about right," says Brian. "You can help build if you like. We're short of volunteers currently, although we might have another person coming out soon."

My ears prick up. More hands on deck would be amazing.

A half hour later we're on the road to the village, arriving an hour later to a buzz of activity. This school will be only the second in the region to have real toilets, and local excitement is high at the prospect of avoiding the diseases that debilitate so many of the people here. The women are tending to open fires, cooking breakfast for everyone, and our community coordinator, Kiwale, waves as we make our way to the building site. Brian confers quietly with him, presumably discussing the day's tasks.

When lunchtime rolls around, two women set up tables and serve hearty stews and *akara*, a fried bean cake, and my mouth waters as I shake out my aching arms. The full smiles that greet me encourage me to try out some French and my limited Swahili, and they laugh and clap at me. How glad am I that I escaped that law degree? God knows what I'd be doing now. Defending some corrupt corporate, probably. I examine the lady stirring the oil in the big metal wok and my throat tightens. They work so hard, overcoming the insurmountable odds of life out here. We're helping them, but sometimes I think we get more out of it than they do.

I gather my food and find a space on the ground. And after washing his hands in a pan, Dan plonks himself down in the dirt next to me, under the shade of the rustling raffia shelters. We've got a bit of a break now from the heat of the midday sun.

I examine him out of the corner of my eyes.

"God, I need this," he says, shoveling food into his mouth. "Hard work, isn't it?" It comes out in a mumble through a mouthful of stew.

I stretch out my hand and tense my bicep in front of his face. It bulges in a very satisfying way. "It's done wonders for my muscles."

He turns to me fully and grins, putting his lunch down and wrapping his hand around my arm. His palm is dusty and dry, long fingers kneading into the aching muscle, with his short, neatly trimmed nails, dirt caked in every crevice. *God, the sheer manliness of him.* My gaze drifts up, over the dusting of blond hair on his forearms and the sleeves of his khaki shirt rolled up to his elbows. When my eyes meet his, he's watching me look at him, clear blue eyes warm on mine.

Emma appears over his shoulder and breaks the moment, dropping down on the other side of him, clutching a bowl of stew and bean cake. Brian is right behind her.

"Are you comparing arm strength?" she asks, staring at his hands on my arm, but Dan laughs easily.

"I'm like some soft, academic weakling that joined an elite team. How do you guys haul so much stuff all day?" he says.

"Yeah, yeah," Brian waves dismissively, sitting on the other side of me. "Stop with the flattery. I saw you chucking bricks around."

Dan shakes his head grinning, and now Emma's watching the pair of us. She puts her food down and pushes at the cuff of his shirt.

"Let's see your muscles then."

Dan laughs and shifts away, but she keeps pushing at his sleeve and my chest tightens as she wrestles with him, smiling up at him.

"Alright, alright," he says eventually, batting her away and rolling the cotton up his arm, tensing his muscles so they bulge out impressively. Emma giggles and squeezes. Ugh. *She's so obvious.* I look down at my bowl and fork in a mouthful of food as Brian grins and folds back his shirt and tenses his biceps, too.

Dan leans over and rolls up the sleeve nearest to me, shoving his left arm in front of my face.

"Seems only fair that you test my biceps as well," he says softly, and I turn to find his face inches away, warm breath gusting over my shoulder, dust clinging to the side of his face. A smile bubbles up as I take in his flexed bicep, and I put down my food and circle his arm with both hands. His skin is unreal, velvet wrapped around iron and heat. The impulse to run a hand all the way up under the edge of his sleeve is almost overwhelming. *He seems so nice, Liss—don't mess this up.*

A smirk dances over his mouth as his gaze meets mine. His lips are firm, the stubble on his chin rough where he clearly decided that shaving this morning was a step too far. An ache starts up deep in my body.

"Well? What do you think?" he says.

It takes me a beat or two to work out what he's referring to. I squeeze hard, digging my fingers in.

"Pretty impressive."

All I can think about is having my hands wrapped around his arms as he's above me, looking down.

A faint trace of pink tints his cheeks as he briefly meets my gaze. Are his thoughts as X-rated as mine? I want to go back to where we were this morning, but Emma's curious stare zips my mouth. His eyes flit over me, and he clears his throat and, turning to Brian, asks him what he was doing before he came out here. And I hold my breath. Brian was quiet when I first met him on the build. He was six months into his contract here managing volunteers, having ditched his life in the US, and all I know is that his wife died. But Brian skims over it all easily with Dan, and, as they talk, the promise of Dan burns all the way down my right side.

Later, when we're in the back of the jeep heading back to the house, Dan's long, tanned legs stretch out next to mine in the back seat, and I can hardly contain the impulse to place my hand on his thigh.

CHAPTER 7

Liss

Saturday, January 19, 2019

A makeshift set of raffia walls in the yard conceals a scoop and a rain barrel where we wash. A gap on one side faces the bush, but it's high enough that you can only see a person's head and shoulders. We only get to wash properly here once a week, one after another, when Alain from the village brings pumped water to replenish the collection tank. Three days after Dan's arrival, on Saturday, when Emma comes back to the room grinning with the sheer pleasure of being clean, I head out. When I spot Dan's blond head sticking out over the top of the walls, his towel slung over the raffia wall, I groan to myself. I don't need to watch him shower. But my feet won't carry me back inside, so I sink into a chair that's been left out. He won't take long, surely?

I've caught Dan watching me once or twice when I've been talking to Brian, and I've been careful to keep things appropriate. I don't want to fawn over him like a puppy.

But as I sit down, I realize the seat gives me a perfect view through the gap in the fence where you enter. Fortunately, Dan's head is down, but as I move to get him out of my line of sight, he strips off his shirt and shorts and picks up the scoop and pours water over his head. My mouth dries. The water streams down his torso causing the blond hair to clump and matt into darker whorls, his happy trail forming a sharp stripe down the middle of his body before disappearing into his boxers. The wet fabric clings to him, accentuating the long line of his cock. I lick my lips. *Holy shit.*

When he lifts his head and opens his eyes, he spots me. *I can't move now.*

"Are you going to join me or carry on gawking? If we washed together, I'm sure we could save water," he says, grinning as he lifts his chin.

Heat crawls up my throat into my cheeks. Ugh. Is this some kind of flirting revenge? God, I'm not sure I'll survive. And where has my usual sass gone?

Dan laughs and shakes his head, droplets flying everywhere, and something thrums in the air like a thread pulled tight.

"Would you like a show?" He reaches for the soap and lathers the bar between his two large hands, rubbing it roughly down his arms and into his armpits as his forearms flex. I was right, he is muscled everywhere. Then he's washing his chest and down his stomach, delving into his boxers as he washes his cock, which is quickly becoming hard. *Jesus Christ.*

"Fuck, that's good. It would be even better if you were doing the soaping. Maybe if I was soaping you too?" As he laughs, it takes me back to three days ago on the veranda, the gleam in his eyes as he was as filthy as I was.

He scrubs down his legs, head dropping down as he turns away and pushes his boxers down and steps out of them. His ass is small, tight and perfect. I want to wrap my hand around one hard cheek as he's over me, pushing inside. Everything swims for a couple of seconds, and I drag in a sharp breath, watching as he soaps himself in that way men do, roughly, getting into all the crevices with a wonderful familiarity that makes my palms itch.

Reaching into the wooden barrel, he grabs the ladle and pours water down his body, scoop after scoop. Soap streams down pooling and running into the brown, caked earth. His feet are broad and splayed as though they need to be to keep his large frame upright. The water runs in rivers down his torso creating patterns in the hair as he turns this way and that, tipping more over his head, and I can't tear my eyes away from his cock. It's perfect, half hard as he skims his hands over his skin, feeling for soap, throwing more water over his body. He bends down and picks up his boxers, his eyes meeting mine as he grabs the old striped towel and roughly towels himself off, wrapping it around his slim hips.

With a grin, a couple of steps bring him closer, until he's a foot away, his gaze lazy as it wanders from my face to my feet. Everywhere it lands lights me on fire.

"Sorry you didn't join me. Next time maybe?"

His hand lifts as if he's going to touch me, but then he drops it and leans in, damp golden skin glistening a few inches away.

"Are you going to treat me to a show, too? I'd be happy to join you." His lips curl. "What did you say about a flirting duel?" He tuts and his eyes roam my face and my mouth, as his hand comes out and moves a strand of hair out of my face. His eyes narrow. "You're suspiciously quiet."

I shake my head, mute. He's too close. Too damn attractive. I'm not sure that starting this flirting game was such a great idea. I let out a long controlled breath as he walks off toward the hut, whistling.

*

Later, when we're digging into plates of stewed meat with vegetables and rice, Dan leans over.

"Did you enjoy watching me wash?" he murmurs into my ear, taking an ample bite of the local bread Gloria makes. Seeing his teeth sink into the soft crumb, all I can imagine is them sinking into me.

A flush climbs up my cheeks. "You put on an excellent show," I mumble.

He laughs, his mouth curling, the muscles working in his throat, the blond scruff disappearing down his neck into his checked shirt.

"Anytime you want to join me, be my guest," he says.

CHAPTER 8

Dan

Monday, January 21, 2019

Two days on from the outrageous flirting, the idea of Liss's graceful hands all over me keeps invading my head. Watching her easy laughter, her good cheer in front of anything she's presented with, and how damn hard she works, has slipped into my bloodstream. I'm certain she wasn't wearing a bra yesterday, and I spent the whole day trying to avoid looking at her chest under the thin fabric of her shirt. Too obvious in shorts. No doubt every other guy was thinking the same thing. But my impression isn't that she did it intentionally; she doesn't come across as manipulative at all. In all the heat and the sweat, a bra must feel like the devil's work.

I'm sitting in a chair at the table outside when Brian steps out through the doorway carrying two bottles of beer. My notes about the build and the village grind to a halt, and I take a bottle from his outstretched hand as he peers over my shoulder at the information about local politics and fighting that one of the elders told me this morning.

"You said you wanted to go to some other villages," Brian says, swallowing his beer. "Kiwale talked to me about a guy from one of the health charities that you could travel with. It would take a few days and could be a bit rough accommodation-wise, but the elder you chatted with today could accompany you, and show you some of the areas he mentioned."

I squint up at him. "More oral history would be amazing. Could you arrange that?"

He inclines his head. "Easy enough to do."

"That's very kind of you. Thanks."

"Perhaps Liss could go with you?" His eyes twinkle at me, and I look at him sharply.

"Liss?"

"Another volunteer is arriving in the next week or so to help, so after that might work. Liss is good with the local people." He smiles. "She understands all the nuances and pays the important people the respect they expect."

He's right. She's the one who always talks to the locals with Kiwale.

The call "Shower's free!" comes drifting from the back of the building, and he gives me an easy smile before ducking back through the beaded curtain.

Has he noticed this attraction between Liss and me and is he encouraging it? I'm not sure I should be encouraging it myself, but every time I'm near her, common sense seems to fly out of the window. I sigh. I need to draw a map to understand the land and the migration of people with all the fighting. Google Maps gives just the big picture; none of the local tracks are on it. Extraordinarily little is recorded anywhere. A trip around the nearby area will give me so much more: alliances, rivalries, and politics.

Cicadas are providing a background chorus in the evening heat when Liss pushes through the beaded curtain and slumps into the seat next to me, a smile curling her pink lips. How is she still smiling after the brutal lifting we did today on site? As she leans into me and peers at my notes, I inhale a whiff of warm woman and sweat, and a bolt of pure lust shoots down my body and settles between my legs.

I examine her sideways. Liss is oddly flirty, like it's something she does by default as a fun distraction and it's not really a reflection of who she really is. I'm not sure what to make of it. It reminds me of the women back home that hang around my dad. Maybe she flirts all the time and it doesn't really mean anything. If that's true, I really overstepped a line with my display in the shower a couple of days ago.

"Which college do you go to?" she says, eyes scanning over my notes, oblivious as I examine the smooth skin on her arm. My brain crawls, hot and slow, and caution slips into my bloodstream. My life outside of here isn't something I can really share.

"Zimbabwe. I live in Harare," I say. I chose to go to college in Harare for one reason: to be out of my father's reach … The fact that the professor and the programs were renowned was an added bonus.

"What's that like?" If she's picking up any hesitation in my voice, she isn't showing it.

"Awesome actually—it's a fascinating place." *Being careful with strangers.* It's always been part of my life and I've always hated it.

"You don't have much of an accent."

Now we're really on thin ice. I don't have much of an accent because I went to an international school. "I think I lost it over the years. Where are you from?" I counter.

"A good question," she murmurs. "When I go home, I go to New York, because that's where my two best friends are." No mention of her parents. *Interesting.* But I can't probe further, because then she'll ask me about my family and I can't give her that.

"What do you do when you're in New York?"

"I work at one of the universities."

Safe ground. "Really? I'd like to do something like that."

She eyes me. "Delivering classes was part of my master's program, and I've carried on working for them on an ad-hoc basis doing admin. I'm not experienced enough to teach."

I nudge her shoulder with mine. "But you'd like to do that eventually? Teach?"

She shrugs. "I'm not sure I'll ever fit into a full-time job."

I'm curious. "Why's that?"

She leans away from me, and cold washes down my left side. Damn. Part of me wishes I'd looked at her lips when they were close to me. When I glance at her again, she's staring off into the distance.

"I like being out here. I studied Environmental Sciences, and got to come out here in my first year of college on a summer voluntary program and loved it so much I kept coming back every chance I had." She smiles at me. "I haven't worked out how to make all the parts of my life fit together." Spreading her hands, she laughs. "Clearly I need to start earning some money at some point."

I nod, grinning back at her. I'm not sure I'm so positive about the nuances of living in Africa with all the endemic corruption, but I identify with trying to make all the bits of your life fit together.

And escape. I can definitely relate to that.

I really like Liss, but I need to be more measured in my interactions with her.

CHAPTER 9

Liss

Wednesday, January 30, 2019

The streaked window of the jeep obscures the view of cattle and low-lying buildings as we bump along the dirt road, heading back to Adebe's from our day on site. Dan has been away for almost a week, off with one of the aid workers to some of the outlying villages. The new volunteer, Henry, is asleep on the back seat next to me with his mouth open, his head lolling backward. He's been a welcome relief workwise, but I've missed having Dan's quiet voice and thoughts of an evening, watching his muscles flex in the hot sun.

Dan was perfectly friendly with me before he left, but there was a hesitancy there and I got the impression that I had mis-stepped somehow. *Ugh.* Dan's so solid, so grown up, and as he's shared more about the work he's doing, I like him more and more. I let out a long sigh and pull at the stitching on the car seat. My usual approach to men doesn't feel right out here; it's out of kilter with working on site and sharing a house. That hasn't stopped Emma, though—she's been flirting with Dan any opportunity she gets. I study her blonde strands curling around the headrest of the seat in front of me.

As we draw up to the house, Dan is sitting on the veranda, scribbling away in his notebook. He raises his head and squints at the vehicle in the sinking sun as we pull to a halt, and I clench my teeth as Emma squeals, "Dan's back!", and shoots out of the jeep repeatedly calling his name.

His grin aimed at her makes something sour curl in my stomach, but when his gaze shifts over her shoulder and his eyes meet mine, something comes over his face, a warmth that causes my insides to twist in a different way. A flock of small birds flutters under my ribcage. Has he missed me, too? As he rises from his chair, Emma flings her arms around him and presses in, and I turn to Henry who's appeared next to me. He's been sticking by my side all through the build, eager to learn whatever I can tell him about how to do things right.

When I blink back toward Dan, I find he's extracted himself from Emma and is heading toward us looking pointedly at Henry and back at me. An introduction. Right. I wave out my hand.

"Henry, this is Dan, our resident academic," I say, grinning up at Dan's tight smile, as his eyes flit over Henry's face.

Henry's an easy guy, a bit earnest and young, but completely solid. And he's clearly a little intimidated by Dan's size and … what is that expression on Dan's face?

"Good to meet you," Henry says.

Dan nods at him in that way guys do. "You too—how long have you been here?"

Henry laughs. "A couple of days. I still feel like a total newbie, but Liss has been teaching me everything I need to know." He turns toward me with a grin, and a frown drops over Dan's face.

"Not sure I'm adapting to the lack of washing facilities, though," he adds with a chuckle.

"The showers when you get them become even more valuable, especially if you have company," Dan smirks, narrowing his eyes at me. I raise my eyebrows.

Henry's forehead is furrowed. "You have to wash in pairs?"

Dan laughs. "Not really, I was yanking your chain. Why don't we go and find some beers?"

"Beer o'clock," I say with a sigh. "My favorite time of the day."

Later, when we're all crowded around the makeshift dining table, Dan slides into the seat beside me, cutting Henry on my other side a glance.

"How's it been, while I've been away?" he murmurs as he settles on the stool.

"Okay," I say, wolfing down a piece of soft bread and chewing. "Having more hands on deck is a relief." I incline my head toward Henry. "With this extra help, we'll start the roof next week I think."

"How long are you here for?" Dan leans over me to address Henry.

"The summer, hopefully. I'm studying plant science. My plan was to understand the strains and stresses on the flora here, the demands of farming, but I've discovered the local doctors use indigenous plants for medicine, and that's much more interesting. Because Liss talks to everyone, she's managed to arrange for me to meet one."

Shaking my head at him, I grin. "It was easy enough to do. If you want anything done, you just ask Kiwale."

Henry leans in and nudges my shoulder. "It's greatly appreciated. I might even be able to build my final-year dissertation around it."

Dan's eyes flick between us before he goes back to his stew.

"What happens when we finish this toilet block?" Henry asks.

"Brian's got a list of other villages in the region desperate for construction and advice, so we'll move on to the next project, hopefully another school. You should go and visit the last one we helped. It's had a huge impact. So many girls came back to the school after we built water collection facilities and toilets where they felt safe."

Henry nods and gets up to fetch some more food from the dishes on the side table, and I surreptitiously watch Dan's jaw as he rips some kwanga bread apart with his teeth. He glances at me sideways and laughs. *Busted.*

He nudges me with his shoulder. "Do you like him?" he says quietly.

"Who?"

"Henry."

That wasn't what I was expecting him to say. "He's a hard worker, and good company, too."

"He seems pretty into you."

My eyes flicker over his face, but his expression gives nothing away. I bet he's an awesome poker player.

I shrug. Henry's a puppy next to Dan. "He needs someone to look out for him. I remember being a clueless newbie and how brutal it was adapting to the physical work in this heat."

Dan nods and shovels another forkful into his mouth, like he's thinking about something. I don't know what to make of it. Why did he ask about Henry? Regret settles over me like dust.

I take a mouthful of stew. "Why did you ask if I liked Henry?" I say. I've never asked a guy a straight question like this, but maybe if I understand what I'm doing wrong with guys, then …

He swallows and gestures toward me. "I think I misinterpreted your flirting."

"Misinterpreted it?"

"I've never been comfortable with women who string men along for all the wrong reasons. You gave me the impression that …"

Panic curls in my stomach. "I wouldn't do that. I mean … I'm not like that."

He nods. "No, I can see that."

God, do I really give off those vibes?

He studies my face for several beats and must see something there because he smiles and leans into me, nudging my arm. "I've got to go out to visit some more villages the day after tomorrow. Brian suggested you might be a useful addition to the trip. Charm the locals. Do you want to come with me?"

Go away with him? All my worry curls into something else as a depth charge explodes inside me. "Of course," I say with a grin. "That sounds like fun."

His eyes rove over my face. "I think anything with you would be fun, Liss."

CHAPTER 10

Dan

Friday, February 1, 2019

Two days later, I'm in the middle of the bush examining a rough narrow wooden bed with a thin lumpy mattress, two candles burning on a couple of crates. This has to be these lovely people's best room, and my chest expands. It's humbling how little they have and how much they share.

Liss runs a hand through her dark curls and dumps her small backpack on the bed. I examine her small frame. Henry has stars in his eyes every time he looks at her, whether she realizes it or not, and I can't believe how territorial I'm feeling.

I put my backpack down too and pull out my self-inflating mattress. It's dusty and crumpled, but I roll it out and start unscrewing the valve on the end of it.

"What's that?" Liss says.

"A mattress."

Her body slumps. "You're kidding, right?"

And it makes me laugh. "I slept out rough a lot when I was younger." *Maybe I can give her* tiny *snippets of my life.* "And believe you me, this is the best money I've ever spent on anything."

"God, I wish I was that organized," she says.

"You can have it."

"No way, Dan, you're not doing that."

"Yes, I am."

"Don't do the looking-after-the-lady thing. I don't like not being treated equally."

Is she really turning down a more comfortable sleeping option?

"Big surprise," I say, grinning. On the building site, Liss has the propensity to lift a lot of weight and I love teasing her about it, particularly demonstrating how much more I can lift than her. She calls me an asshole when I do it.

"Let's put it on the bed and share it," she says.

My blood heats as I peer at her and raise my eyebrows, grinning. "Are you asking, or telling me you want to sleep in a bed with me?"

She looks down and fiddles with a thread on her shorts. "Seems like the best solution to me."

God, could I sleep with her and not …? Her gaze comes back to mine, and I press my lips together, eyes fixed over her head. "I'm not sure I …" I start.

"Whatever," she says, sinking down on the wooden edge of the bed. "I'll take the bed, you can sleep on that contraption on the floor." She gestures at my inflatable.

She lies back on the lumpy mattress on the bed and winces. What's in that thing?

I loom over her, placing my hands on either side of her body, and she blinks up at me.

"It's not a question of not wanting to, Liss, it's that I wouldn't be able to keep my hands to myself." I glance at the thin wall of the building above my head and the sheet covering the door.

Her mouth goes slack, and my lips twist, eyes flicking over her nose and cheeks. "… Or stop myself from getting hard," I add. I want to be *direct* here, I want her to understand just how much I like her. She was direct with me about Henry, and I think it took courage to do that.

"As long as I can stroke your biceps, I'm up for it," she says, a smile radiating up at me.

My eyes drift down to her lips. Does she want this? I lean back and drag her to her feet, removing the lumpy mattress and lifting the inflated mattress onto the bed, pulling a mosquito net and a hook out of my backpack. Climbing onto the bed, I start fixing the hook into the low roof. It's a well-worn routine.

"God, you're organized. I'm impressed," she says.

I study her for a beat before going back to screwing the hanger into the wood. "You brought a net too, though, right?"

"Yes. One'll be enough, won't it?"

"Yeah." I step down and pull my shirt off over my head, folding it and putting it on the crate. The candlelight casts a golden glow over everything as I unbutton my shorts. Liss stares as I strip right down to my underwear and climb beneath the net. I try not to watch as she removes her pants and takes her bra off under her T-shirt. It's a level of shyness I wouldn't have associated with her, and something warm burns through me. I like this thing I have with her. I like who she is under the sass and the liveliness.

As she shifts beneath the netting, I get a tantalizing glimpse of gray boy shorts. There's nothing special about them, but at this moment nothing has seemed sexier. My mouth waters as we shuffle around trying to get comfortable.

"We should sleep head to toe," she says.

"No fucking way," I say, moving so I'm tucked into her back, and I slide a forearm over her chest. I breath out into her curls, and the warmth of her seeps into me, her hair tickling my face as my stomach turns liquid. She places a tentative hand on my arm.

The rustling and snuffling of animals drifts in through the makeshift doorway. We're so close to nature and all its dangers and raw elements here, so far away from the heat and honk of the city. She shifts and I groan into her hair, hardening at the feeling of her small hips tucked into mine.

"Don't. Move."

"Sorry," she whispers.

"Sorry about the hard-on," I add.

"I'm flattered," she says, and that isn't fucking helping. I want to pin her to the bed, under me.

She sighs and strokes a hand over my forearm.

"What are you doing?" I whisper.

"Sorry," she says again. "I'm a bit obsessed with your arms."

"Don't say things like that."

"Sorry."

"Stop saying 'sorry.'"

"Okay."

"Knowing you're thinking about my arms doesn't help."

"Okay."

I can't get her scent out of my nostrils. Burying my face in her hair, I say, "You smell amazing."

She laughs. "What? Sweaty?"

"Yeah, funnily enough." I lick her neck. "You taste good too." She exhales a shaky breath, and the idea that I'm having an effect on her too makes my stomach tighten. "Fuck, I shouldn't have done that."

I harden more and I can't help the loud groan that slips out into the silence of the hut.

"Shhh!" she says.

"You feel far too fucking good." I kiss her just under her ear, sinking my teeth in, nibbling, arm tightening on her like a vice. "Okay. You were right. This was a mistake. It's like sleeping with chocolate cake."

She snorts. "Chocolate cake? Are you high?"

"It's my favorite thing to eat."

She starts giggling. And I can't stop myself from laughing too. "I'll have you know I taste better than chocolate cake," she says.

I groan. "Lying here thinking about how you taste isn't helping either."

"I've been told …"

My hand clamps over her mouth. "Shhh, woman, sleep."

"Little hope of that now," she says, moving again.

I tighten my arm. I'm never going to be able to sleep either. Despite the heat and discomfort and the feeling of her small body tucked securely into mine, I close my eyes on a long sigh. And it seems like only seconds later that my eyes blink open to daylight seeping in around the cloth over the door. How did that happen? A cat that's appeared from somewhere jumps down from the bed and stretches. I move out from behind Liss and climb out from under the net.

"Is everything alright?" she whispers.

"Time to get up."

"*What?*"

Her eyes dart to the door, and she grimaces before she curls in on herself.

She's so cute in the morning, sleepy eyes and her dark curls in some mad disarray. I smile at her. "Sleep well?"

She sits up and swings her legs over the side of the bed. Groaning, she rubs her hands down her face and pouts and regret burns through me. How could I have had the chance for more with her and nothing occurred, not even a kiss?

I squat down in front of her. Her face is so close, lips pink and plush, so I lean forward and skim my mouth across hers. Her lips are like velvet, and I instantly want more but I don't want to push my luck.

"Did I fuck up?" I mumble.

She shakes her head. "No, you made the right call."

CHAPTER 11

Liss

Friday, February 8, 2019

On Friday, at the end of a hard few days, Brian offers us a night out in Kiwanja. The local town is a collection of old colonial government buildings and a shanty town, and he's promised a bar and beer. The weariness in my arms and the dryness in my throat do nothing to dampen the adrenaline pumping through my veins. Every day has been eat, sleep, build, repeat.

Emma is singing loudly along to some pop tune on the radio, and I sway next to her. Dan turns from the front to grin at the pair of us, and I want to lean forward and plant a kiss on his firm lips. The soft brush across my lips he gave me after we shared a bed has been playing over and over ever since we got back, though I have no idea what's going on in his head. *Maybe tonight, Liss.*

"I don't want to have to rescue you girls this evening," Brian says from the driver's seat. "So don't go overboard."

I wink at Dan, and he grins back, before turning to face the road again, slapping his hand on the roof and opening his mouth for the chorus. *Not bad.*

With a glance at Brian, he nudges his arm and Brian groans, but belts out the words too, tapping the wheel with his fingers. And I carry on swaying from side to side, grinning. A hard day's work and close friends—is there anything better?

When we arrive, the bar is full of local people, military guys, and aid workers. Five men are huddled around a pool table in one corner, and one of them catches my eye as I soak in the chatter and laughter. With a nudge to his friend, he glances over, and I grin to myself and look away. Tonight is going to be entertaining—lots of men to flirt and have fun with—maybe that will get some reaction from Dan. His broad shoulders and tumbling blond curls are like a wall in front of me as he heads to the counter with Brian, and a shiver runs down my spine. *I want to have fun with him.* Emma bounces forward and waves her hand in my face.

"Jukebox!" she squeaks, pointing over the floor and heading away. A guy detaches himself from the crowd and moves toward her, and I laugh. Tonight is going to be crazy. As I reach the bar, Brian peers at Emma and rolls his eyes, then points his finger in my face.

"No trouble," he warns. "Or this one here will be bailing you out." He jerks his thumb at Dan.

I grin at Dan and raise my eyebrows at him, and he laughs.

An hour later and I'm leaning against the side of the pool table surrounded by the five men I clocked earlier. After we'd been at the bar for fifteen minutes, Dan disappeared, and they came over and dragged me off, protesting.

"Woohoo, darlin'!" one of the guys shouts as I hit a ball.

They're all standing too close, slurring their words and being a little handsy, so I've kept moving round the table. The one who eyed me up has laid claim to me by leaning down and coaching me through each shot every time I line up the cue.

Glancing around, I spot a head of blond curls. Dan's seated at the other side of the room talking to a woman with bleached hair and curling red lips. My stomach sinks. He's chatting up someone *else*? A sharp pain stabs through my chest. After sharing a bed with him, I thought things were good, but maybe, like a lot of guys, he just wants sex. *And I did go off and play pool with five other guys.* I stare at the green baize of the table. Honestly? I think I'd be down for whatever he was offering.

Emma and Brian have disappeared. The pool table guys are whispering and looking at me. *Damn.* I make my last shot into the pocket, which gets me raucous cheers, and I wave at them cheerfully before heading back to the bar. Sweat trickles down my spine. What am I *doing*? Tequila. That's what I need. Two arms land on the counter on either side of me, and a body presses into me from behind.

"I'll buy you a drink, darlin'." Ugh. My friend from the pool table.

He nibbles my ear. An hour in and I'm already in trouble. *Why, Liss, why?* How am I going to extract myself from this one? When I turn around, his face is inches away as he grins a drunken grin at me. I lean into his ear, and he bends toward me.

"I'm a transvestite," I say quietly. "You okay with that?"

With a start, he rocks back, eyes like saucers, and scans down my body. I place my hand on his chest, digging in my fingers and purring at him, "I like to be honest and upfront, so you know what to expect."

He nods, licking his lips as his eyes flick sideways. Then gestures behind him at the pool table.

"I'd better go and …"

He lurches off, and I turn back around, hot with relief. My eye catches Dan's blond head again still dipped down to talk to his lady. *Don't stare.* The bottles are lined up along a shelf on the back wall of the bar, and I purse my lips and gesture at the bartender for a tequila shot. If Dan's picking up another woman tonight, then I'm getting wasted. I knock back the alcohol and slide onto a vacant stool. *You should have kissed him back, Liss.* Gesturing at the barman again, I tap my foot against the wooden counter.

Without warning, Dan appears at my side and leans over the battered counter, raising his hand and asking for a beer and a tequila. *One for the lady.* Ugh.

"What happened to your fan club?" he asks, tipping his head toward the pool table, and when I turn to look at him, he seems as open and friendly as normal. The words have no sting in them, nothing to indicate he's jealous. Maybe he flirts with everyone he meets. *Like me.* And my first impressions of him come roaring back. He's good-looking and charming; he probably sleeps with all the women he can. *Like Nick.* Ugh. I've only myself to blame. This is a game I started. I flirted with Dan the first morning I met him.

Shaking my head, I say, "I think I've managed to put them off. Nice lady?" My question is way more loaded than his. I'm failing to be cool.

Nodding, he turns to face the bar and studies the bottles behind it. Then he leans sideways toward me and says quietly, "I don't play games, Liss."

I examine the side of his face.

"I don't really flirt or expect a woman I'm with to flirt with other guys either."

"Okaayy," I say, drawing out the word. *What was all the flirting he did with me, then?* And is he saying he's *with* me?

A long breath seeps out and he laughs, shaking his head. "I'm sorry, maybe I've read you all wrong." He shrugs. "Perhaps I'm totally out of line here."

With a sigh, he picks up his beer and turns to leave. I grab onto his arm.

"What do you mean, read me all wrong?"

Heated eyes roam mine for a couple of seconds. "Are you interested in me, Liss?" he says.

My eyebrows rise. Isn't it obvious? But alcohol is steaming through my blood, so I grin up at him. "Possibly," I say, but he shakes his head.

"I said I don't play games."

My stomach sinks, and I swallow, pulling up my courage. "Are you interested in *me*?"

He frowns. "Liss." My name is a hard reprimand on his lips. "Answer the question."

I let out a long sigh. "Of course, I'm interested. Who wouldn't be? Look at you," I grump, gesturing down his body and turning away on my stool to face the bar again.

His drink lands on the polished wood beside me, and he moves in behind me, hands resting on both sides of me, one next to where my hand is cradling my empty shot glass. The tequila he ordered is still on the counter: Why didn't he take it with him?

Pressing in, he nuzzles my ear. "See, that wasn't so difficult, was it?"

"It wasn't much fun either." My voice is sulky, but my body is shivering with his hot breath on my neck and his warm chest pressed into my back.

"Watching you flirt with a whole bunch of guys wasn't much fun for me."

Oh.

Oh.

Oh.

I melt into him and find he's hard at my hip. *Oh my God.* "Why didn't you say something?"

"Are you going to behave? Give me the right to rein you in?" Pain radiates out as he nips at my ear.

How well he's read me already. I roll my lips together and nod.

"That fucker touched you," he growls. Am I bad for being utterly thrilled by how possessive that statement is? Teeth graze the skin on my shoulder. "Do you know how difficult it was to witness that and not wade in?"

Licking my lips, I turn my head to find his mouth inches from mine.

"I'm very pleased you're touching me now."

He groans and kisses my neck below my ear, trailing downward. "You smell so fucking good."

"What about your lady and her drink?" I nod at the tequila.

"That's for you."

"*What?*"

Easing back, he moves around to lean against the bar again and cold washes over my back.

"She works for an NGO here. Brian introduced us. I was arranging to go on a day trip with her out to one of the villages."

Oh, God. Busted.

"And you say you don't play games?" I say, looking at him sideways.

"At no point did I flirt with her," he says with a frown, reaching out and running a hand down my back to my butt like he's claiming me. Blue eyes narrow on mine, and I stare at his pulse thumping in his neck, the firm line of his lips. *What were we talking about?*

"You flirted with me," I say.

He grins. "Why might that be, I wonder?"

I'm melting like that chocolate cake he likes so much. I move my bar seat around, widening my legs and pulling him toward me. A deep rumble vibrates in his chest. "Careful," he says, "or I'll throw you over my shoulder and fuck you in the alleyway."

Laughter bubbles up as my ribs expand, and I lean forward smiling. "Please," I say, perhaps to be outrageous, but I'd also be down with him carrying me outside to do just that.

He laughs and runs a hand down his face. "You're a bad girl."

"I'm really not," I say, but he grins down at me and takes a strand of my curls and winds it around his finger, shaking his head.

"How come no guy has tied you down in New York and tamed you?"

Tamed me? "A few have tried ..." I say honestly. "But I'm not sure I'm up for a lot of taming. My dad's a control freak, and I don't respond well to men telling me what to do."

"No kidding. They must have been doing it wrong," he winks, grinning. "Are you this much of a firecracker in bed?"

Tongue in cheek, I say, "Absolutely. Boom." I make a big explosion motion with my hands, and he laughs again, leaning in to kiss my neck before pulling back and looking over my shoulder.

"Do we have to be careful about Brian?"

Tightening my hand on his side, I shrug and say, "Not sure, but he'll tell us if he's not happy. He's pretty straight."

Dan shifts away, adjusting himself with a shake of his head as Emma suddenly materializes behind him.

"Someone's pestering me," she says, and he turns, eyes scanning the room.

"Who?"

Emma blinks up at him, a smile curling over her lips. "It's fine," she says, squeezing his arm with a giggle. "No fighting over my honor. He won't pester me with you here." Her hand lingers on his forearm.

The urge to roll my eyes is almost irresistible. Didn't she just see him kiss my neck?

Henry appears next to her. "Shots anyone?" he says, with a wide smile.

*

When we arrive back at the house hours later, Dan falls out of the front seat nearly hitting the dirt, and Emma doesn't fare much better. Henry weaves his way unsteadily toward the door. How did Brian drive? I collapse down onto the sofa on the veranda as Henry lurches through the beaded curtain, closely followed by Dan. Then Dan reappears with a bottle of tequila in one hand and shot glasses in another.

"Henry's passed out on a bed," he says.

Brian flaps a hand at him. "Is he okay?"

"Yeah. He's fine. Can't stand, though." Dan laughs as he stands waving the glasses around. "Anyone for tequila?"

"Just one drink!" Brian protests, but Dan dumps the booze down on the low table and pulls a pack of cards out of his pocket with a flourish.

"Poker!" he says, and I groan. How am I going to focus on a game?

And we keep playing it all wrong, getting drunker and drunker as one round turns into three. Or is it four?

Emma leans into Dan as he deals, and after a couple more hands, she shifts to sit on his knee, putting her head on his shoulder. Dan's eyes meet mine with a rueful smile. *Shit.* But eventually, she slides sideways and lies down on the grubby sofa, closing her eyes. Brian moves over to her and takes her pulse, examining her face.

"I'll take her inside," he says and picks her up and carries her off to our dorm, mumbling that he is going to bed as well.

Dan smiles and crooks his finger. When I lurch upward, he hooks his hand into the waistband of my shorts and pulls me onto his lap. I rub a thumb over his lips, trailing my palm over his jaw and down his neck, rough under my fingers.

"Are you growing a beard?"

Laughing, he says, "Shaving is a pain in the ass out here. Do you like it?"

"I like all of it," I whisper, because the tequila has loosened my tongue.

He runs his hand down his face. "I've drunk too much."

"Me too. Obviously."

He slides his hand into my curls and pulls me down to him, lips feathering across my mine, tongue reaching out briefly. The taste of warm alcohol lingers on his lips, and he smells like hops.

"I've been wanting to do that all night," he murmurs, as I chase his mouth, his hand running down my thigh from my hip to squeeze my knee. Then he shifts back on the sofa pulling me sideways and down as he stretches out on his back. I curl in beside him, my hand on his chest as I stare at the out-of-focus stubble on his chin and his face swims in and out.

"Fuck, I'm drunk," he says.

*

My eyes blink open again to birdsong and a cool dampness to my clothes. The sun is starting to lighten the sky, not yet high enough to warm the air. Pushing up, I shiver and move my head gingerly, blinking blearily as Dan groans next to me.

"Did we just fall asleep on the sofa?" he says, sitting up and rubbing his arms. "Fuck, it's freezing. Let me go and find a blanket."

"Let's go inside, it's too cold out here."

When he pulls me through the kitchen into the boys' dorm, Brian and Henry are stretched out snoring on two of the beds.

And he clearly glimpses something in my face because he shakes his head. "They're not going to wake up. Both of them are out cold."

He tugs me down onto the bed which must be his, grabs a sheet, and throws it over us, curling around and pressing his erection into me.

His eyes drift shut and he yawns. "Couple more hours' sleep, yeah? Sorry about the morning wood."

Smiling, I close my eyes. With the heat of his broad chest behind me and the heavy weight of his arm, my thoughts float and the next thing I know is that I'm far too hot. A noise like someone is rattling pots in the kitchen drifts through the walls. Dan is a furnace at my back, and still hard, but as I peer over at the other beds, Brian's and Henry's bunks are empty. Dan's breath tickles my nape and the faint whiff of coffee and the sound of somebody whistling reaches my ears.

I snuggle back, enjoying the peace and being held by a large male body, and he groans in my ear. A giggle slips free, and I wiggle my hips against him. Lifting his head, he peers across the room.

"Morning," he murmurs, hoarse and thick as he kisses my neck and his fingers slide up and slip under the edge of my top to my breast.

"You feel amazing," he whispers, his work-rough hand stealing my breath.

"Shhh," I gasp, laughing as he presses his length into me, huffing quietly.

"I was never any good at keeping quiet," he mumbles, and this makes me laugh even more.

A voice drifts through and the beads of the outside curtain jangle. The whistling fades away, and a few seconds later a car engine starts up.

Dan's fingers brush over my nipple as he nibbles the back of my neck. "I think Brian's taking Henry to meet this witch doctor guy."

"He's *not* a witch doctor."

"Whatever, I don't care right now." Teeth scrape across my skin. "They're out of here. You wanna come?" he murmurs.

Sliding a hand up and over my head, I play with the soft curls of his hair as he kisses my shoulder.

"Yes, please," I exhale on a silent breath. Emma will still be in our dorm, but I can be quiet.

I reach behind me to find his cock, but he bites my ear.

"Let me do this before you touch me," he whispers. "I'm too turned on. If you touch me, I won't be able to wait for you."

His hand trails down my stomach as I unzip my shorts and wriggle them loose. Long fingers trace the edge of my panties and slide them down, brushing my folds and delving into my slick heat. A shudder rolls through him.

“I want this all over my face,” he mumbles as he parts me, and tingles run through my pelvis from the firm pressure of his fingers as I widen my legs to give him better access. With a practiced ease, he slides a teasing finger down and inside me, his thumb flicking over my nub and making me shiver. I squirm against him, and he tips forward, pinning me to the bed, thumb still moving underneath me right where I want it as I gasp into the rough cotton of the sheet.

“Stop wriggling, woman,” he growls, pushing his hips downward. “Oh God, this is so hot.” And he sinks his teeth into my shoulder.

The pressure of him behind me and the swirl of his fingers make the tingles morph into a warning tightness that builds far too fast. He rubs his erection against my ass, so I push my legs outward, but he stills me with a hand on my hip, reaching over the side of the bed, his heavy length pressing into my butt as he roots around in a bag on the floor. A kiss feathers across my hair, lips at my ear. “Condom,” he whispers. “Is that okay?”

All my words are stuck in my throat, so I nod, mute. He puts the wrapper between my teeth, and I bite down as he tears it. Lifting back, he drags my shorts and panties down over my ass to the tops of my thighs as his hands move, rolling the latex down.

“Fucking hell,” he mumbles into my ear, warm hand spanning my butt cheek, squeezing. And before I know it, the hot hard length of him is pressing in. “Are you sure this is okay?” he whispers.

“More than okay,” I manage to wheeze out.

“Good.”

With a tilt of his hips, he pushes forward, probing. But I can’t widen my legs, I’m held by his weight and hobbled by my shorts. He grips himself in his hand and explores with his fingers, and then settles into my entrance with a sharp stretch. A gasp bursts free, and he clamps a hand over my mouth.

“No noise,” he breathes on my ear. “Fuck, Liss, you’re so *wet*. You like being held down like this?” he murmurs, easing into me inch by inch, his breath coming in ragged gusts across my shoulder.

When he’s seated right in, his chest vibrates against my back in a long silent groan. I'm half crushed under him, and I'm not sure whether the difficulty I'm having breathing is because of his weight or this ridiculous heat that's burning through me.

"You rippled around me all the way in. Fuck." He nuzzles my neck. "How come you're so wet?"

I shake my head, drooling into the mattress. The stretch of his cock, along with his fingers playing softly with me, makes prickles run from my toes to my scalp.

"Oh, yeah," he whispers. "You're close." And he shifts his hips back and thrusts back inside, soft curls tickling against my backside. "So good, Liss."

All his whispered entreaties and I'm on the verge of shattering. After all the wondering about whether he likes me enough, I can't believe I'm pinned under him, how right it feels.

The bed squeaks ominously, and I groan behind his fingers as an amused breath huffs over my cheek.

"Do you like having to keep quiet?" he murmurs.

"Dan," I lick his hand, and he groans.

"I'm there, Liss ... Oh Jesus."

Hips falter as he grinds into me, and his thumb on my clit takes on a desperate, uncoordinated edge.

"I can't ... I ..." he says.

And the shivers that have been running up and down my body coalesce into a white heat that explodes right between my legs and behind my eyes as I tighten around his length, pulses moving out from my core and making my knees jerk.

He thrusts and grunts in my ear. "Oh fuck, oh fuck," he mumbles and his cock jerks inside me as he comes.

CHAPTER 12

Liss

Saturday, April 20, 2019

As the weeks burn into months, we finish the build with a village party. There are lots of giggling children trying out the new toilets and learning the importance of soap and handwashing, and discussions start on helping another community. Dan regularly disappears off to other towns and villages nearby, and Brian is happy for me to go with him sometimes. The opportunity to travel and meet more local people lifts my heart. And Dan writes feverishly late into the evening as I read over his shoulder about the causes of war and long-held resentments passed down through generations.

Dan and I settle into an easy camaraderie, living in a bubble of denial like there's no time limit to this, with my head on his shoulder and his slender fingers woven through mine. The opportunities for anything more are limited, apart from Dan occasionally trapping me against the wall in the house or a hut in the bush when no one's around and kissing me senseless. Sometimes we find a few quiet hours where we escape to a single mattress, where he pins me down and sets my skin on fire.

Dan seems so self-contained. He doesn't talk much about his life outside of Congo, and perhaps he wants to forget about it for now. And God do I have some sympathy with that. I have no desire to talk about my shitty upbringing or what happened before I came out here.

April arrives in a flurry of thunderstorms, and one rainy Saturday morning Dan and I grab a ride into town so he can spend the day talking to people, arranging trips, and negotiating transport. I sink down into a seat in the local café and pull out my laptop, clicking to join the Wi-Fi. This is the only place that provides it here—at a cost. My gut churns as I log into my bank account. Drinks, my mobile contract, toiletries, occasional food purchases: Even though I'm careful, it all adds up. *I have not been keeping track of this.* And sure enough, only a couple of hundred dollars are left on the bottom line. *Shit, not even enough to buy a ticket home.* I'm going to have to go overdrawn. I've never done that before.

I gaze out of the dirty windows at the brown earth of the main street. *How can I leave him?* But Jesus, I've got to go back and earn some cash, probably in the next few days. Why was I ignoring it, hoping it would go away? That's an epic money management strategy right there. Rolling my eyes at myself, I examine my watch. It's a precious day off, and Dan is coming to meet me for lunch. I let out a gusty sigh, and the café owner, Jafari, glances over at me with a full, guileless smile.

"Miss Liss! You are not happy today, I think?"

People like Jafari run these amazing places that provide everything in the small towns here. Food, booze, coffee, internet, cash transfer, a poker game, a live chicken: You name it, they do it. So much entrepreneurship, looking after their customers, and particularly the Westerners who, he's well aware, have more to spend.

I shrug at him. "My money is running out, Jafari." And he makes a face, nodding as he shifts from behind his counter and slides into the seat opposite me. Any excuse for a sit-down and a chat.

"This is the problem all over the world, I think. The thing everyone struggles with." He smiles. "No one has enough money."

And here I am, sitting among all this poverty when I have the option to jump on a plane and head home, sign up for a job, and make more than he's probably seen in his entire life. Somehow, I want to give him all my money, and see what the entrepreneurial Jafari could do with an injection of cash. I want to help the people who have no clean water or schooling, but I also want to assist people like Jafari too, the enterprising ones who, with the input of a few hundred dollars, could expand their business and do so much more. *Why does my father think I'm wasting my time here?*

"The balance in my bank account won't cover my ticket home. I'm sorry to be a whining Westerner," I say, and his eyes widen.

"Miss Liss, we all have our money problems! Whether it's a fifty-dollar loan I make to someone or your ticket, it still stops you from doing what you must do. This is why I lend. People think I'm a loan shark, and yes, I am, but I also want to help." He cocks his head at me. "You, too, are a helper I think. People have to realize their dreams."

Patting my arm, he says, "If you need to buy a plane ticket, I can give you an advance." White teeth beam at me, and I laugh—ever the businessman. The interest rates on his loans are astronomical, way more than a Western bank, but they are better than most of his competitors in town.

"What's this snake lending you money for?" Dan's voice brings my head up, and my stomach flip-flops as I latch on to slim hips in khaki shorts and a biscuit-colored shirt that makes his tanned skin look edible. He runs a hand across his stubble, a lazy grin curling over his mouth as his other hand lands on Jafari's shoulder with a squeeze.

Jafari twists his head to look up at him. "Miss Liss can't afford her ticket home. I was offering to lend her a hand. But I am not offended you call me a snake: Here in Africa, they are revered!"

And he waves his hands so dramatically that Dan laughs, but I shrivel inside. I've had no time to prepare what I was going to say to him or think about how soon I might have to go.

Jafari rises from his seat. "I give my place up for the better man." He winks at me, strolling off to help someone who's appeared at his serving counter. Dan eases into the chair, frowning.

"What's this about a ticket home?" He cocks his head.

"I've got to go home, Dan," I say, ripping off the plaster as I wave at my screen. "I haven't been keeping an eye on my bank account and now I don't have enough for my flight. In fact, I'll have to borrow money to get back." My embarrassment at my lack of funds is deeply ingrained—it's like that when you're from a family that thinks that what you earn is everything.

"You can live off me for a while, yeah?" Warm eyes roam my face, and the hope in them makes me blink at him. Does he mean it? God, what a generous offer. But … *I can't do that … can I?*

"Living off guys is a bit of a problem for me," I say, as a shiver runs down my spine. "My father held money over me for years."

Dan pulls a face like he gets it but doesn't like it. "Not sure I'm ready for you to go home yet, Liss," he rumbles, sliding his fingers over the table to trap mine as he stares off out of the window. My stomach starts up like a washing machine. "Not sure I'll ever be ready."

Oh God. My hands shake. We haven't talked about how we feel, what this is. He's kept his counsel, and I've … done what I always do: *I've been cool.* But I like him, I more than like him. Being with him is amazing and … *damn it.* I am in too deep.

"Not sure I'll ever want to leave," I burst out.

Something shifts in his gaze like he's thinking something through. "Then don't. Come back to Zimbabwe with me when I've finished my thesis."

Oh, wow. Could I quit my wanderlust life and do that?

CHAPTER 13

Liss

Saturday, May 4, 2019

Two weeks later I'm at the airport, my throat on fire with everything I'm holding back. My battered backpack seems out of place on the conveyor belt as the lady efficiently organizes my seat and tags my bag. Dan stands stoically at my side staring off into the distance, blood thrumming in the vein at the base of his neck. *I'd give anything to know what he's thinking.* Grabbing my boarding pass, I incline my head, and in minutes we are heading away from the desk and toward security, my heart thumping like a piledriver as the tickets-only section draws near.

Dan's been noncommittal since I told him I needed to go, the early easiness of our interactions morphing into detachment, and I've started to loathe this decision, to hate myself. *Why do I need to do this exactly?* I *could* go to Zimbabwe with him, after all. My head shrieks at me that I'd be dependent on him in a foreign country, trapped, and at the very least I have to have my own money. My heart screams back that I'm risking the best relationship I've ever had.

As we head across the marble floor, his hand finds mine, fingers weaving through, and I squeeze his palm.

"God, this is awful," I say. "Like the shittiest decision I've made in my entire life."

With a reciprocal press of my hand, he says, "We'll survive it, Liss."

And my breath stalls as I gaze up at him. *What does that mean?* Is it a comment about us getting through this, or is he implying we'll recover on our own separately? Where is my relationship radar? I mess up every one I have, and by God this feels like a mess to me.

When we reach the barriers, he turns, pulling me to the side and into his body, arms wrapped all the way around me. He hasn't done this much in the last two weeks, and an ache starts deep inside me.

"I'm sorry I've been distant," he mumbles into my hair. "I've found it very hard to be okay with this decision, but I understand."

Words rush up my throat and spill out. "Have I fucked this up? Forgive me, I …"

He shakes his head. "I know you need to go."

Pulling back, I say, "This is real, right? You feel it too?" And I am out on a limb now, I've never taken a risk like this.

And my stomach is like a hive of bees as he stares off to the side, mouth tight. But when he cups my face in his hands and his eyes come back to mine, I'm shocked to see they're bright with tears.

"Of course, Liss, Jesus. All we've done these four months? You don't even have to ask. It's been the best time of my life."

Tears spill over and down my cheeks. "I'm so sorry I'm going."

"Promise me you'll come back."

I nod. "I promise. Nothing will get in the way of this. Once I've got some money, I'll come back, and we'll work out what we're going to do."

"Or I'll come to you, whatever works."

"Whatever works."

He squeezes me tighter, groaning. "I can't let you go."

Laughing, I slide my hands into his back pockets. "Me neither."

With a shaky exhale, his lips find mine and I open my mouth under his, heart beating like it wants to explode out of my chest. Warm palms cradle my face, then he steps back abruptly, eyes still wet, as he jerks his hand through his hair.

"You'd better go. I don't want to make you miss your plane."

I nod, picking up my backpack that's slipped to our feet. The hum of the airport returns, the banging of trays in security, the murmur of voices.

"See you, Liss," he says, eyes bright on mine, deep grooves bracketing his mouth, and I think I will remember the look of pain in his eyes for the rest of my life. He turns abruptly with a flap of his hand and strides away. My lips part as I stare at his retreating back. *But, God, I understand.* Tears blur his outline, and my last glimpse is his shoulder and blond head before he's enveloped by the crowd.

"I love you, Dan," I whisper, too scared to say it to his face. The urge to chase after him and tell him is overwhelming, but I turn toward the lines of people, wading through molasses as I'm swallowed by the system that flings us far away from the ones we love.

CHAPTER 14

Liss

Monday, May 6, 2019

Jo's spoon falls into her saucer with a clatter. "Remind me why you came back here again?"

I growl at her, and Kate laughs. But something warm burns in my stomach for the first time since I landed with these two sitting opposite me. It's been a very depressing twenty-four hours back with my parents in New Jersey so far, but at least Kate thinks I can move back into the apartment.

"You finally find a decent guy, spend four months with him, have a tearful farewell where you basically tell each other they're the one …"

"Well, not exactly …"

"Where you basically tell each other they're the one …" Jo repeats loudly over me, garnering some stares from the table next door.

"I've no money, Jo. Nothing to live off. I can't just 'stay out there.'" I make air quotes with my hands as I glower at her.

Kate's eyes flit back and forth between us and then soften on me. "You probably just need to plan it all out, so you have a date for when you're going back," she says, ever the pragmatist.

"She doesn't need to work it all out! She needs to get her ass back on that plane and show him she's committed to making it work. Running away won't find her a decent guy, and some other woman will move in and snap him up!" Jo exclaims. "Like that Emma woman you were telling us about."

"Like you moved in on Janus so fast," I say, as she scowls. "I seem to remember …"

"That was different."

"No, it goddamn wasn't."

"My reputation was at stake. I think you're forgetting …"

Leaning over the table, I open my mouth to tell her why she's just as relationship jumpy as I am, when Kate holds up her hands.

"Guys, come on. Liss has just got back. My job is stressful, and this is my lunch hour. Patients might be dying as we speak."

Jo and I glower at each other. She's got no right to criticize me when she danced around Janus for months. But damn it, Kate's always been an expert at cutting to the chase.

She pats my hand. "You need the security of earning some money and not relying on a man. Totally understandable, but Jo is right: We have to get you back out there asap. How fast do you think you could do it?"

I shrug. "This six-week maternity leave I'm covering is admin work, but they said they might use me to teach some international aid modules for one of their courses since I'm here and available."

"They're going to pay you extra to do some teaching?"

"Possibly."

"That's fantastic, Liss."

"It does sound great," Jo says. "It's amazing they'd add some stuff into a course based around you."

I was thinking this too. My brow furrows. "Yeah, I'm not sure why they're prepared to do that. Maybe it suits them because they don't have to take on a full-time member of staff."

"They've done it because you're smart and talented," Kate says staunchly.

I love that she thinks this, but before I went out to Africa, I'd just finished my master's and I fumbled through every seminar they let me teach.

Jo's head is down as she stirs her coffee, and I curl my fingers into my palms. I shouldn't be grumpy with her. But I can't help feeling hollowed out, like a tornado has ripped through my insides.

When he worked on site, his blond curls used to turn dark with sweat and cling to the back of his neck, and a smile would twist over his lips when I made some joke about him being a weakling. *Why didn't I stay?* Depending on him when we were so new felt so wrong, and I didn't want to set that tone to what we had.

"Sorry," I mumble, eyes prickling. "I didn't want to leave him."

Jo's head lifts, and she reaches out and grabs my hand over the table.

"I'm sorry too. You've had so many awful experiences with men, and I'm so happy you've finally found a good one, I got carried away."

I squeeze her hand. They lived through every one of those bad experiences with me. "I'm glad you and Janus got together."

Kate and I turn to look at Jo when I say this, and Jo examines both of our faces and starts to laugh.

"Look at the pair of you, you're all starry-eyed!"

"Jo, you landed the most eligible guy on the planet," Kate mumbles.

Enough of this sappiness. I slap my hand down on the table. "We need details. I come home, I'm all depressed about Dan, and it's not acceptable that you're not cheering me up by telling me what Janus is like in bed. Every woman in New York has been drooling over him for forever, and you owe us"—I gesture to Kate and myself—"as your best friends who've always had your back, detailed descriptions of what that insanely hot man can do."

Jo is still laughing as she rubs her palms up her face. "Kill me now."

"Oral?" I say.

"Arrggghhhh," Kate groans, as she and Jo try and slap their hands over my mouth simultaneously. A man at the table behind Jo turns around. Raising my eyebrows, I catch Kate's eye and Jo frowns at us, half-turning as I shake my head, starting to giggle.

"Keep your voice down, Liss," Kate grumbles as we all lean forward over the round table between us.

"So?" I whisper.

"Yes, alright," Jo says through clenched teeth, widening her eyes at me meaningfully and Kate grins. "He does that," she adds, and I groan.

"Come *on*. Is he any good?"

The color rises in her face, and Kate giggles again. An unrestrained smile breaks over my face like a wave. These girls. Honestly.

She nods at me, and I growl.

"I'm not giving you details, Liss."

"Okay. I'll ask the questions, and you just answer yes or no."

"I'm not doing that either."

"Does he make you come?" I say with exaggerated slowness. The man behind Jo leans back toward our table.

Jo nods, and I hold up five fingers. "Number of orgasms a night?"

Kate's eyes bug out, and I grin. Some guys set great store on their ability to give orgasms: One guy gave me three once. He turned out to be another asshole in the long line of assholes, but the sex was amazing. *Story of my life … until Dan.* Damn, I'd forgotten how sad I was in the joy of this conversation.

Jo shakes her head.

"No orgasms?" I say with mock horror, and she frowns at me.

"You're a minx."

"Tell me or I'm going to text him right now," I threaten, snatching her phone from where it's resting on the table in front of her. *She should never have given me her PIN number.*

She tries to snatch it back, but I hold it way up over my head, and she gives an exaggerated sigh.

"Okay. Okay. It varies."

"Between what and what?"

Pursing her lips, she leans forward to whisper, "One and four."

"*Four?*" Kate squeaks.

That's impressive. Points for the boy. The guy behind Jo has turned around, so I wink at him, and he blushes before turning back to the other man at his table.

Jo laughs and waggles her hands at us. "Magic tech fingers."

"Why do I feel like I'm missing out?" I say.

"*You're* missing out?" Kate says with a deep frown. "You've just had a hot summer fling in Africa. What about me?"

"Miss Missionary Position."

I grin, and she snorts. Kate's always been relaxed about the fact she likes straightforward intercourse. She says she doesn't want to have to think about an orgasm, and that it should be as unchallenging as possible. I think she hasn't had sex with the right guy yet.

"There's always Fabian," Jo says with a sly smile.

"Moving on!" Kate says pointedly. *Interesting.* Just as I open my mouth to ask more, she says:

"Tell us about Dan. How many orgasms did he give you?"

Definitely deflecting.

But I can still feel the heat of him pressing into my back. "It was always so difficult! The accommodation was arranged in dorms, so we were always hurried." Jo's lips turn down. "He had a thing for pinning me down, though."

Kate blinks. "Really? Did you like that?"

I grin at her interest. So unlike her. "Seriously hot being pinned by a big guy like him." I hold my hands up. "No lie, I'm surprised how much I liked it. You know me, Ms. Independent; it's not likely I'd be into that."

"It's the right guy," Jo mumbles.

"What?"

"When you're with the right guy, he could do anything to you, and you'd love it." She clears her throat. "It's being with the *right guy*."

CHAPTER 15

Liss

Tuesday, June 4, 2019

I never imagined I'd hate a sultry June in Manhattan, but a month in and every day is like climbing a mountain. Even the few lectures I've got at the university are dragging. Getting on my bike, weaving through traffic. I sigh and grab my phone from the nightstand and glare at it. Nothing from Dan in the last twenty-four hours. Cool your ass, girl, he'll be out in the bush and out of coverage. It happened all the time when I was out there.

The sound of the apartment buzzer goes, and I peer at the clock. Who's buzzing at 7 a.m.? And, goddammit, Kate will have gone to work already. Staggering to the door, I blink blearily at the camera on the intercom. *What the hell?* I rub my eyes. A head of tousled blond hair fills the viewfinder. *Dan?* He straightens up, and I can't hold back my gasp.

It's him.

It's him. It's him.

Oh my God! I flap my hands and press my knuckles to my mouth. His head turns toward the street and then he peers back at the camera with a quirk of his eyebrow, leaning in with a hand on the wall.

"Hello?"

"Dan?" My voice is an incredulous squeak.

A heartbreaking smile breaks over his face, and o*h my God.* I can't believe it. He's here? *He's here.* I bend over to ease the tightness in my chest, to pull some goddamn air into my lungs before straightening up to the intercom. "What the hell are you doing here?"

He laughs. "Had to come after my girl," he says, and my hand flutters up to my throat. *Be still my crazy beating heart.* I press the buzzer and his familiar curls disappear from view as the door clicks. Shit, he doesn't know what floor I'm on.

Wrenching the door open, I fly out of the apartment, barefoot, and I'm in the concrete stairwell in seconds. It's only three floors down. I can catch him.

When I burst through doors into the brown wood of the lobby, he's examining our mailboxes with a frown, and I laugh as he straightens and turns. In an instant, I am across the old tiles and flinging myself on him. He lifts me up and swings me around, hands sliding under my ass as my legs circle his waist. The smallest movement and his lips are on mine. And oh! Heat and warmth and stubble and …

He pulls back, and I bury my head in his neck.

"Damn, woman, that's a welcome. What floor?"

"Third," I say, tilting back to beam at him. He came to Manhattan. For me. *My God*, no one has done anything like this. I take his face in my hands, kissing his cheeks, his forehead, his nose.

"I can't believe you're here!"

He chuckles as he presses the button for the elevator and brushes his mouth over my lips, tongue reaching out to tangle gently with mine, licking along my lips. When it dings, he shuffles us inside, leaning around me to press the button behind my back as I kiss his throat, his hard length is pressing into me right where I want it. So I shift my hips against him, and a groan rumbles in his chest.

"Goddamn, woman, let me get us somewhere decent."

But I laugh, still moving, and his grip only tightens on my butt as I nip his neck, trailing my lips up to his ear.

"You feel amazing," I whisper, wriggling and giggling, and his fingers dig in to the point of pain.

The elevator shudders to a grinding stop, and he steps out into the hallway as I incline my head to the right. The apartment door is still ajar from my crazy race down the stairs, and he kicks it wider, stepping into our open-plan lounge.

"Left. Second door," I gasp as he strides down the corridor, shouldering through my bedroom door and tossing me onto the bed.

Big hands land on my stomach and peel my pajama pants down, leaving me naked from the waist down. And he's a vision standing here staring down at me, his khaki shorts and his sleeves rolled up like he just stepped out of the African bush. The hard outline of him beneath the fabric. He scans the room.

"Nice apartment. I'm looking forward to laying waste to you on a proper bed at last."

He grabs the bottom of his shirt and wrenches it over his head. The smattering of blond on his chest and the trail of hair down his stomach are dappled in the light seeping around the blinds. *I want. I want. I want.* His hands go to the buttons on his shorts.

"I want to do that," I say.

"Come and undress me then," he says, stilling.

So I push myself up, walking across the covers on my knees, breathing quietly as I kneel in front of him and examine his muscly arms, tight shoulders, and perfect nipples. Memories bloom of watching him lift wood and bags of cement on the build, sweat running down his torso, wanting to follow the trails of water with my tongue. *Maybe I spent the last five months in a sexual haze.*

Bending down, I press my lips once against his happy trail where his shorts have slipped down, feeling the hitch in his breath through his tightening stomach. His eyes track me everywhere. And I don't want to touch him with my hands; I want to worship him another way. I straighten to kiss him, but veer off at the final second to his shoulder, working my way across his collarbone with my lips, around the base of his neck to the other side. His hands hang loose at his sides like he's enjoying the show, chest rising and falling, not touching, the tension building in his body like a spring about to explode. My breath comes out on a huff—he often surprised me when he pinned me down.

He touches my throat lightly with his finger, trailing it down my throat to the hollow between my breasts, pushing down my sleep shirt, his knuckle grazing the curve.

"So, fucking hot," he says, voice hoarse, his stare a laser down the front of my top.

The finger moves from my neckline across the checked fabric to my nipple, flicking upward, making a zing of heat run down to my sex. *So sensitive.*

"I'm feeling a little crazy right now," he admits on a groan.

I laugh-gasp at this, already wet and aching.

"I want my hand between your legs, followed by my mouth; but really I just want to"—he sucks in a long breath—"think about doing all of that to you first."

The way he talks about sex before and during, the way he talks about me, my body, is a revelation. I sink my teeth into his pec below his shoulder, and he growls, properly this time, like a dog, so I bite harder. Give me some action. *Surprise me, Dan.*

"Fuck!" He says, not moving.

Crawling my hand up and under his shorts, I tease the rough hairs on the outside of his thigh, then slide around to the inside. This isn't easy. His shorts fit him too well, and his thighs are strong and muscly, but my fingers eventually find their way up, grazing the hot skin between his legs. When my thumb rubs back and forth, he grinds his teeth.

Why is he standing still? I trail my other hand down over his buttock in a soft caress. Biting my lip, I lift my hand up and bring it down with a hard crack. His hips jerk forward as he grabs my waist, and I shriek as he spins me and pins me down on my front in the bed, one hand twisted behind my back, his other hand spanning my bare ass cheek, squeezing painfully.

"Do you want to play rough, Liss?" he says, breath hot on my ear, using his size to keep me pinned down, knees straddling my pelvis. The heat of his erection presses into my ass right next to his hand. *Holy shit.* I move my hips to ease the ache, slippery at the top of my thighs.

"Please," I choke out.

This gets me a sharp nip on my earlobe. "Are you begging, Liss?"

His mouth trails down my neck and around until his teeth are at my nape, biting in, his weight pushing me farther into the sheets. I'm reminded of lions mating, how they hold on to the female from behind. Fire races through my blood, and a moan slips out as he shifts against my buttocks, pressing his cock into me.

"Answer the question."

"I want you to ..."

"Liss." His voice is a stern reprimand.

"I want you inside me," I gasp, desperately dragging in air as he crushes me.

He chuckles. "You're going to have to wait. You dished something out, and you need to accept the consequences."

His big hand squeezes my ass, and in my mind's eye I imagine his long fingers, the short nails, the tension in his grip. Despite the bruising throb of it, his thumb is absent-mindedly brushing the crease at the top of my thigh, and every time he comes close, I tighten up inside—the burning hold mirroring the building ache radiating down my legs.

Nuzzling into my neck, he says, "I want to tie you up." Is there a question in that statement? The sheets blur, words stick in my throat.

He rubs his cock against me as he moves, hand releasing my ass, and I've just time to register the hot relief of it when he brings it down with a slap then massages the sting while the pain spreads. In a flurry, he's up and off me, throwing open drawers in my dresser and rummaging as I turn my head. A pair of black tights emerges from the back of the drawer, and he holds them up triumphantly, making me laugh. And they must be the only ones I have because those torture garments disappeared from my wardrobe a long time ago. Climbing back over me, he grabs my wrists and ties them above my tailbone, fingers trailing along the crease of my ass.

"Lovely," he says.

Another slap, this time with real force. And a sharp cry tumbles out, my mouth falling open against the soft cotton sheets. *He's never done this to me before.* All we had was a furtive and stolen sex life and this is … this is…

I'm pulled up to kneeling by my tied wrists, while Dan snugs up tight behind me, knees on either side of mine as he trails his fingers over the front of my shirt. There's an indent in the bed where I was face down, and his rough hands rest on my stomach, a pink tinge from red earth still obvious in his nails and cracked skin. He starts to unbutton my shirt from the bottom, stroking over every inch of my ribs that he bares. My head goes back, drooling, and he rubs himself unashamedly against me.

"*Oh God, Liss.* This is so fucking hot." Lips and breath dance across my shoulder, trailing goosebumps in their wake.

"I need my skin against yours," he mumbles, shuffling off the bed, and I turn my head as he shucks off his shorts and boxers. His cock is perfect—tight, swollen, leaking precome at the tip—and I swallow as I gawk at him, his eyes snagging mine in a sear of molten blue.

"You want this?" he grunts, gripping his length and jacking himself twice, exhaling on something that sounds like relief. *No such luck for me.*

"Touch me," I say, voice shaky as my throat tightens. I *never* beg guys.

This gets me a smirk. "More begging, Liss? You need to be a little patient."

Whatever. I stick my tongue out as the only line of attack open to me, and he laughs, climbing onto the bed behind me. A whimper leaks out when he presses his bare cock into my ass.

"I love how you think you can abuse me and not pay for it," he says, chin on my shoulder, still trailing his hands over my stomach, rubbing the crease where my abdomen meets the top of my thighs. "Your muscles are so well defined here: I can tell you're a runner just from these."

"Please, Dan."

"What?"

"Touch me."

"I am touching you."

I growl at him, and he chuckles.

"You mean here?"

His thumb rubs over the smooth skin between my legs, and he rests the tips on my folds, not delving in to where I'm hot and wet, so I tilt my hips forward to press into his hand. "Stop teasing me."

He groans. "You're soaked all over here."

"Please, Dan," I whisper, turning my head and kissing his cheek.

Teeth sink into my shoulder. "It's all over my fucking fingers." He brings his hand up to my lips. "Lick it off."

I swirl my tongue and nibble his fingers like I would his dick if he'd let me anywhere near it and hadn't tied me up. Will this make him move faster? *God, I hope so.*

A little choked noise seeps out of his mouth as he shifts behind me. *Excellent.*

"Jesus, Liss, you're going to set the building on fire."

I give a half laugh, half strangled whimper.

"Anyway, you're distracting me. I was busy arranging your shirt." He strokes my stomach and undoes another button. "So fucking sexy."

My breasts ache as his fingers coast up to the bottom of my ribs, rubbing against him as he laughs.

"Has it been a little while, Liss?" His voice drops. "For me too. I've been dreaming about this. About you. But the more impatient you are, the longer I'm going to take."

Fuck. But … *Maybe* … My mouth curls up. "Don't you want my hot wet pussy around your cock? Aren't you thinking about how tight and slick I'll feel when you stretch me?"

Silence. The movement is quick when it happens. My face is in the sheets, and his hand slaps my ass so goddamn hard my eyes water. But God, *I like this.*

"The key to getting what you want here is obedience, sweet girl, not rebellion."

"You like the goading, though," I say, shifting my sore ass against where he's notched in the crease. "I don't do obedience, Dan, you know that."

The laugh he makes is deep like I've said something funny. "You've always obeyed me in bed," he says.

Frowning, I open my mouth to disagree, but … ummm … *my God, he's right*. Every request, every single thing he wanted, I've handed control right over. *Holy crap*. Have I ever done that with a guy before?

He chuckles into my silence. "Don't overthink it, Liss. It's the hottest thing to have a woman who's as strong-willed as you are obey everything I want to do to her."

Okay, then.

Pulling me back up, he undoes another button and strokes down my torso. "Fuck, I love that you're not wearing a bra. I can't wait to play with your nipples." He grunts into my skin. "How wet are you now?"

Rough fingertips find my folds, and when I shift, his other hand grips my stomach to hold me still.

"If you're good, I might touch you here next time," he says, tapping my mound and lifting his fingers, and I moan as he puts them in my mouth, sucking the juices off them. Thoughts about trying to turn him on, about giving him some relief, have gone out the window; I'm so needy.

"I've never been able to take my time with you, Liss. It was a constant struggle walking around the building site, half-hard."

He nuzzles up my neck, kissing my chin, my cheek, my temple. The blood in my body zeros in to where his fingers are brushing the underside of my breasts as he fiddles with one of the last two remaining buttons.

"Can't you do that with your cock inside me?" I gasp.

"We've got hours to play," he says. *Hours?* "Once I'm inside you, it's going to be over far too fast."

Another button pops open, and he runs his finger up and caresses the side of my breast with his knuckle. But he snugs up to my back, his erection nestling securely between my legs, and I'm so wet it must be all over him. *He's not in as much control as he'd like me to think*. Perhaps I can … His cock twitches, and I tighten my thighs as he rubs against me, once, twice.

"You're going to pay for trying to speed things up," he mutters, a large hand settling in the middle of my back, tipping me back into the sheets and bringing his hand down hard on one buttock then the next, over and over. *Holy shit*.

"Stop, stop. Oh my God." Sharp needles of pain radiate outward, but he stops, hand resting on the small of my back.

"You okay?" he asks, nuzzling into me.

"Just wait until I tie you up," I grumble into the bedclothes.

He runs his hand down my ass and pinches me. "You just got more for that little statement. Apologize." His hand comes down on me again.

Fuck, no. I shift, but he grips my hip as my skin burns. Hotter. Tighter. *Goddammit.*

"Sorry," I wheeze, and he grunts in satisfaction.

"Let's find out how wet you are now, Liss, hmmmm?" he says, his fingers trailing from my burning ass to brush my folds, inching toward my clit, and my whole body lights up, legs widening on a gasp.

"Mmm, I think you liked that." The combination of his fingers skating over me and the pain is so sharp, I drool into the bedcovers.

His hand stops moving. "Now where were we before you distracted me? Oh yes, buttons." A smile twists his voice, goddamn him, as he pulls back and moves around to my front. His cheeks are flushed, blond hair in crazy disarray like he's run his hands through it, and I drink in his toned torso and the tensed muscles of his thighs. It's like he's been running, chest heaving, a faint gleam of sweat visible in the dim light. His lips curve up as he meets my gaze, eyes trailing down to the gap in my shirt.

"Even hotter now," he says, and I blink down. My curves are straining against the last remaining button. "I want you to text me a picture like this every day," he says, and I suck in a stinging breath.

The reality of what we are, no longer in the same country, shakes something loose in me. *We haven't talked. Why has he come here and for how long?* A sharp stab pierces my chest and I close my eyes. Without warning, his hand cups my cheek, and I open my eyes to find his, soft and earnest, warm, remorseful, like he understands what he said.

"It's okay, Liss. We just need to work it all out. You know that right?"

He sounds so *sure*. I could fling myself on him. *He wants this as much as I do.* I nod at him as he leans forward and kisses my cheek.

"Don't look so worried. I'm serious, yeah?" His mouth finds mine, and it's probing and gentle in contrast to the manhandling of earlier. I tangle my tongue with his and I want to disappear into the heat and the desire that's waiting just around the corner, but he backs off, nibbling my lips.

"I missed you," I gulp out.

He groans, pulling me into a warm hug. "God, I missed you too. You have no idea."

He pulls back and trails his hands down the front of my shirt, his fingers brushing my nipples. He cups my breasts over the fabric, thumbs skimming over the exposed curves. His face is serious, as he stares down stroking my stomach gently.

"I want to see you pregnant with my children," he says, and my insides drop through the bed and several stories below.

"Oh crap, did I say that out loud?" He closes his eyes like he's in pain. "I did, didn't I?"

I laugh-gasp at him. "Did you mean it?"

"Of course, I meant it," he growls. "I'm crazy about you, Liss, ever since that first day …" He swallows hard. "Those mischievous eyes laughing at me when you tried to talk me into taking off my shirt—I'd never met anyone like you."

I'm so weak I could crumple onto the bed.

Stroking farther down, his fingers brush my sex, and I do collapse forward. My forehead lands on his chest, and he laughs, hand invading my hair to hold me as his long fingers delve in, finding my nub and dancing over it, slipping on wet skin. He groans, pulling my head back as his lips find mine, and his cock presses into my stomach.

"I want to touch you," I moan into his mouth.

He pulls back, laughing. "I'd come in seconds if you did that."

Leaning back, he undoes my last button, and my breasts swing free. He bends his head down to nuzzle my shirt to one side, taking an erect nipple in his teeth. His hand between my thighs moves, exploring, and I push my hips forward.

"How many times are you going to come for me, hmm?" He slides a long finger in deep, and my breath whooshes out as tingles travel down my legs. Hooking into me, he presses upward and finds a spot that makes everything tighten up. *God. Small circular movements.* I gasp, wobbling as I try and find my center, but he's having none of it, his touch is relentless. I want him filling me, the stretch and the pressure.

"Please, Dan, please, I need you inside," I whisper, and he groans into my breast, sinking his teeth in as he plays with my nipple. A beat goes past. One. Two. And a shiver rolls through me.

"Fuck this," he says, and he leans over the bed and snags his shorts, pulling a packet from his pocket and ripping it with his teeth, then rolling the condom down as he squeezes the tip. He swings around behind me, and … *oh God* … the roughness of his legs brushes the inside of my thighs, the softness of his pubic hair and the hardness of his length against my ass before he widens his knees. I tip forward but his hand on my stomach stops me.

"Like this," he mumbles into my shoulder.

"Yes," I gasp.

Cock in hand, his fingers find my entrance and he pushes forward, sliding in my wetness. *Not quite the right angle.* I shimmy my hips but his hand clamps harder on my hip.

"Stay still, woman."

It makes me giggle, and he stills. I turn my head and kiss the side of his.

"I love your cock," I mumble, and now it's his turn to laugh.

"You're filthy."

Then we're giggling like a couple of teenagers as he kisses my hair, hand and erection poised between my legs, pushing a little as my entrance stretches and gives and … *Oh yes.* I groan and he moves from one knee to the other like he can't wait, hand stiff on my stomach and suddenly I want more.

"Hard," I gasp.

"What?" He presses in a little and my muscles flutter. That's so *good.*

"Go in hard."

"Jesus, Liss, don't say things like that …" But he grabs both my hips and pushes in, and I tip forward with the force of it, but he flattens me back against his big body. A long rumble reverberates through him and into me as he presses up tight, buried deep, stretching me, all the way in.

"Oh yeah," he says, rubbing his forehead over my shoulder. "Yes, yes. *Fuck*."

I've no idea what comes over me—perhaps it's that he's clearly losing it too. "Fuck me," I say.

He wraps one arm around my chest and one around my hips and starts to thrust hard, releasing a litany of filthy words that sends heat burning up my legs.

"This wetness … it's all over me, making me really, really slick." He presses his nose into me and rubs it up and down my neck. "Oh God. Oh God. Fuck, Liss. I'm not going to last. You feel fucking amazing. Holy shit, you're so tight. *Jesus, fuck*."

God, I love how verbal he is. Hot breath gusts down my body, his hand snaking down my stomach, holding me for his thrusts, and when those long magic fingers find my nub, my bloodstream is like liquid fire. I give him my weight with a groan. His fingers are erratic all over my wetness, sometimes where I want it and sometimes not, as we drown in a haze of heat and sweat. Tightness climbs from my knees on the bed, to my pelvis, to where his finger's touching me. I widen my legs, wanting more of everything.

"I'm close, Liss. *Oh no. Oh no.* Fuck. I can't … I can't …"

Too much. Too much. This whole teasing build. I start to come, mouth dropping open, a long wail slips up and out. He gasps into my throat as the first shudder rattles through me, and I lurch forward, almost losing his cock, but he thrusts back in fast.

"Oh fuck, you're there. You're tightening *everywhere*. Holy shit. *Oh God. Oh God*. I'm fucking *coming*. Oh Christ."

His cock jerks as we both fall onto the bed, and he climbs me like he can't push in deep enough, burying me into the covers as the hottest groan rasps in my ear. He convulses and shudders over me, tremors bringing goosebumps out on my skin.

"Oh. Oh. Oh."

As he grinds against me, an aftershock rolls through him, making him jerk, sweat sticking his chest to my back, the sheer size of him crushing me down. I want to laugh. I want to cry. I want to lie here forever under him and be unable to breathe.

He turns his head and nuzzles me, panting in my ear, licking and nibbling, rubbing his nose into my throat. *Cats.*

"Jesus, Liss." A hot hand runs down my side as he lifts his weight off me. "You okay?" His hand works at where he tied my hands behind my back, loosening the knot and jerking the tights free.

I smile into the sheets, sucking in a breath. He's still inside me, and I don't want to lose him just yet.

"Come back down here," I mumble.

He cocoons me with his big body, flush against my back. He's still hard, and I wiggle my hips as he lets out a long groan, before sinking his teeth into my shoulder.

"Stop, woman, are you trying to kill me?"

*

When I wake in a dim half-light, he's sprawled face down on the bed next to me. I take in the rounded curve of his butt, exposed by the white sheets halfway up his thighs, and I'm practically drooling. I can't believe what we did last night, what he said to me, how different it is to *share a queen bed. He's a sprawler!* I sit and lean over, kissing him at the base of his spine and up each vertebra to the curls on the back of his neck. Then I give in to temptation and run my hand over his ass, and lower between his legs.

"If I'd been lying on my back, I'm thinking I might have liked this wakeup more," he mumbles into his pillow. "Not that this isn't pretty sensational in its own right."

I want him in my mouth. This one night in Africa, with the sound of the bush all around us, I knelt and pushed his knees apart, unbuttoning him. A hungry expression overtook his face when he realized what I was doing, and the groan he made when I put my mouth on him was unreal. My breath stalls. Have I really only had the opportunity to do this *once* before?

He shifts and rolls over, and I eye his impressive erection, ghosting my index finger up the underside, concentrating on the sensitive area under the head. He adjusts his hips, and I grin at him, leaning forward to lick the tip.

"Oh God, that's good," he says, eyes fixed on my mouth on him. I suckle a little, and his pelvis lifts off the bed on a soft growl, so I pull back, blowing across the wet skin, and he groans, eyes closing.

"Don't tease," he says, voice tight.

My eyes widen. *After what he did to me?* I stretch up his body, kissing him on the lips and his hand invades my hair, holding me still as he plunders my mouth. When I draw back, his hand on my neck tightens.

"After last night, you expect me *not* to exact revenge?" I say.

He laughs at this, eyes softening. "You might be strong-willed and feisty, Liss, and I love it, but I'm calling the shots in bed."

My eyes flick between his. There's no amusement in his gaze. Sure enough, he was dominant the few times we found a private corner in Africa, but last night took it to a whole new level. *What do I want here?*

"You like that?" I ask.

"We can have some ground rules, but yeah, I want to be in charge. Of your pleasure and mine."

His jaw juts out, eyes narrowing. But he looks nervous too, like he's not confident that I'll take this the right way, and my heart flips.

"Are you saying I can just lie back and enjoy myself?" I joke, and the tightness around his eyes disappears as he laughs.

"I might want to torment you a little," he says, voice rough, and it takes me straight back to how much he got off on it.

"Sounds good to me," I mumble, starting to kiss down his chest, but his hand tightens in my hair.

"Liss."

I blink up at him. "What?"

His eyes slide to the side. "I'm serious about this."

When his eyes come back to mine, I say, "I understand. You want to be in control in bed. In case you didn't realize it, last night was good for me too. I'm down with that. Can't say I won't fight you sometimes, though."

He closes his eyes. "I like the resistance," he says, sotto-voiced.

I grin. "Don't be shy about it," I say, leaning forward to kiss him as his eyes pop open. "I like resisting, and last night was amazing."

He groans, hand tightening in my hair. "For me too. God … the playing with you … so fucking hot."

Never has a guy been so honest with me about what he wants.

"I'm not sure how much I want to dominate. I've never been with anyone …" He lowers his voice as my eyebrows rise. "Someone who was prepared … who responds like you … I …"

"We can have some words for when it's more than I can stand," I say.

"I don't want to be an asshole." He slides a hand down my side to my butt. "You're not sore?"

I laugh. "In all the right places," I whisper into his mouth, and his fingers tense but then he releases my hair as I restart my journey down his chest. *Placated for now.*

"If you don't like something I do, tell me. I don't want to step over the line," he adds, watching as my lips trail over his abdomen. He lets out a warning growl, and my lips curl, shifting down to take the tip of him in my mouth and trailing my tongue over his saltiness. His hips come off the bed on a sharp snap, so I sink right down, taking him to the back of my throat.

"Oh God, oh God, that's perfect," he groans, hands in my hair again holding me tightly so he can see what I'm doing as his pelvis gives an involuntary stutter forward.

"Holy shit, *so good*."

I tighten my teeth around his length, and his mouth falls open as his hold on my curls tightens painfully. "Let me play for a bit," I say, but all this gets me is a glower, and I grin. "Not to tease, just to enjoy tasting you."

"Okay," he grunts grudgingly, fingers easing.

"Watch," I whisper as I roll my tongue over his tip, pushing his thighs apart on the white sheets and stroking his balls, the sensitive skin behind his cock.

"Oh, yes! Jesus," he gasps, head tipping back on the headboard, eyes closing.

"Watch me, Dan." His head snaps up, eyes hot and fierce. "I want to see you come. Last night you were behind me," I hum, letting all I'm feeling about him being here bubble up through me and out.

"Okay." He nods, swallowing hard. Not looking away. His chest rises and falls as his breath gusts, fists clenched by his sides. I sink down on him, and he lets out a long groan.

"Fuck. I cannot stay quiet," he says, eyes wild, and he groans again as I inch my lips back up his length. I keep up the tortuously slow pace until his hips are lifting off the bed every time I slide back up, like he can't bear to be out of my mouth. He is groaning loudly through each thrust, his hands everywhere: My scalp to hold me, the sheets, his hair, the pillow, clenched by his side. Never taking his eyes off me.

"Oh God, look at you," he grits out.

I pull off to admire his gleaming wet cock. "Look at *you*," I say, grinning. The dark red color reminds me of ripe plums, and it moves in the morning air with his pulse, quivering as I rub him all over with my thumb, suckling his tip and sliding all around it, wet and slippery as I play with his foreskin.

His jaw clenches. "I want to come in your mouth," he grinds out, and I nod. I'm down with that. I'm red hot just from watching him. He thrusts up, groaning loudly. My fingers explore down to his base to find his balls tucked up tight. *He's close.*

Then he holds my head firmly and rocks his pelvis, faster now, against my teeth and lips, hitting the back of my throat. The lines etched into his face are almost cruel.

"Oh yes, Liss, so good. Too good. Fucking hell. Oh … Oh … *God.* Oh … Oh … *I'm coming.*"

He starts to jerk in my mouth, and I swallow and swallow as he thrusts, making an unreal noise as I hold him, playing and sucking every last drop. He shudders and shudders, pushing his ass up on a groan. I shift my hips restlessly as he collapses back, and I nuzzle his cock, licking him clean. He jerks, moaning each time I touch his tip.

A ridiculous sense of pride burns through me as I sit back on my knees and take in his big body sprawled on the sheets, sweat sticking his hair to his forehead. His chest is heaving, eyes closed and face pale behind the pink tinge high on his cheeks. I crawl up the bed to tuck into his left side, and he wraps a shaking arm around me. I fling a thigh over the sprawl of his legs.

"Holy shit," he gusts out. "You've ruined me."

He sounds so breathless that I rub a hand over his chest, and he shifts his hip into me cracking open an eye. "You're wet."

I grin pressing into his hip. "Of course, how could I not be, watching that?"

He rolls into me burying his face in my neck, groaning.

"Has anyone ever told you what an incredible woman you are?"

I laugh. *Such a giver, always.*

"Not recently," I say. "I haven't seen you in a while."

His hand invades my hair, and he groans.

"Too long, Liss. When are you coming back to Africa?"

It's been a miserable month. Usually being back here is a joy, stepping into my life, seeing Jo and Kate, helping students and enjoying the cut and thrust of the city before the traffic and the aggression pisses me off, and the pressure builds to be back among smiling faces and in the hot sun.

I wrap my arms around him squeezing tight. "I've missed you," I say.

He draws back kissing my cheek, satisfied eyes searching mine. "I've missed you too, but answer the damn question: When are you coming back to Africa?"

"I've got to save some money."

"*When*, Liss?"

"A couple more months."

He groans when I say this. "You have to get a proper job out there so you can stay. Stay with me."

"You want me to give up this incredible lifestyle for a guy?" I'm joking, but he pulls back with a frown.

"We need to find a compromise that works for us, Liss. Would you consider coming to Zimbabwe? Living with me?"

I was too scared when he offered this before. I'm skittish, I know I am. He's pushing, and I'm thrilled he's pushing, but to put myself in his hands so thoroughly …? Well, it kicks against something very elemental in me.

Then he says, "Polishing up my thesis is the last thing I need to do, and I've nearly finished. I've got to hand it in, get everything organized, and find a job, which could be anywhere, maybe here if I could get a visa."

The walls seem to tilt in toward me. The idea he could come here warms my stomach, and my reluctance to answer his question is not because I don't want to go to Africa, that's an excuse, it's because the whole thing terrifies me. I've known him, what? Five months? He appears genuine and straightforward, but I've been fooled before. A shudder runs down my spine.

"You know I'm coming back." That I can give him. I'm not quitting volunteering in Africa ever.

"But are you coming back to be with me?" he whispers.

I have to be honest; he's laying it all out here, and I'm not giving him much in return.

"I'm scared, Dan. I have a terrible history with guys. I'm terrified of trusting you, terrified of fucking this up. I want it, oh God, I want it, but I just …"

He hugs me close and kisses my temple. "I understand."

He reaches down and pulls the cover over us, and we lie curled around each other in the ticking silence of the apartment. Traffic hums in the street below, a door closes down the hallway. I'm drifting off to sleep when I hear him say,

"Just know I'll always be waiting for you."

CHAPTER 16

Liss

Monday, June 17 to Wednesday, June 19, 2019

Two weeks after Dan's visit, the seminar room is quiet, heads bent over laptops as the summer students all work on the task I've given them, and I bounce my foot as I stare down at my phone. No messages from Dan in six days. We normally email every couple of days, send a text or photo daily, and talk once a week. I've tried calling him multiple times since he didn't answer my first call and each time it's gone straight to voicemail. I blow out a long breath. *You know how communications are in Africa.* He could be somewhere remote, out of reach. There's nothing on his Facebook page; it's still the post he made while he was here with me. I type in another message:

> Getting worried about you now. Let me know you're okay.

But I receive no response all morning. After my lecture, I head over to the café in the central university buildings to grab some lunch, taking it out to the park over the road to sit in the sun. But my stomach is queasy, and I pick over my sandwich and grimace, placing it on the bench beside me. Aside from his email and phone number, the only other thing I've got is an address in Harare he gave me before he left.

I fire off a message to Jo as I set my coffee down next to me. I don't want to interrupt Kate when she's in the ER, and after about thirty seconds my phone vibrates in my hand.

"You've still not heard from him?" Jo's soft tones fill my ear as she moves about and a door closes. "How many days is it now?"

"Six. I just … I don't know what to do. It's so odd."

She hums a little. "I think you've got to go out there."

I take a sip from my cup.

"I just don't see any other option," she adds.

"Going to Zimbabwe after six days? It seems a little extreme. There could be a simple explanation. He could be out in the bush somewhere, visiting a village or …"

"Wouldn't he have told you he'd be uncontactable?"

I scuff my foot on the concrete of the quad. "Yeah. Yeah, he would."

"I'll pay, Liss. Don't be thinking about that."

"I've got money. It's just I haven't got enough to go out for any length of time."

"My business is doing well. A flight is nothing to Janus. He flies to Asia for a two-hour meeting. Just …"

"I'm not getting into debt to Janus." I run my free hand through my hair. "I sent Dan another email yesterday, and it bounced back, like it's no longer working. All the others went through. That's odd, isn't it?"

"Emails can bounce for a lot of reasons. Servers can be down, the mailbox can be full, or your address could be the problem. Did it send you a message?"

"Yeah."

"Forward it on to me."

I take the phone from my ear and tap on my email app.

"You don't think going out to Harare comes across as a bit crazy lady? Like turning up at a guy's office because he didn't offer a second date?"

She laughs. "I think you and Dan are way beyond second-date territory. He told you he'd be waiting for you. He's going to be delighted if you go and see him. Hang on and let me check why it bounced back. Hmmm. It says the email address no longer exists."

"*What?* He deleted it?"

"Not necessarily, they can be taken down for all sorts of reasons."

I scuff the floor again. "Maybe he got fed up with waiting. You were right, Jo; I should have left everything to be with him. I'm kicking myself." Yet again, I've fucked up a relationship with a guy who's dropped me like a hot potato.

"You've known him what? Five months? If he's done waiting, then he's the most impatient man on the planet. No one gives up something good after five months. If you were two years down the line and had had a series of conversations about how difficult long-distance was, then maybe. But not after such a short time."

I let out an extended sigh. "Yeah, yeah. I guess."

"You've had a succession of awful guys, Liss, but the good ones are solid. Trust me. They don't buckle after five months."

Has something happened to him? I chew my lip. An accident or illness or … he could be in hospital. How would I know? His life in Zimbabwe is a mystery. What do I know about him really? His family? My willingness to sweep things under the carpet is looking like a really dubious decision now. *Stupid, stupid, Liss.* Is he gone forever? *Oh, God.* Is he okay? *So many questions.*

"Liss. Book a flight, or I'm going to do it for you."

"All right. All right. Mrs. Bossy."

"Do it now."

"Not sure I like the new Jo who's business has taken off and now she's ordering everyone around."

"Yeah, yeah. Just do it." And she hangs up on me.

He could be lying in a ditch. My stomach churns. A group of students head across the quad, books and laptops tucked under their arms. Fuck, I'll need permission to leave my job if I'm going to go out to Africa. I'll have to talk to the head of department. Tapping on my phone, I search for flights and find several seats available tomorrow. So I gather up my stuff and head over to the offices and knock on the warm wood of John Arnold's door. He glances up with a wan smile and gestures at me to come in. How do I begin? I sink down opposite him and chew my lip.

"I'm aware it's unconventional to request time off when I'm covering for maternity leave," I start. "But a friend of mine is in trouble in Zimbabwe, and I need to go out to Harare for a short time."

John appears worn down, like the whole department is weighing on him, and he runs a hand through this thinning hair. He's going to refuse, *goddammit*. But, to my surprise, he nods.

"You're a hard worker, Liss, and you never ask me for time off. Of course, you can have it." His eyes scan over my face. "Is your friend okay?"

"I don't know. I've had some difficulty reaching him, but communication can be tricky out there anyway."

He purses his lips. "Yes, it can."

"I can talk to someone I know here, Ekon, who can cover the summer course for a week if you like. He's not an academic, but he's worked for aid agencies in a lot of African countries, and if I briefed him, he'd give the students an eye-opening view of how things work out there."

John smiles at me. "That's just like you to solve the problem for me, Liss, sounds great. Send me his details, and I'll talk to him."

I sit on my hands to stop them shaking. *Thank God*. Such a nice guy. *Most guys are not my father.* John's matter-of-fact, cooperative approach is the polar opposite of my dad's. And perhaps I shouldn't worry so much about Dan. There will be some normal explanation, some stupid tech glitch, or he had to be out in the countryside.

All the arrangements happen in a blur, and I'm pleased to be doing something after so many days of waking up every morning hoping to find a text from him. Twenty-four hours after my conversation with John, I'm settling myself in my seat on the plane, and I scroll through my phone as the flight attendant hands me a menu card.

But three hours in, after meals are served, I can't settle. I spot a head of blond hair about ten rows in front of me, and all the fear comes crowding back. What if something has happened to him? Getting everything organized has calmed me down, but what if he doesn't want to see me? I try several films, flick through some books on my Kindle. Nothing seems to work. Eventually, I give up and stare into the black ink outside the window, the plane's lights flashing in my peripheral vision. Most people have bedded down, and the cabin is dark, quiet. But I will go mad trying to sleep in this tight seat. The flight attendant offers me something to drink, and I nod, mute, as she comes back with a large glass of wine. Anything to knock me out. I almost feel like a storm should be raging out there to match the turmoil inside me, but it's all calm and peaceful. *Thank God.*

And I must have fallen asleep because my head jerks when we touch down in Harare, and I blink blurrily at the other passengers and then stare out at the hot tarmac. The only thing to do is go straight to Dan's. I'm too antsy, and if I can answer some questions now, why not? It's 6 a.m. Who's not in at 6 a.m.? My gut tightens. What will he say? What explanation could there be? I ring his number, and it goes through to voicemail again. *Damn.* I left a message before leaving the US telling him I was coming.

"Dan, I've just landed in Harare. I'm really worried about you, and I'm on my way to your place. If you get this, call me. I want to know you're okay."

I pull up the maps I've downloaded onto my phone and study transportation options for ten minutes. No organized routes run in the city, it all appears to be ad hoc, and I quickly realize that talking to local people would speed things up, so I head outside the terminal, eventually finding a minibus into the center of town. When I consult with people on the bus, everyone tells me to catch another minibus out to the suburbs and then walk. I can do that. As the bus gets closer to his address in a leafy area north of Harare, my stomach is like a cauldron, and at long last I trip onto the sidewalk, nausea bubbling in the back of my throat. I examine the neat row of low bungalows, the hot sun beating down on my shoulders and through my hat. What am I going to find out here?

CHAPTER 17

Liss

Wednesday, June 19, 2019

I eye up the painted houses with their trimmed lawns and plants in pots as I walk down the street. How little did Dan tell me about his life in Zimbabwe? At no point did I imagine where he lived and what it might be like. He talked about his PhD and his thesis, but never mentioned his home, his friends, his family. It's odd, now I come to think about it. Most people would chat about how they grew up, things they'd done at college in passing, wouldn't they?

Eventually, I arrive at number 134. The front yard is dry, the grass just about hanging on but in dire need of a water. I walk up the cracked concrete path to the main door. It's not glamorous, but it's not a dump either. It's a little run down like it needs some care and attention. *A typical rental property.* I pull in a deep breath and glance at my watch: 7.30 a.m. Hopefully, I'm not too early. Where's the bell? Finding none, I lift the knocker and it falls back with a sharp rap. Voices call inside. *Voices?* Then a man's voice, more distinct. "I'll answer it!" and the door is flung open by a Black guy wearing suit pants and a smart shirt, collar unbuttoned like he was getting ready for work. He frowns at me, but his face is still polite.

"Can I help?"

"I'm looking for Dan Andrews?" I say, clutching my phone like it will give me credence.

His frown deepens.

"Dan Andrews? Ummm ..." I take in the lines on his forehead, and my heart sinks.

"He doesn't live here?"

"No, just me and Marjorie, my wife."

My mouth falls open. Of all the scenarios I imagined on the plane, this wasn't one of them.

"That's ... that's ..." *Very odd.* "134 Pretoria Drive, right?" I say, peering down at my screen at the address. I can picture him typing it, blond curls bent over the phone.

He nods at me, leaning over to examine the address, and I turn it toward him.

A smiling woman appears behind him.

"What's going on?" she asks.

"This lady here is looking for someone named Dan Andrews." The guy turns, taking my phone and showing it to her.

And the whole story comes tumbling out, of meeting Dan in Congo, of him coming to Manhattan and then not hearing from him. Their expressions morph into interest and sympathy.

I stretch my hand out. "I'm Liss, by the way," I say with a smile, and they both shake my hand.

"Masimba and Marja," the man says, gesturing to himself and his wife. "And we actually only moved in at the weekend, so I guess he could have lived here before us." He smiles.

That's just a few days ago. My heart leaps. "Was there any mail when you got here?" I chew my cheek.

The woman shakes her head. "The university cleaned it and cleared it all out. This is one of the houses they let out to people. Everything is registered with them."

"Oh, so it's university accommodation? Dan was doing his PhD there."

"Marj works at the university," Masimba interjects.

The woman nods, and my heart lifts. Perhaps, once Dan handed his thesis in, he had to move out. But … But … I sigh. It still doesn't explain why he's not responded to any of my messages, and why he didn't say anything to me. He still could be in a ditch somewhere.

"Actually, a letter came the day we moved in …" the guy starts, tapping his lip.

"Oh yes!" Marja cries. "A circular thing addressed to a company. I'm so sorry, we threw it out. I didn't think it was important."

"That's okay." I squint down the rows of front lawns, shimmering like a mirage in the heat. "Maybe I'll try the university," I say.

"Definitely. They'll have records of previous tenants, I'm sure." Marj's head bobs.

"Thank you so much. I'm sorry to hold up your morning routine."

"Give us your contact details," she says suddenly, disappearing into the house and coming back with her phone. "Just in case. If any mail comes through, we could get in touch with you?"

"That's very kind of you," I say, tapping in my number and taking theirs as well.

"Best of luck!" she says.

"I hope you find him," Masimba adds.

I smile at them both and lift my hand as I head off down the brown earthen road toward the bus stop, sun beating down on my head. The university must have an accommodation office, and of course they'll have records of Dan, perhaps even a forwarding address. My nerves flatten out. I'm not sure what I'm thinking: He didn't tell me anything but maybe it's okay that he's not here. *If he was here, it would mean he'd been avoiding me.* But Jesus, has something happened to him?

*

When I get to the accommodation office, I throw myself on the mercy of a woman named Jaya behind the desk, throat dry. She leans on the wood between us and gives me raised eyebrows and says, "Oh, honey!" when I tell her my story, so I play up the romance angle because she seems like the kind of person who might love that. I'm not sure if they'll have any privacy restrictions, but she doesn't seem worried and just turns her monitor toward me as she searches for Dan's name.

"Ah yes, here he is. Dan Andrews …" Her long purple nail rests against his name on the screen, and I let out a large breath I didn't realize I was holding. *He does exist. He's not some figment of my imagination.* Maybe this will make him magically appear from somewhere. And … he wasn't lying about being a student here.

"… He was doing a PhD here." She makes a few more clicks. "He's handed his thesis in. There's nothing odd on his record."

"He's not in the house he rented from the university any longer," I say.

"Yeah, that would be right." She nods, looking at me over her thick frames. "It's policy that students have to leave at the end of their time here: Only staff have extended accommodation rights in university housing."

"Would you have a forwarding address or anything for him? Perhaps a home address?"

"Yes, we usually do," she says, and my heart leaps as she clicks through tabs on the screen.

"Hmm, that's interesting." She pauses, eyes narrowed.

"What is it?"

"We've got no other address for him on here … Oh, you're in luck. I've got an email and a telephone number."

A small part of me dies as I lean forward and examine her computer, pulling out my phone to compare the details. Damn. They're the same ones I've already got.

"I'm sure if you email, he'll respond …" she starts to say, but I shake my head.

"The emails started bouncing back around three days ago saying it was no longer a valid address," I say, blowing out a long breath. "There's nothing else on his record?"

She flicks through screens, but it's all stuff about his PhD. Surely, this can't be a dead end? I was so convinced this would lead me to Dan. Surely, surely, there must be *some* way, some other information on him.

"Why wouldn't you have a home address?" I ask, hand fluttering as I place it on the desk.

He told me once his mother had died, but nothing about where he grew up. Despite the heat of the day, I feel cold all over. I press my hand to my chest. Where is home for him? He never mentioned his father, never even alluded to him, and we had *four, five months* together.

Jaya sighs, eyeing the screen and clicking through the records.

"It's unusual, but not unknown. Sometimes we find out the information is wrong and we take it off their record, but don't have an alternative to put in."

I sigh. What else can I do? "Do you have his bank account details, for paying rent?"

She eyes me dubiously. "Well, it's possible, but finance isn't my responsibility. I couldn't access that part of the system, and to be honest the university couldn't give you those details. Someone would be fired."

I smooth down the cotton of my pants. "Could I at least talk to somebody in finance?"

She purses her lips, sympathy morphing into a frown.

"I'm really worried about him," I mumble at her, feeling my throat tighten as disappointment begins to bite. "I keep thinking of him lying in a ditch somewhere. This wasn't some flash-in-the-pan affair and I'm not some obsessed woman, I swear. It's so odd he's disappeared like this. He's not that kind of guy." I blink off toward the corridor out the door, swallowing as tears gather in my eyes. "He said he'd always be waiting for me." The confession slips out in a faint whisper.

Her whole face changes, and she presses her hand to her chest, before patting my hand and picking up the phone, holding up a hand. I can hear it ringing as she holds the receiver to her ear.

"Lucinda, I've got this American woman with me ..." she starts. There follows a long detailed explanation of my story with lots of "uh-huhs" and "I knows" and a "yeah, terrible right." She twirls the phone cord around her index finger. "He said he'd be waiting for her, Luce." And a raised voice echoes down the line.

She grins, placing her hand over the mouthpiece. "She's going to have a look."

"Thank you so much," I gulp out. "This is so kind of you."

She shakes her head at me. "I'm worried about him too now," she murmurs.

Her mouth goes back to the phone. "Yeah?" She raises her eyebrows. "What's the name of the company?" She scribbles something down on a pad. "Spell it for me? Okay, uh-huh, un hunh. I get you. Thanks, doll. We need to do another Tuesday-night cocktails."

The chat on the other end of the call sounds like distant squawking, and Jaya laughs. "I hear you. Thanks, hon." She hangs up and purses her lips.

"I'm not sure this is going to be much help," she says, and my stomach sinks. "All she could tell me was the rent was paid by a business. She gave me the name of it, but that's all she had."

And the piece of paper she's turned toward me reads "HORIZON HOLDINGS" in neat block capitals.

It might be a small something, but it's something. This company was paying his rent, ergo he must have *some* link with them.

"What do you think would be the best way to find out about this company? Would there be some sort of register?"

"Yeah, sure. If it's a limited company, it'll be registered. The library has an online database."

"The university library?"

"I can give you a temporary card," she winks, and my mouth goes slack.

"That's incredibly kind of you."

"As I say, girl, I'm worried about him too. You have to come back and tell me what happens though. I have to hear the end of this story."

I laugh. Way to go, Liss, you're a badass for making things happen with people. I've been doing this in Africa for years, persuading people to help. No matter where you go here, it's like this. The people are easygoing and not too concerned about abiding by the rules. They appreciate that security leaks and fraud are not caused by a random person who turns up in your reception looking distraught.

"I will. I promise. Give me your number."

She chuckles at this and wanders off to find her phone. We swap numbers by texting each other. I lean over the desk and envelop her in a tight hug.

"Thank you so much," I whisper, and she pats my back before stepping back and wiping under her eyes with a long nail.

She points at me as I leave the accommodation office. "Don't let me down," she says.

CHAPTER 18

Liss

Wednesday, June 19 and Thursday, June 20, 2019

I arrive at the red brick and concrete of the university library by late morning. How much more of the city will I need to cover before I find Dan? Funny how it never occurred to me that he wouldn't be in his house or he'd be difficult to locate. I'm kicking myself for all the things I didn't think about before I got here.

The woman behind the desk is efficient and helpful and logs me into a computer to trawl through the registered company database. But she bustles off, skirt swishing, as another student approaches her, and I have no chance to tell her my story and gain her sympathy. I scroll through a number of databases, finding thirty different companies with the name Horizon Holdings, spread all over Africa, and I spend ages going back and forth, checking each one. I start a spreadsheet on my laptop and put all the details in, but four hours later I begin to wonder what I'm doing. What does this tell me? I don't have anything to link Dan to any of them. I concentrate on the ones in Zimbabwe, of which there are four. There's only one in Harare, and its address is out in the suburbs. The other businesses in Zim would take days to visit, but I could ring them. I glance at the clock on the wall and gawk at the time: 6 p.m.

Too late to call, but the library is open in the evening, so I crawl through the newspapers for the time Dan disappeared, from his last message to date, as the sun sinks slowly outside. I read about elections, flooding, someone being attacked by a lion, ongoing corruption investigations, and some high-up politician who's been shot in South Africa—no surprises there—and yet more politics, politics, politics. I even go through the obituary columns, but no one seems to match Dan's age or description. I sit back and examine the wooden desks and the now-dark sky outside the window. Would the police or a private investigator be able to help? Or is that insane?

My eyes start to prick as I search for PIs. The online reviews make for interesting reading: Someone has left a glowing review about for one of them where they tracked down a long-lost sister, and on impulse I phone them. To my amazement, a lady answers. The PI is out, but I make an appointment for tomorrow. I'll go to the police in the morning too.

I rub my eyes and look at the clock again: 9 p.m. now, and a huge yawn stretches my face. The library will be closing soon. I close my eyes before dragging myself to my feet and heading out into the warm night air, walking the ten blocks to the backpacker place where I've managed to book a bunk, last minute. I'm asleep as soon as my head hits the pillow.

*

The private investigator's offices are in one of those old concrete blocks in downtown Harare that are full of small businesses and sit over a ground floor of shops. I make my way up a well-kept set of stairs, passing several glass doors with names engraved on them before I reach one that says, "Masters & Co." When I press the intercom by the door, it buzzes open. An older woman in red is sitting behind a wooden desk on a stained gray carpet, a white wall with a number of framed certificates above her head. She gives me a bored once-over over the top of her screen.

The private investigator is just what you'd expect: a Black guy with thinning hair and a direct gaze like an ex-cop. A smile creeps over my mouth.

"Boni Masters," he says, returning my smile as I shake hands with him and sink into the seat opposite and spill the whole story, including my visit to the police this morning. He scribbles away on his pad. He's keeping notes, that's good, right?

"Dan Andrews, you say?" He studies me over his glasses. "A white guy, yes? Is that his real name?"

I pause, swallowing. It's almost reassuring to have someone else voice this question.

"He was registered at the university with that name," I say. "I know that at least. He also used it when I met him in Congo."

I relate to him the day I had yesterday and what I've done so far, and he raises his eyebrows.

"That's an impressive trail you've followed," he says. "Have you tried to find anyone from his department, someone he might have worked alongside?"

My eyes widen, shaking my head. "That's a great idea," I say, and he gives me a wry smile. Okay, he *is* a private investigator.

"You did well to obtain information from the university. They've been quite cagey with me in the past."

"Thanks." Perhaps I didn't waste my time yesterday.

"Yes. You've ruled out some lines of enquiry, certainly. Okay." He pauses, scratching the stubble on his jaw. "Date of birth? Any nicknames?"

I groan internally. "No date of birth, I'm sorry."

He purses his lips at me. "That's unfortunate. Birth records are always a good place to start. But I can check into the register for a Dan Andrews anyway. He was from Zimbabwe?"

I swallow. "I mean … I presume so. He never talked about anywhere else."

"Any idea of age?"

I pause, mentally running through conversations with Dan. He never said anything to me about how old he was or his birthday. He never even mentioned his star sign.

"Around twenty-seven I would guess, but he never told me directly."

"What was his thesis about?"

I tell him the long, complicated title, and he writes it all down, checking he's got the exact thing right.

"Any photographs?"

I show him a few on my phone, and he nods, asking me to email them to him.

"And you know nothing about his family?"

"I know his mother's dead. That's it."

"Did he mention the names of anyone at all? Parents, siblings, friends ..."

I shake my head. How weird does this sound? He's looking at me as if to say, "Lady, this guy told you nothing."

"I'm sure you must be thinking I was just a fling to him, and he didn't want me to find him, but honestly it wasn't like that."

He nods politely. How many times has he heard that before? Desperation tightens my throat.

"You talked to the police you say?" he adds.

"This morning."

"Did they check any records you're aware of? Reported deaths?"

"No." I blow out a long breath. "They were so unhelpful."

"Yeah, they're like that with members of the public. The opposite of the university. I work with them a lot: I can review arrest and death reports. If you think he hasn't done a runner on you, that's as good a place as any to start."

At least he believes me, but maybe that's his job. He's probably being encouraging so he gets his fees. He drops his pen on the keyboard and leans forward on his elbows on his desk.

"I'll be honest with you, there's very little information here to go on. I'll do what I can for you and rule out a few things, but I'm gonna be straight when I tell you the chances are not high."

Ugh. "How high?"

"Five to ten percent chance of finding anything. The odds of you actually tracking him down?" He runs a hand over his hair and grimaces. "Lower than one percent."

I stare at the dusty window behind him. *One percent?* What can I do, though? I have to try. I have a line of credit at the bank. I have friends. The thought curdles in my stomach. I've never crossed that line, borrowing from people I know. But I can still hear Jo's voice echoing in my head. I'm going to be honest with him too.

"I don't have a lot of money, but I want to do everything I can. I can pay, but I need you to keep me up to date about how much you're spending so I can monitor it."

He nods. "I'll do a few hours, make some basic checks, and let's see what we can achieve from that."

CHAPTER 19

Liss

Friday, June 21, 2019

The next day, a message from Boni appears on my phone telling me he's tracked down two people from Dan's department whom he's arranged to meet at the café in the university this afternoon. He's also matched the company that paid Dan's bills to the Horizon Holdings I found on the outskirts of Harare. He asks if I want to ride along with him to visit the place, and I text back a yes with shaking hands. An hour later a rusty, beaten-up old car pulls into the curb outside my hostel and, as we pull out into crazy traffic, he tells me that Dan's phone records came through before he left. The last call he made was one to me from Zimbabwe, then *nothing since June 11th*, which is … wow … I don't know what it is except extremely odd. I guess it means that Dan's not just ignoring my calls, but it worries me more. Unless he went out and got another phone, of course. But … but … why would he do that?

When we get to the industrial park, the grass is growing up through the concrete of the empty parking lot next to a four-story office block. We head over and peer through a grimy ground-floor window—there's a dirty carpet and two dusty-looking desks and an old filing cabinet but, otherwise, it's completely empty. Boni looks around at the four other buildings on the estate that are in varying states of disrepair. There are a few cars dotted around nearer some of the other buildings.

"Come on, let's go and see if we can find anyone and ask some questions."

We walk across the parking lot, and then skirt a couple of other buildings, peering in and finding one or two occupied offices. A couple of people look up from their desks. The third building has what I assume is a security guard sitting at a makeshift reception desk inside, so we head in. It's a hot and grimy space, and the guy couldn't look more bored if he tried.

Boni raises his chin in greeting and hands over his card. "We're looking for a company called Horizon Holdings. My information tells me that they're based in the end unit."

The guy narrows his eyes on him. "There are hundreds of companies based here."

"Hundreds?" Boni says, frowning and staring out the window at the buildings we've just walked past.

"Yeah. Landlord runs a virtual address service from here." He indicates a bank of mailboxes all along one wall that I'd totally missed. There are literally hundreds of them, white numbered boxes running from the floor to the ceiling. My stomach drops.

"You mean these companies aren't physically here?" I say.

He shakes his head.

Boni cocks his head. "Have you worked here long?"

"Ten years."

"And how does this work?" He gestures to the white boxes.

The guard shrugs. "The mail comes in, I sort it into the boxes."

"And do people collect it?" Boni asks.

"Sometimes. Sometimes it gets scanned and forwarded on."

"And if we wanted to find out about the mail for a particular company?"

The guy shrugs again. "You'll have to ask the landlord about that."

Boni purses his lips. "Okay. If anyone comes in asking about Horizon Holdings' mail, could you let me know? Happy to pay a reward if it leads to anything."

The guard writes Horizon Holdings on the back of the card, then looks at Boni. "Why you interested?"

"Missing person case," he says, and the guard nods.

"Lotta that around here."

"Really?" I pipe up.

He shrugs. "Gangs, drugs, crime. People get sucked in. Disappear. A body turns up in the river."

Oh shit. Nausea roils in my gut.

"Is that true?" I say as we head out of the office and across the hot concrete back to Boni's car.

He shrugs. "No more than any other city in Africa, I'd say."

As he settles behind the wheel, Boni calls the landlord and explains that he's a PI investigating a missing person case. When he asks about Horizon Holdings, he puts the phone on speaker and the landlord says he'll check his records. And there's quiet on the line for a while, but eventually his voice comes back. "That company's been registered there for six years. No forwarding email or mailing address," he says.

Boni frowns. "And why wouldn't they supply that?"

"If they're not expecting any mail, or know it will just be irrelevant mailers."

"Is that usual?"

"More common than you'd think. They just want an address to look legit or make it look like they're based here. I don't care, to be honest, as long as they pay."

"Okay, thanks," Boni says. "I'll call you if I have any more questions." And he hangs up.

"What does that mean?"

"It means the company is a dead end," he says, starting the car engine.

What? No! "But how can it be a dead end?" I say as we pull out of the lot.

"Well, physically it's a dead end. It's probably a holding company of some kind. There might be a money flow, but …" He looks over at me. "We'd need a court order to find out about that. Happy to do it if you want to, but it would be expensive. You can hide money flows through any number of different companies and accounts and jurisdictions around the world if you're really committed."

I want to groan. "Yes, I want you to look into it. Goddammit," I say, slamming my hand down on the dashboard.

He eyes me sideways. "Horizon only had one director, and that was Dan Andrews."

What? "So he had a company that paid his rent but he was the sole director? That just has to be suspicious."

"It's not uncommon for people to legitimately have a business that they put things through. It's just an alternative to a personal bank account."

"So it was just like his bank account, but he used a company name?"

"I suspect so. He probably just needed an address for it that wasn't the university."

"Damn."

The PI jerks his chin up. "Let's go and meet these guys from his department and see if we can learn anything more."

But a half hour into the journey to the university, Boni is frowning and glancing in the rearview mirror.

"Is something wrong?" I say.

"There's a car that's been following us since we left the industrial park." He frowns. "Let's stop off and grab a coffee, see if it stops with us."

He pulls into a parking space in front of a store and he climbs out, indicating to me to do the same. He watches as the cars go by on the road, then his eyes follow a tan-colored vehicle as it disappears around the bend up ahead. "That was it."

"Were they following us?"

He shrugs. "Maybe, maybe not. If they're good at their job, they will have seen us stop and know they've been made. They'll pass the tail on to somebody else. I got the registration. I'll check it out when we're back in the office."

Is he paranoid or do I need to be more careful? The security guard's comments about drugs and gangs wash through my head. Shit! Was Dan involved in something? I'm so glad I've got Boni on my side. I like his realistic no-nonsense caution more and more.

When we reach the university café, a short white guy with close-cropped hair and a good-looking Black guy greet us warmly, introducing themselves as Jeff and Tanaka. And as we make our own introductions of who we are and what we're doing, their faces fall.

"Has something happened to Dan?" Jeff says.

"We don't know as yet," Boni says, pulling out his notebook. "Liss hasn't had any communication from him since June 11th. I'm treating this as a missing person's case."

Jeff's eyebrows shoot up. "Well, it explains why I didn't hear from Dan this week to arrange our weekly squash game. I hope we can help. But I have to say that I didn't know him well outside of that. He kept himself to himself."

"Did Dan tell you anything about himself? Age, family, maybe where he was born?" Boni asks.

Their smiles falter a little. Jeff looks at Tanaka with a frown, and Tanaka sucks his lower lip into his mouth and looks back at him.

"I'm doing a PhD like he did, same department, slightly different subject area," Tanaka says. "We talked about research, how we were getting on but not much else. He was a good guy, friendly, always concerned about me."

This is achingly familiar. Sometimes he answered *my* questions with his own questions. I want to groan out loud. This is so much more than being self-contained. *He shared nothing.*

"I don't remember him ever talking about where he was brought up or his family." Jeff laughs nervously. "I don't know what we talked about. *My* family I think. He was always asking questions, and I have a very big family." He shakes his head.

Boni asks a few more things about them and their background and what they had in common with Dan, but I can see from how little he's writing down that it's fruitless. They probably know less about Dan than I do. Both of them express concern and ask us to let them know if we find anything, and Boni takes it all down, making a note of their phone numbers.

When we leave the university café, Boni blows out a long breath and glances over at me. He pulls out his notebook as we get to the car and flicks through the pages.

"This doesn't feel good to me, Liss."

I roll my lips together, staring off over the parking lot shimmering in the lingering afternoon heat.

It doesn't feel good to me either. Where do we go from here?

CHAPTER 20

Liss

Saturday, July 13, 2019

I lay down my phone and study Kate's and my small Manhattan apartment: the chipped Formica cupboards of the kitchen opposite Kate's bedroom, the worn wooden floors. After ten fruitless days in Zimbabwe, I came home two weeks ago. The car license plate was just an ordinary guy in the suburbs driving into town. We put Dan's picture in the *Harare Tribune and Herald*, which resulted in a flurry of calls and "sightings," mainly crackpots looking for money, other private investigators, and people promising to find "Mr. Dan." Boni has managed to track down another couple of people at the university who knew Dan, but got a similar story. He's reported Dan as a missing person, which is standard in a situation like this apparently, but the police aren't too interested. They think he's left the country and that explains his switch to a new phone. *Yes, but if it's just that, why hasn't he contacted me?*

It's in my court to decide if I want Boni to keep digging, but I've spent over four thousand dollars already, which is money I don't have. I've read about people disappearing in the past and always wondered how that could be possible with the trail left by smartphones and online. I've never thought tracking the last place someone was would be that hard. And I guess we have tracked Dan to where he was last, but it hasn't helped. *But this can't be the end of the road.*

I pick up my phone again and scroll through the photos. My favorite is a joint selfie we took in a bar, both a bit drunk, two smiling idiots, Dan's chin on my shoulder. A lump forms in my throat. *God, he could be dead.* I would rather anything than that, even if he had lied about everything. I blink fast, trying to hold back the tears, but they well up anyway, and I curl into myself on the sofa hugging my phone to my chest. Lying on the couch, I stare at the thin surface of the coffee table, the TV from next door chattering away in the background, and everything blurs as my tears track down my face. My whole chest is tight, my heart squeezed in a vice. I have no idea how much time passes, but eventually a key rattles in the lock and Kate barrels in, dropping her backpack down when she sees me curled up.

"Liss." Her feet hurry across the floor, and her warm hand wraps around my shoulder. "Are you okay?"

I roll onto my back and peer up at her. Her face swims.

"Oh God, what's happened? Have they found him?" She studies my blotchy face intently.

I shake my head, tears starting up again as she plonks herself down next to me, pulling me up and into the slightly antiseptic smell of the hospital.

"Tell me what's going on," she says, sitting back and smoothing my hair with her hand.

"Just another update from the PI: still no trace of him." I briefly gulp out the details.

She slumps into the back of the sofa, and I shift to make room for her.

"Oh God, it's all so weird," she says.

"I can't bear the thought he might be dead."

She shakes her head. "There'd be some evidence of that, surely? Your guy has examined the death records, hasn't he? No one matched his description?"

"He's checked it all out, yes. There were a couple of people who were about the same age, but he talked to the families and got photographs and neither of them are Dan. What if he's lying in a ditch somewhere?"

"We overestimate the chances of someone dying because of all the cop shows on TV. Usually, people don't die unexpectedly and anonymously in ditches. They pass away in obvious ways like old age, car crashes, drug overdoses, or at the hands of their spouse. The police are always involved in those." And I know she's trying to provide some hope in her matter-of-fact way.

"The Harare police think he's left the country, that that's the most likely thing."

"Then they're probably right."

"Yeah, but why hasn't he got in touch with me? I mean, that I don't understand."

"It's pointless speculating about things you can't answer, like *why*. I think the real question is *where* he might have gone."

"Well, if he lied to me, then he could have been from anywhere. Not Zimbabwe. Not even Africa."

"Didn't he have an accent?"

"Not really." I sit up, somewhat buoyed by her straight, analytical approach. "I'd say it was African of some kind, but to be honest it was one of those indeterminate accents you get with people who've moved around a lot or watched a lot of American TV when they were kids."

"Okay, well why don't you see if you can find a Dan Andrews somewhere else in Africa?"

"I'm starting to doubt that that was even his real name."

She grimaces. "If he gave you a false name, Liss, he could have lied about everything."

That's the logical conclusion of all this. Of course, it is.

What we had was real, I want to say. *I know it was.*

I'm not a quitter. What else can I do but keep looking? Perhaps I've reached the end of the road with Boni, but there must be something I can do from here.

CHAPTER 21

Liss

Saturday, July 20, 2019

The script tattoos run like chainmail all the way down Fabian's arms, and stray curls have escaped from the messy bun on his head. How did Kate land *this* guy? He's got trouble written all over him with a capital T. But also nobody better matches the phrase *sex-on-a-stick*. There's a knowing tilt to his body, the way he leans in when he talks with one of those smiles that make you want to hand your heart over to him on a plate. I watch as he winds his long, battered fingers through the leather bracelets on his wrist, leg bouncing under the table.

"So, you and Kate, hunh?" I say.

"Is that what this is?" He squints at me. "The best friend intervention?"

I laugh. "No, I …"

"Listen, I know I've put her through a roller coaster." He blows out a long breath. "Believe me, I know. I've been in hospital more than any sane man should be. My behavior has been"—he runs long fingers along his unshaven jaw and leans forward over the café table—"at best, erratic." He shakes his head. "But we're good now. I promise."

His eyes meet mine in a flash of silver, like a sword. Like a knight in armor. I stare down at my coffee. Did he slip something into my drink?

A smile curves over my lips, and I lean back in my seat.

"What?" he says.

"That's not actually why I wanted to see you."

He frowns away from me at the queue at the café counter. "Fuck. All that worry before I got here, and that's not it? I'm not going to be given my marching orders?" The gleam of silver turns back to me, amused.

I slap his arm where it's resting on the table. "Don't be a numbskull. You think I have that kind of power?"

He squints out at the busy street again. "You and Jo, yeah. Yeah, I do."

I laugh, shaking my head. "With Kate? About you? No. On other things, yes. But you, no. I've never seen her so invested."

Something rolls through him and his gaze warms. "Fuck, Liss. It's …" He presses his short-trimmed nails into the corner of his eyes. "I've never seen that kind of commitment, not directed at me."

I grin. "That's Kate. She's a terrier. An ocean of caring and drive."

He nods. "I thank God every day … She's everything to me, Liss." His eyes are soft now. "I won't let her down. You have my word."

His eyes meet mine and then his lips curl up in a shy grin … and oh, that look of his … Goddamn you, Kate. How did you lasso the sexiest guy on the planet? And make him settle down? She's a quiet, unstoppable force.

"So why did you want to meet?" he says.

"I want you to find someone for me."

His eyebrows shoot up his forehead. "Find someone?"

"You're quite the tech wizard, I understand," I say.

He hums. "Kate mentioned some guy who you met in Africa that disappeared. I'm really sorry that happened to you, Liss."

"S'okay." And I take him through the whole story. My time with Dan, my search in Zimbabwe, what Boni and I did together, and where we got to. His eyes take on a faraway look.

"You know people don't just disappear like that," he says.

"That's what Kate said."

He nods. "Because it's true. Nowadays everyone leaves a footprint: They use computers, they use phones, they're on social media, they get tagged in social media. And if you don't have a footprint ..." He pauses and picks up his spoon. "It takes a lot not to have something out there, if you understand what I'm saying. So it's always premeditated. Always. Once it's there, someone can find it, even if you've tried to get rid of it."

Fuck. I mean, I knew the stuff with Dan was weird, but hearing it confirmed like this from someone who probably knows more than anyone about this kind of stuff makes a large boulder turn over in my stomach.

"Was he white?"

"Yes." I pull up a picture of him on my phone. "Why?"

"It'll influence where I go looking for information. I'm happy to do some digging—try and match his photograph maybe. Hack into a few places. See if I can find anything useful."

"You think he was hiding something?"

"Oh, there's no question." My God, he's so certain. "Send me everything you've got, and I'll take a look."

I should be mad at Dan, but I somehow can't be. He took my heart, and until I find him, I can't get it back.

He squeezes my hand. "I'll see what I can do."

I nod and gather up my stuff, lean over, and kiss his cheek. It's rough under my lips. "I've got to go and do a lecture now, but thanks for meeting with me and thanks for this." I squeeze his shoulder as I get up to go. It's rock-hard under my hand. "I owe you."

"No, you don't. It's my pleasure."

I narrow my eyes at him as I hitch my backpack over my shoulder, then I lean in to whisper, "Make her life amazing," I say, and his eyes widen at me.

Make it what mine should have been.

CHAPTER 22

Liss

Thursday, October 17, 2019

The bus lurches down 2nd Avenue, and I shuffle robotically toward the doors. The last month has been round after round of wake up, teach, come home, watch mindless television, collapse. I can't let any feeling close to the surface for fear the whole dam will burst. Fabian's keeping me abreast of how he's doing, but it's been slow progress—apparently something to do with ancient African computer systems.

As I step out onto the sidewalk, I think longingly of my Netflix subscription and the *CSI* episodes downloaded on my laptop. I've got years of missed episodes. Kate and Jo insisted on dragging me to a bar tonight, forcing me to ditch my lounge pants. I'd be happy with a life spent addicted to dubious TV shows.

When I arrive, Kate and Jo are sitting at the bar in silky dresses and full makeup. Jo's dress is covered in lace. I glance down at my ripped jeans and casual jacket. *At least I showered.* In the past, I would have been tricked out too, anticipating a night of flirting and a fun guy to spend the evening with. But as my eyes meet Jo's, her forehead creases. Shit. I'm now *that* friend, the one adding to the list of worries. And Jo has a business to run, and Kate has a daily menu of life-and-death decisions.

"Thanks for persuading me out," I mumble, and Kate rolls her eyes. I bitched at her last night about not wanting to do this. "Sorry. Fuck. Sorry," I say, my hand on her arm as I hitch myself onto a bar stool. A lump starts in the back of my throat, and I swallow.

"This place is the best for cocktails, so I'm told," Jo says, a bright smile flitting across her face as she leans over and squeezes my hand. I look down at the extremely long cocktail menu. "The tab is on Janus, so we don't have to worry about how much we drink," she adds.

Kate turns to her, mouth falling open. "We can't do that."

Jo's face grows rebellious. "Look, my company's doing okay now, and he wants to give us this, so yes we can."

"Can I get you ladies anything?" the barman says, appearing like a genie and spinning three mats onto the bar in front of us.

"Three Hammered Hulks," Kate replies.

Now Jo's mouth falls open. "What on earth are those?"

"No idea. Someone at work recommended this bar and these cocktails, so that's what we're starting with."

Jo rummages around in her purse and pulls out a piece of paper, smoothing it out on the glossy surface in front of me. Dense text surrounds a large picture with tall palm trees and a pristine beach. The headline reads: "POVERTY IN PARADISE."

I narrow my eyes at her.

"It's an article about volunteering in the Philippines, about the problems there and …"

Kate straightens in her seat. "We think you should volunteer, but go someplace else other than Africa."

Jo slaps her arm. "Stop jumping the gun! I was going to work her up to it …"

I smile at their bickering. Thank God I've got two friends who care enough about me to put something like this in front of me, annoying though it might be.

"I love you both," I say, and their wide eyes swing to me. I shake my head. "But Fabian's working on some stuff for me and …"

Kate and Jo exchange glances. "Do you think he's going to find something you don't already know?" Kate says softly, and I scowl at her. Has she talked to Fabian about this?

"I'm just not ready to go volunteering again."

Jo fiddles with a coaster on the bar. "Either something happened to him or he deliberately cut off all contact. Neither of those things is good."

Whenever they talk about Dan now, it's in the past tense.

I chew my lip. "I can't just abandon him," I say.

Kate rolls her eyes. "You're not abandoning him. You're moving on," Kate mumbles into her glass, and something fires in my blood.

Moving on? What the fuck? "Like you moved on from Fabian when he messed up?"

She opens her mouth and shuts it again. "That was different," she eventually says.

Why? Why was it different? She's with him now: She forgave every one of Fabian's disasters. "I'm not going anyplace else," I say mutinously.

"But maybe it would help," Jo says.

"It would be a positive change," Kate agrees firmly.

"I'm doing okay."

Kate frowns. "Look, Liss, you're …" She focuses over my shoulder. "It's not good." She waves her hand toward Jo. "We've never seen you …"

"I mean sure you've been down about guys …" Jo chips in.

"… But we've never seen you down like this. Something needs to give, and you like radical change. Jo saw the article and thought it could be just what you needed."

I shake my head again.

"I don't want to …" I trail off. My mind is fuzzy like my thoughts are reeling away, just out of reach. "I need someplace familiar, where I've got friends."

"I don't think you do. Not you, Liss." Jo squeezes my arm. "Manhattan is routine and safe. You can function on automatic pilot. But you need to give your brain something else to think about. Some challenge that will stop you moping."

Moping? "I quite like the moping," I mutter.

"You're getting worse not better," Kate says, with a stubborn shift to her jaw. And goddammit, Kate is fiercer than Jo when she's on a mission. I hunker down into my body. I'm going to have to live through this onslaught, or intervention or whatever the fuck is happening here. I'm happily digging a hole for myself—why can't they leave me in it?

"I'm just trying to get through the day," I say. Maybe some honesty will deflect them.

The barman appears with three sickly-green drinks, and we all eye them dubiously.

"Who was this friend who recommended these?" Jo asks, and Kate grins.

"An anesthetist."

"Jesus, was his judgment skewed by what he does to people every day?" Jo mutters.

We sip cautiously, and as the sweet lime liquid slides down my throat my tastebuds explode. *Oh, that's fabulous.* I smile at Jo. "Clearly a guy who understands the value of the anesthetic properties of alcohol," I say.

This is actually nice, being here, with them, apart from the rabbit-caught-in-the-headlights nature of it.

"I think it's just a question of time," I say, mumbling into another syrupy swig. And my stomach drops, the disloyalty burning down my throat. I don't want to forget Dan or what he was to me.

"Trying something different can't hurt. Even if you only do it for a little while. Even if it's shit and you come back. You could come back in weeks," Kate assures.

"They're desperate for volunteers," Jo adds.

Kate bites her lip. "Thousands of people are starving."

"Is this to do with all the typhoons they get?" I know very little about the

Philippines, apart from the fact that they get a lot of tropical storms.

Jo nods. "Typhoons, earthquakes, volcanoes, you name it."

Of course. *The Pacific ring of fire.*

"A lot of the endemic problems haven't been addressed. A mountain of aid is not reaching those who need it most." Kate taps the paper.

"Corruption," I mumble into my drink. I've seen it all before. "And a significant degree of desperation too."

I eye the pair of them sitting on their stools like a couple of chipmunks. "I don't want to forget him."

Jo reaches over to squeeze my hand. "I understand that, sweetie, and you don't have to forget him. You could go, do something useful, and still remember him." She squeezes my fingers with a grimace. "Promise me you'll think about it."

I'm not going to get out of this. "Okay."

The picture I have of him in my head is already fading. The last thing I need is to be distracted from remembering the unchecked grin that would roll over his face that made me feel like I was looking at the sun.

One thing's for sure, though, I'm not fucking going to the Philippines.

CHAPTER 23

Liss

Friday, October 18, 2019

The next morning, I crack an eye open as a vice tightens around my temples. It's been a long time since the throbbing in my head took over my whole skull … *Congo* in fact. I roll onto my back, and the whole room swings. *God.* Stretching out my arm to grab my phone, a piece of paper flutters to the floor and I scrabble at it with my fingertips. *That goddamn article.* I groan, screwing it into a ball and throwing it across the room where it bounces off my closet.

I peer at the time on my screen: 10 a.m. dammit. I shuffle out into the hall, past Kate's door as I remember Jo drunk-dialing Janus, lurching on her stool as she whisper-shouted what she was going to do to his penis with her mouth. I laugh. I hope he had a wild night. *Goddammit.* I am *not* thinking about penises, guys, sex, or any of that stuff. In the bathroom, I throw down water and tablets with gay abandon. *Food.*

The kitchen's tidy, and a note on the countertop tells me that Kate has gone to work. How the hell did she get up early? Flicking the switch on the coffee percolator, I inhale the smoky bitterness as I grab a bowl of yoghurt. Then I curl up in bed with my laptop and press the play button for my next *CSI* episode.

Four hours later, I click pause and rest my head back on the headboard. The ceiling is as stained and peeling as it always is, and my tummy gurgles as the quiet of the apartment tickles at my senses. *I'm starving.* Once I've rustled up some cheese and crackers, I potter back to my room and flop onto the duvet, my eyes landing on the scrunched-up article. Damn that thing. I lever up and head over to put it in the trash, stopping to collect yesterday's outfit where I shed it on the floor last night. I dump the clothes in the hamper and unwittingly smooth the paper out on the bed, eyes skimming over the page, latching on to a picture of a group of sickly-looking children. *What's wrong with them?* I scan up the article and before I know it, I'm reading. Cholera, typhoid, no clean water. In ten minutes, I'm through the whole thing, gut churning. Still so bad so many years after the tsunami.

I pick up my laptop and start clicking, calling two friends in aid organizations and reading through a multitude of articles before the sunlight tracking across the ceiling makes me glance at the clock. Jesus, it's 4 p.m. And yep, it's terrible out there. One of the managers was delighted to hear from me, and gave me the number for Care Philippines, who, she said, would know a lot more.

The *CSI* video is still hovering on the screen, and I release the pause button. I'm forgetting about this crap right now. I grind my teeth. I don't need another problem to chew over. But somehow I can't stop my mind drifting to starving children and conversations about water and cholera. *Goddamn Kate and Jo.* How well they know me. Urgency starts to thrum through my blood, and I toss back the covers, diving into the shower and scrubbing at my skin. The local rep for Care Philippines in the USA is someone named Letty, and when I call her, she squeaks excitedly at me, telling me to come in, so I throw on something presentable and head out the door, gathering a coffee from my favorite barista before jumping on a bus.

Letty's cramped and shabby office makes my jaw drop. Files are everywhere, old bits of paper fixed to the walls with yellowing Scotch tape like they've been there since the 1970s. A dead plant graces the gray plastic desk in front of me as I take it all in, somewhat awed.

"I'm sorry about the mess. I'm the only person here, and somehow fundraising is always more important than this," Letty says, waving a hand around, and stands to clear a pile of papers off a chair so I can sit down. She stacks them on top of other files, and they instantly slide to the floor. She ignores them and plonks herself back down on the other side of the desk from me.

I nod. People are dying. Who puts admin or decor above that?

"So, I think you said on the phone that you normally volunteer in Africa?"

The smile that breaks across my face catches me unawares. "That's right." I give her a potted history of what I've done to date and how my life works: how I earn money by working at the university before periodically heading off to Africa. I'm not telling her about Dan, so I waffle on about how I've read about the problems in the Philippines.

She nods, sighing as she glances around the office. "As you can probably tell, I'd be grateful for any help you can give me. Even a few hours in here would be amazing. It seems impossible to keep on top of everything."

"I really like this place, Letty," I say, and she blinks at me.

I don't want to leave New York right now, but I could help Letty for a couple of hours a week at least. It would get me out of the apartment and get Kate and Jo off my back. Despite all my protestations to Jo and Kate, I know I've got to pull myself up by my bootstraps and get myself out of the hole I'm slipping into. I examine the bun that's falling off one side of Letty's head and the pilled brown cardigan pulled over a floral dress. I don't have to make a big commitment here.

I smile at her. "I'd be very happy to help."

She grins at me, and we arrange that I'll come in the following day for a couple of hours.

As I'm heading out my phone vibrates with a text. Fabian:

> Hundreds of thousands of matches on Dan's photograph. You could wade through them, but it'd be a long checking job. Probably take you years, I might be able to write some software to speed things up, but the bottom line is, it's a very long shot.

My stomach drops. Oh God. I feel my eyes start to tighten, but the dots start again:

> Still working on hacking into a few places to see what I can find. Will let you know when I'm in there.

I stare across the street, and the red gleam of a Coors sign catches my eye. A bar. Alcohol. Perfect.

*

Friday, November 8, 2019

Three weeks later, Letty's office is looking considerably better. I've cleared the space, found all sorts of funding applications buried in the piles, and organized her entire filing system. I've bagged two office chairs from other offices in the building, and yesterday I brought in plants. And Letty has turned from this frazzled person into someone calm and capable. She's the most amazing networker I've ever known. She spends all her time on the phone, making contacts, and going to events and meetings to make more connections. There's so much to do, and I'm amazed that she's pulling it all off.

She puts her hand over her phone and whispers at me.

"Could you do a meeting on Tuesday with somebody at Google?"

My eyes widen. "Yeah sure, but I've never done …" I start, but she just nods and goes back to the person on the other end of her call.

When she's off the phone, I clear my throat. "I've never done anything like that before."

"We'll do a run-through before you go." She glances at her wrist. "Oh my God, I've a meeting uptown. I'll see you this weekend?" She says as she grabs her purse and flies out the door as I'm nodding.

I stare around at the quiet office. "What am I doing?" I ask out loud to no one.

I inspect all the bids sitting on Letty's desk. I've printed them all out to keep her on track, ordered by submission date. As I scan down them my heart jumps: One of them has tomorrow's date on it. *Shit.* I fire off a quick text:

The deadline for the USAID bid is tomorrow.

What comes back is:

Oh no!

followed by:

Can you have a go at it?

Oh God. I don't have to be in the university for the rest of the afternoon, but I had planned to go home and have a marathon session with ice cream and some boxsets. I purse my lips. I'll read through it quickly.

But I'm still sitting at my desk four hours later when Letty arrives back, and her eyes widen when she catches sight of me, and I give her a rueful smile.

"Okay," I say to her as she walks through the door. "I've pulled lots of bits into the proposal from previous ones you've done, particularly the applications which looked like they'd been successful. I've read the criteria, added some sections of my own ..."

"Great!" she says, smiling.

"Can you read it?"

She unwinds a scarf from around her neck. "Sure. Leave it with me. I'll add anything I need to and send it off to them. How complete is it?"

I screw my face up at the words on the screen in front of me. "Probably about 80 percent finished?"

"That's fantastic, Liss. Thank you so much."

I grimace. "Don't thank me until you've read it. You might have to rewrite the whole thing. There's a lot of money up for grabs, though. I've put together something similar to a project I worked on in Africa."

She nods enthusiastically. "Great. Let me take a look."

"Okay," I say, getting up and stretching. "If you're alright to take it from here, I might head off. I could do with some fresh air." I wave my hand at the screen. "I'm not so happy sitting indoors at a desk for hours." *But somehow, I manage with being chained to* CSI *just fine.*

"Thanks so much, Liss. I don't know what I would do without you now." She smiles at me in the most touching way possible, and my heart squeezes with how much I miss this when I'm home. These committed people who work so hard, day in, day out, to help others. It warms something up inside me that I don't like to examine too closely nowadays. I enjoy the university, but it doesn't set me alight like this.

Two hours later when I'm slumped on the sofa, a text appears on my phone:

This is great!

I laugh to myself. I'm sure it isn't, but it was fun to step out of my comfort zone for an afternoon.

Glad to help.

Then three dots start:

I'm putting it in. Fingers crossed.

CHAPTER 24

Liss

Monday, December 9, 2019

I step out of the front door of the apartment building onto a freezing Manhattan street, and pull my collar around my neck as I head down the sidewalk. The satisfying thing about checking out of life is it's a cheap way to live. I've got money stashed away for a rainy day, something I've never achieved in my whole life. Who knew that heartbreak would be so profitable?

As I head off down the street, my phone vibrates in my pocket and when I pull it out, it's Fabian.

"Hey."

"Hey, Liss. I don't know whether what I've got to say is good to be honest, but let me tell you where I've got to." He launches straight into it.

My heart sinks. "Why not?"

He hums in my ear. "Because I can't really explain what I've found, if anything. There's a strange lack of records."

"A lack of records?"

"Bank records, phone records, immigration. There's *nothing*."

"Nothing?" Am I a parrot?

"I talked to Boni, and got him to pull immigration and airline records. Then I wrote a script to collate information about every person on that list. Nothing matches Dan. I also can't find any phone or bank records for a Dan Andrews or Horizon Holdings."

"But Boni got the phone records from Econet, didn't he?"

"Yeah, I've got what Boni had, but they're not on Econet's system anymore."

"How do you know that?"

"I hacked into their system. Sorry it's taken so long, but … yeah … very obsolete technology." He hums. "I've been wondering whether they'd delete records for a number that's no longer in use."

"Sounds logical, I guess." I chew my lip. "You said bank records … Wait a minute … how did you know where he banked?"

"University payments. I hacked into the university's financial records first."

I almost want to laugh. I didn't need to sweet-talk Jaya that day, did I? Fabian could have hacked into any system I needed.

"Can you hack into anywhere?"

He laughs. "Well … there's always a back door into a system."

"Are you serious? That's just scary."

He laughs again. "It's actually awesome if you know what you're doing. You can find out anything. Anyway, Horizon banked with Standard Bank, and the payments for Dan's rental were paid from there, so I hacked into Standard Bank which has taken a hell of a long time because the system is like twenty years out of date and I had to put some serious research into how to do it."

I snort. "God, that sounds tortuous. I don't know how to thank you."

"S'all good, Liss. I've learned a lot. But the depressing thing is that I've found nothing. No account for Horizon Holdings. I had the account number the payments came from. That doesn't appear to exist anymore, but I also checked more widely than that. Right across all their records."

My God, he's thorough. "Wow."

"Clearly they deleted everything, but why? They'd have no cause to unless someone asked them to close the account, and who'd ask them to close it? Dan was the sole director, wasn't he? And even then I think they'd keep a record on closed accounts for a certain amount of time. There was nothing there, Liss."

God everywhere I turn it's a dead end. But there could be a simple explanation for this, couldn't there? "Maybe Dan closed it when he left the country."

He hums again. "I guess. But the records would still be there, Liss. It's weird." He lets out a long sigh in my ear as I stare unseeing down the street. I'm just numb these days. Maybe in my mind he's already gone, like Jo and Kate said, and my throat tightens uncontrollably.

"Anyway, I wanted to let you know because I've kind of reached an impasse. I'm so sorry, Liss."

"S'okay." I stare up at the skyscrapers like big square fingers reaching up into the sky above my head. "I've kind of been not getting my hopes up anyway. The radio silence from him, for so long … it's all been …" My throat is too tight to continue.

"Are you okay?"

Maybe he can hear something in my voice. "I'm good. Maybe I'll see you later with Kate?"

"Bank on it. Let's have dinner tonight at your place. We'll bring food. I'll let Kate know. I'm so sorry, Liss."

"Thanks for everything."

"My pleasure," he says and hangs up.

I turn my head and blink down the road toward the subway, trying to stop the tightness in my throat taking over my whole body. I can make no sense of it. I've never been able to make any sense of it. My eyes drift over the people on the street, a blond man heading up the sidewalk. Something about his loping walk sends my heart into my mouth as he negotiates the cars at the intersection, and the honking noises of Manhattan traffic fade out. He turns to head along a crossroad, and I trot down the street, narrowly catching the lights. I'm a couple of hundred yards behind him now, catching glimpses of his curling blond hair through the sea of people. He rounds the railing at the top of the subway stairs, and I push through the crowds as my heart leaps and then goes into freefall as I see his face. *It's not him. It's not him.*

The flow moving down into the subway threatens to sweep me down, so I flatten my back against the wall of the building on the corner as people stream past into the station. I close my eyes. *Breathe, Liss. My God.* There's no way he'd be on the streets of New York. I know that. Why am I acting like a lunatic? I open my eyes again, the tide of human traffic washing past me. One or two eyes flick over me in the checking-out-the-Manhattan-crazies way, and I start to count my breaths. This is getting worse, not better. But what do you do when you can't climb out of the hole you're in?

The phone in my hand buzzes, and, grateful for any distraction, I peer at it. *Letty*.

Where are you?

I press call, breath slowing as I'm pulled back into the real world.

"Hi, Letty, how are you doing? I'm on my way in."

"Oh God, Liss. They liked the proposal we put in!" Her voice vibrates in my ear. "We've got some money."

"Seriously?" Despite everything, a hot spike runs through me. I did most of this bid. Perhaps I'm better at this writing gig than I thought.

"Can you come into the office?" Letty says.

I blink at the mass of people. "Of course, I'll see you soon," I say and hang up.

When I get to the office, Letty is a grinning, arm-waving mess.

"I'm so pleased!" I say, as she pulls me into a warm hug.

"We're going to have to travel to DC to meet them next week," she bubbles. "I was wondering what day you might be able to do."

Travel to DC? "Me?"

"Yes, of course! It's your idea, your project." She grins.

I stare at her, internally groaning. I've got a lot to do. I don't need five-hour road trips south.

"They're talking about funding it for eighteen months. We could establish a base out there, maybe a permanent one. They loved the proposal. *Your* proposal." Letty squeezes my arm, a broad smile on her face.

"They did?"

She laughs. "We're an awesome team. You're going to have to go out there."

My heart plummets. "What? *Me?* No way, Letty. I don't know the first thing about the Philippines or their problems or …"

I can't leave here at the drop of a hat, that would be insane.

"I don't think it matters, Liss. I mean someone has to set it up, and I've got kids in school and …" She pauses, biting her lip. "At least to start off with …" She tails off.

Oh, God! I'm an idiot. That's why she wanted to see me. "But I have no experience of management, of doing something like that. I'm a volunteer, not a manager."

She shrugs. "You had no experience of bidding either. You've got to learn sometime."

I open my mouth to object, to say I'm good with people, but of course that's what management's about, isn't it? Also, where am I going? I can't stay a volunteer forever, much as I love it. Am I going to build brick walls and dig wells for the rest of my life? No. At some point, I'm going to need to find another way to help. I just hadn't expected it to be so soon. And I don't want to go to the Philippines. What if Dan …?

Letty is watching me, eyes pinched. I've stupidly created a big opportunity for me and her. Ugh. This is awful.

I screw my eyes up and stare at the winter trees behind her head, out the window, black arms stretched up into the cold blue sky.

"I'll need to think about it, Letty, I can't just up and leave everything. I'll have to talk to the university."

She reaches out and squeezes my arm. "Of course! I'm sure we could time the project to fit around you. If you even want to do it."

I look at her then, really look at her. The lines surrounding her eyes, burning bright with commitment and drive. I think of palm-fringed beaches and disease and poverty. It'd be very different from Africa, that's for sure. And

Letty burns with what I burn with: We haven't known each other for long, but I love her for it.

She tilts her head. "I'm so sorry, Liss! I just assumed because you volunteer a lot you had no family keeping you here, and that's so presumptuous of me!"

And I open my mouth to object but shut it with a snap and close my eyes. She's right. There *is* nothing really keeping me here. All the stuff with Dan … *He's gone, Liss.* Kate called it. And of course, that's the truth of this: It actually doesn't matter what Fabian found out. Dan didn't want me, or something happened to him. And neither option gives me the happy ending with him that I wanted so badly. Somehow, I need to find the strength to move the fuck on.

CHAPTER 25

Liss

Thursday, January 2, 2020

What the hell am I doing here?

I head out of Cotabato airport, scanning over motorcycles and the hot asphalt. Someone named Ramesh, my interpreter and guide, is supposed to be meeting me here. I was half expecting a guy holding a board with my name on to be waiting in the terminal. I scan down the three cars lined up outside the tiny terminal. A gorgeous Indian Filipino guy in shades is leaning against the hood of a beaten-up old jeep, scruffy jeans and a tight T-shirt outlining his toned body. *Now there's a man I would have flirted with in a past life.* I press my lips together. He's engrossed in his phone, not even checking whether anyone is coming out of the building.

Once I reach him, I clear my throat, and he looks up, pushing his glasses into his curly dark hair with a smile like sin itself, and I can't help the answering curl of my mouth. Not a man who has to try too hard with the ladies, I suspect.

"Hi! Ramesh?"

His grin gets impossibly brighter, brown eyes widening in delight. "Yes! You are Liss?" His eyes scan down my body slowly and appreciatively and I want to laugh. Could he be any more obvious?

"What about this?" he says excitedly, thrusting his phone in my face as his long fingers fly over the screen, and a cat runs repeatedly into a mirrored garbage can.

He shakes his head and laughs as he studies it with me, leaning over my shoulder. "I love these things. Memes. Yes?"

I giggle too. *What a flirt.* But also, clearly delightful.

"Yeah," I say, turning my head toward him, and he stares at my mouth.

My jaw drops. Seriously? "Stop doing that."

"What?" His eyes flick to meet my gaze, frowning then giving me the full-wattage smile again.

"You know fine well what," I say, heading around to the passenger side of the car.

He waves at me. "This is not my car."

He gestures to a motorbike with a sidecar sitting farther down the sidewalk. Rust makes up 50 percent of the bodywork. How is the sidecar still attached?

I turn back toward him, and he leans into me. "I was trying to appear cool for the gorgeous American lady. How did I do?"

"Very good, Ramesh," I say, a reluctant grin breaking forth. *Definitely too cute for his own good.*

He jumps on the bike, grabs my backpack, and gestures at the sidecar. I hesitate. This is crazy, but some thrill is already bubbling away low in my gut. As I slide in, he secures my bag on the back of the bike, swinging a long leg over the seat and fiddling with the starter. I have no idea what's coming next, no clue where I'm staying, what I'll end up doing here, and it all fizzes through my veins like sunshine. The engine kicks, and Ramesh shoots out into the traffic, narrowly missing a minivan packed with tourists. I send a thank you to the gods for my friends back home who understood that I needed this before I did.

Ramesh slides and swerves along dirt roads that occasionally turn into asphalt full of potholes, before returning to dirt. I'm sure I've put more dents in the sidecar from rattling around on the inside, and when he takes a corner at full speed, I almost lurch out into the mud. Every so often, I get a glimpse of white sand and palm fronds and I tip my head back to gaze at the impossibly blue sky. *This is amazing.* When we finally arrive at the small house inland that appears to be our destination, I'm expecting my hair to be white when I next look in the mirror. Ramesh is still sporting an irrepressible grin, still flirting. He's impossible, and in another time and place I can see we would have had fun together, but I think Dan has made me immune to it all.

Ramesh pushes open the door and shouts.

"Mama!"

Concrete and corrugated iron make up the majority of the low-slung building, bougainvillea and palms of all shapes and sizes surrounding it. As we head inside, I can see an open area to the left with a table and benches, covered with a bamboo shade. A lady appears from behind a beaded curtain with a smile so like Ramesh's that there's no mistaking she's a relation. She chatters away in a local language, and I've already read enough to know there are dozens of these here. Occasionally she appears to scold Ramesh with a sharp frown, then suddenly she grasps my hands in hers and pumps them up and down to emphasize something I have no hope of understanding.

"What is she saying?"

"She's welcoming you to her home. She's also telling me that you are very attractive and that I need to keep it in my pants," he says laconically, and I burst out laughing. His mother frowns and lets out a stream of something else.

"Now she wants me to explain what I said to you to make you laugh."

I smile at her, and her expression softens.

"Welcome, welcome," she says in broken English.

"Thank you, thank you," I reply, clasping her hands in mine and bowing my head.

"She will show you to your room." Ramesh puts a gentle hand on my shoulder, and delivers a stream of words to his mother, who nods and scurries backward, gesturing toward some stairs.

"I'm staying here?"

He studies me. "I thought it would be helpful to live with a Filipino family to help you understand how things work here. More useful than the nearby hotel which is full of cockroaches."

I grimace at this. "That's very kind of your family ..." I start, but he leans in and gives me a wicked grin.

"And also, I saw your picture." He winks.

I shake my head. "In my country that would be harassment."

Alarm darts across his face, and I smile at him. "I'm joking."

I don't want to worry him. Being an interpreter, a guide for Western tourists, journalists, and aid organizations is one of the best-paid and most prestigious jobs possible in countries like this. I can already tell from her broad smiles that Ramesh is his mother's pride and joy, despite the scolding.

"Get settled in, and we will have some tea." He gestures for me to follow his mother.

"A beer?" I raise my eyebrows, and he laughs, widening his eyes scandalously.

"I'm afraid you won't find any alcohol in this house, but we're going to be traveling around to the poorer communities, so when we're on the road, I'm sure we will find some." He winks.

"Beer?" his mother questions over her shoulder, frowning. *Shit.*

Ramesh rattles something off to her, and as I consider him, he turns to me and shrugs. "I told her we were joking, and that Americans call hot tea *beer*." I roll my lips together trying to stop my smile and he grins, eyes roaming across my face.

This is going to be fun, but I've clearly got so much to learn. I've never felt more like I'm starting at ground zero. That one conversation with Jo and Kate brought me here to the edge of something different, the start of something new. Somehow I have to put what happened behind me, treat it like one of those curveballs life occasionally throws at you. Which feels ridiculous right now: I don't want to forget Dan. But no matter how hard, I have to move on from him.

PRESENT DAY

CHAPTER 26

Liss

Saturday, January 22, 2022

Adebe and Gloria, the big welcoming family where Dan and I first met over okra and beans, are first on my list of things to do. I have presents tucked in my backpack for their kids, much older now of course. I peer out the window of the car I had to undertake a lengthy negotiation for at the airport. He has driven me for hours along the dirt roads, my chest tightening as we've drawn ever closer. The scent of brown earth and rotting food, the shouts of street traders, mangy dogs lying outside shops hoping for a scrap, all seep into my soul like my mother's hand on my hair when I was little.

My knuckles roll over my lips as I take in the extent of the destruction. Kiwanja is pockmarked with places where bullets have hit. Mortar shells have taken down whole walls of buildings, but among this there is still so much *industry*: a market, a roof going onto a building, people on the street with their baskets and bags piled high with produce to sell, stores open despite the fact they are patched up with pieces of wood and have cloth covering their smashed windows and holes in walls. Parts of the buildings have been painted in bright colors, like flowers in a battlefield.

I'm here to talk to as many people as possible so I check in at the local hotel and chat with the lady who runs the place. She tells me I'll find the local aid workers in a bar down the street. The rooms are basic, and the three-story building is tattered and crumbling, but it's cheap and clean. After I've settled into my room, I head out into the mele. A cold drink beckons like a mirage.

The bar is in an old colonial building that I think was once some kind of community meeting place. Crates are piled high behind the counter, a fridge stands in the corner chaotically wired to a box hanging halfway up the wall in a way that makes me smile, and stools crowd around tables on a dusty wooden floor. As I slide onto a barstool, eyeing up the choice of drinks on the shelf, a smiling barman ducks under a curtain from the back. I settle for a local beer and turn to scan the room, but almost do a double take when I catch a familiar face tucked into a table at the far wall. *Jesus Christ. Brian?* He's still *here*? I grab my bottle from the bar, and as he clocks someone is heading his way, his eyes swing up and his mouth drops open.

"My God, *Liss*!" he says, breaking into a bright smile. He shoots to his feet and puts his hands on my shoulders, examining my face before pulling me into a bear hug.

Am I surprised he's still here? *I guess*. Brian was a well-paid management consultant in the US before he lost his wife, Helen, to cancer. He found his escape here, just as I did.

"I can't believe you're here!" I say, as he pulls back.

He laughs. "Nor I you."

I pull up a chair, and Brian grins at me and fills me in on the last three years of his life. He left the company that brought us both out here after a year of hard graft and now has a management position with an aid organization. He laughs when he tells me that it's well paid and that he's turning the shambles into something better organized and more supportive. I'm delighted he's built something positive here and that his life has moved on in this unexpected way. When he asks me what I'm doing, I tell him about the funding from the university and how they wanted me to work on the project. He listens intently, nodding along. As he takes a swig of his beer, he assures me that it's vital work, really needed here on the ground.

Finally, he brings up Dan, and my stomach curdles. I swirl my bottle watching the last of the liquid morph into a bubbly whirlpool. I fill him in on how Dan came to Manhattan after I returned home, how unexpectedly all his messages stopped. I recount my attempts to track him down, about talking to the police and ultimately hiring a private investigator. He eyes me earnestly, the lines on his forehead growing deeper as I talk.

"My God, Liss." He taps his beer bottle against his mouth. "Do you think he's okay?"

"I don't know. Either something happened to him, or it was his way of ending things with me." I swallow as a lump sticks in my throat.

Brian draws a breath through his teeth, shaking his head. "I never thought he'd be a guy to ditch a girl he liked. He seemed like one of the reliable ones." He stares off into the middle distance, fingers mindlessly toying with the rim of his bottle as he thinks. "Apart from his thesis, I didn't know a great deal about him. I had a sense that he might have lived in South Africa at some point, but he never talked much about his background."

"He lived in *South Africa*?" And I'm speechless for a second. God, if I'd had some starting point on this continent, I could have looked there. "What made you think that?"

He waves a hand. "I'm sorry, Liss, I can't remember exactly. The first time I met him he said something about Johannesburg, and he gave me the impression that he knew it well. But maybe I just assumed something because of that." He shrugs. "I guess he didn't talk much to you either, given the surprise on your face."

"I'm amazed to be honest." My stomach churns. I spent months going over and over our conversations for any hints he might have dropped, ruminating on how little he told me and why that might be. In my worst moments, I think I was a six-month fling, and he was a consummate liar. At other times, I remember when he came to the US, the things he said to me. Most of the time

I can't bear the torture of not knowing, but this conversation is just underlining all he hid from me.

Brian puts his hand on my arm.

"It's probably not my place to say this, but there was always something not quite right with Dan. He avoided questions. I always thought he had secrets."

I nod. Yeah, he did, and I was too besotted to care. There were things I didn't share either. I didn't tell him about my history of disastrous relationships with men. And I never thought his secrets might be big ones, things you'd disappear over; more like awkward conversations-at-a-later-date kind of revelations. Afterward, I wanted to kick myself, but when it's good and you're infatuated, you don't rock the boat.

"I'm so sorry, Liss."

"I've spent a lot of time wondering whether something happened to him, but how would I find out?"

"You clearly tried hard to find him, Liss. Either something happened to him, or he didn't want to be found."

Those are the only two logical scenarios, and neither one makes me comfortable. *This is why I moved on. Stop thinking about it.* I run an exasperated hand through my hair. This trip is going to bring it all back, and I need to face it and move on.

I give Brian a grateful half smile and he nods. "I'm so pleased to have you back, Liss. It's great to see you again." He pats my forearm. "Why don't you tell me more about the project you're doing, and let's work out if we can do some things together."

He's moving the conversation on, thank God. I got myself out of the hole I fell into after I lost Dan, and I'm not going to fall back down.

CHAPTER 27

Liss

Tuesday, February 22, 2022

How could I have forgotten the frustration of trying to do anything in this country? A laugh bubbles up my throat. *You're only a month into this, you Westerner.*

I wipe the sweat off my forehead as I glance around my makeshift office in the backroom of the local pizza delivery place, fans whirring away ineffectually. Brian's given me so much information about how his teams deliver aid, introduced me to his contacts and explained how to get things done. I've sneakily got to know a few of the militia guys, and with packets of cigarettes or chocolates, I can usually find out the location of skirmishes between rival factions. How do you understand anything if you don't talk to people? Brian gives me earache about my safety all the time and has persuaded me to stay living in the hotel. He thinks it's keeping me safe; I think it's cheap and clean. *Whatever*. What I find out is gold dust for both of us.

Locals are eager to earn much sought-after US dollars. A guy I met in the bar one night is a genius with software and has developed an interactive map with statistics on camps and displacement. Lots of local agencies are using it now, and we've had an initial meeting to help people add their own data. *Keep reminding yourself of the good things.* My focus shifts back to the voice of Akai, our contractor, on the other end of the phone telling me why the shipment of tents and materials we've been expecting for days is stuck at the border.

"But, Akai, can't we offer some money to make things move faster?"

I'm not supposed to give bribes, but everything happens this way. Akai starts detailing who's been offered money and why, and I tap my pen on the table with a sigh. When I glance up, James, who works in Brian's office, is standing smiling in the open doorway. I wave him in, and he grins, slipping into the chair opposite, dark curls flopping over his forehead. James is a sweetheart, and he obviously likes me, but he's shy and after Dan and Stéphane cheating on his wife, I want a relationship with a guy like I want a hole in my head. He raises his eyebrows at me, and I put Akai on speaker. Then James grabs a pen and a piece of paper from my desk and writes: *There's a strike in South Africa. They've closed the northern borders.*

I widen my eyes at him. Our main suppliers are in South Africa. It's one of the largest food producers on the continent. And the government was overthrown there recently, and there's obviously still a lot of political wrangling going on. No wonder we've got problems. I scratch the back of my neck. *South Africa.* The desire to go and search for Dan rises up like a drumbeat, and I squash it back down. *Don't be stupid, Liss. He's not there.* Thank God I haven't had enough days off to put *that* mad plan into action. Brian wasn't even sure, and how would you find him, you crazy bitch?

"Akai, I've got James here who works with Brian from FoodAid. I've put you on speaker so he can join our call. He's told me there's a strike in South Africa."

"I did see some chatter online," Akai groans on the other end of the line.

I listen as James fills him in on what they know about routes and the companies involved.

"I'll see what I can find out down here," Akai sighs. "Leave it with me."

Akai has a multitude of contacts with the drivers and the haulage companies;

he'll try and work all the angles. He's committed as I am to getting resources up here for local people.

"Great," I say. "Call me back."

"You got it, chief," he says, hanging up.

I grin at James. "Thanks for that. At least it explains some of the problems we've been having."

He smiles as he avoids my eyes. "I thought I'd come and tell you as soon as I found out." His eyes flick to mine and away again. "They've closed the borders because of the unrest and looting. We think we're going to lose thousands of dollars' worth of perishable goods that are stuck on the border with Uganda."

I groan at him—that's so much worse than my problem.

"The transportation bosses and food producers have organized a meeting on Friday in Johannesburg to discuss the strike. Brian and I thought someone should go down and find out what's going on and how long it might last. We've got to decide whether to source our produce from elsewhere. I came to see if you could go. Brian is in the Nkamira camp in Rwanda at the moment, and I've got to go to Kirumba to sort out a distribution of what little food we've got." He glances at his wrist. "Imminently actually." He grimaces.

Just when I've tamped down my desperate need to go to South Africa, someone puts an offer like that on the table. I have to go, if only to return all Brian's kindness. I could head down there and make some contacts, meet some key aid people. *You're not kidding anyone, Liss.* Electricity hums through me. Goddammit, hope is what finished me last time. And South Africa is a *huge* country. And why would he be there now? The whole search for him in Zimbabwe was fruitless. *Maybe you could hire another private investigator.* I groan and put my head in my hands.

James blinks at me. "You don't have to go," his concerned eyes scan my face as I lift my head to rest on my hands, staring out the window.

"It's fine. I'm happy to help." I turn to meet his gaze and give him a weak smile I pray he won't see through.

CHAPTER 28

Liss

Friday, February 25, 2022

After a few morning meetings, I wedge myself into the back of a dilapidated colonial-style meeting hall behind rows of wooden chairs full of people. Hundreds more people stand against the side walls: Everyone who's trying to get goods out of South Africa is here. Security guards are talking to more people who are trying to cram inside. We desperately need to sort out how to get supplies into Kiwanja, but there's so much reluctance to deal with the DRC given the armed groups and attacks on transportation. Nobody is interested: To them we are another troubled, war-torn region, but it's local people who are starving.

The only thing in our favor is that we're an aid agency, and we have money. Our distributor here has already shaken his head at me and said repeatedly, "Not possible," but if I can find the right people and grease a few palms, things will happen. *The hustler, that's me.* I'm sure I can persuade someone to transport our stuff. Brian's too.

My short pants and T-shirt stick to my skin, and I glance up at the ineffectual wooden blades slowly rotating over the central part of the hall. The top sides are all coated in dust like they belong to another age, before technology moved from fans to something better. A smile curls my lips: Just the sight of this overcrowded place and the creaky old fan makes my heart ache for these chaotic countries with their lovely hospitable people and vital problems. *I'm so pleased to be back.* I survey the room again. It's unlikely I'll spot a familiar face, but you never know, and it might be helpful.

Several people are making their way toward the makeshift platform at the front which holds a long table at which six or seven people are seated. As I follow the line of people down the aisle, my gaze lands on a white guy at the end of the table with long hair and a beard. He looks familiar. With broad shoulders in a crumpled khaki shirt, he's just like … *don't be stupid, Liss* … the number of times I've seen guys I thought were him ... I roll my eyes at myself.

The government official chairing the meeting stands up, bangs the gavel down and the talking begins. And boy, does it go on. There's a lot of speeches about supply routes, ongoing negotiations with the strikers … Gah. I should be taking notes. Then the sandy-haired guy stands up and the chair introduces him as a member of the farming community, and my gaze wanders over him again. Something about the movement of his hands has me riveted. He clears his throat to speak and the way he does it … *Don't be an idiot, Liss* … I wish Brian hadn't told me he thought Dan had lived in South Africa: I'm going to be seeing him everywhere.

But then he starts speaking and my heart stops.

Oh my God.

It's Dan.

That deep rumble …

Surely … surely …

No.

No. It can't be.

I used to listen out for his voice, hear it through mud and bamboo walls. And he's just sitting here, on this platform? Like he popped up from nowhere.

Holy shit. But he's smaller, shrunken somehow, not the smiling person I knew. *Is it really him? That hair and the beard?*

He carries on talking, and I focus down on my hands only to find they're shaking, a buzz of electricity flooding through my body. The hall starts to fade in and out. I'm fucking hot and getting hotter. *I need to sit down.* I raise my water bottle to my lips, banging it against my teeth. Deep breath, concentrate on breathing. In out, in out. *Holy shit.* His face is lined, hidden behind all the facial hair. *I thought he was dead.* I want to wave. I don't want to wave. What happened to his short soft curls? My eyes skip to the long roping arms, so much thinner than I remember. His face creases into a frown as he sucks on his lip, like the whole world is weighing him down.

Oh.

My.

God.

He's saying something about the harvest, about workers. He shifts in his chair, and it's so achingly familiar. I have a hundred images of him sitting on the veranda, taking his shirt off on a build, shifting that exact same way. I groan internally.

I glance at the guys next to me and lick my lips. He's not going to see me in a crowd as big as this. Is that a good or a bad thing? But maybe as one of the few women here, I'm standing out like a sore thumb. The thread of what's being said washes over my head. Fucking hell, he cut me out of his life. *Am I going to talk to him?* He moves to cross his legs. What could I say? So many things I've wanted answers to for so long, like you're not dead and where the fuck did you go? And Jesus, why, why, why? I shake my head. I have to talk to him. After everything, how could I let this go by?

The back-and-forth discussion from the floor is interminable, but eventually the chair calls it closed with promises of action and a disgruntled mumbling rises into the air with a couple shouts of "Shame!" echoing off the walls. People surge toward the raised platform to speak to the government's transportation boss, to talk to *Dan.* But I don't move. I'll catch him when the crowd clears. *Is this his job?*

As he leans down to chat to a man who taps his arm, Dan's head lifts, eyes scanning the room absent-mindedly, running over me and carrying on. Then he stops and his eyes swing back, lips parting and a hundred emotions skitter over his face. He bites his lip and focuses back on the guy who's talking to him, blinking rapidly before looking to the side, clearly not concentrating on what's being said. His eyes meet mine, and he stares.

He's alive.

Alive.

Alive.

An uncomfortable prickle takes over my throat, eyes tightening. I can't hold his gaze. *All this time. I worried about him.* When I look back, he's frowning, and he lifts a hand at me like he's telling me to wait, and my legs go weak, cold flooding through me. After all the torture of the last three years, he's going to talk to me. I can't bear it.

The man he's talking to gestures with his hands, and two other guys butt into the conversation, angry and arms waving, arguing. His eyes switch from one to the other, nodding, patient. The crowd is fading a bit now, and so I scurry down the aisle toward the front. As I look around, a white lady and a small girl I didn't notice before are standing to the side at the front. They're looking at the platform, watching. I shift slightly closer. The girl is gorgeous, with blonde curly hair that reaches the woman's waist and an inability to keep still. Her bouncing and fidgeting almost make me laugh. It reminds me so much of the energy I had when I was younger. She keeps pulling on the lady's sleeve, who bends down to quietly answer her questions. I move nearer and as the noise drops, I start to pick up on their conversation.

"When will Daddy be finished?" she says, and I look toward the people crowded around the platform.

"As soon as he's answered all the people's questions," the woman replies, eyes flickering over me with a smile, before returning to the knot of people surrounding Dan.

Who are they waiting for? My eyes dart from the pair of them back to the group of people milling around at the front. And it all happens in slow motion in front of me. The building pit in my stomach. *They're watching Dan.* My gaze swings from Dan to them. I study the blonde curls and Dan's hair. Oh my God, this, this … what is *this*? My eyes track over the woman, and she smiles at me as my eyes skitter away. I stand like I'm carved out of wood. Is this, is this … was she talking about Dan? Dan is her *dad*? I scrutinize her small, upturned face, the blonde lashes sweeping her cheeks like they hold some genetic clue. How old is she? How can Dan be her father? *Three years.* She's not tiny, the minimum age she could be is … God, I don't know. I inhale and roll my lips together. *I'm going to be sick.*

Dan's head is bent down as he talks to someone, no longer looking at me, and I turn slowly on my heel and walk in a daze across the battered wooden floor toward the exit. *Don't look back. What am I doing?* I'm just going to head away for a bit and think. Get some air. As I push through the old oak doors, a sign for a restroom looms on my right and in seconds I'm pushing through a swinging door and leaning over a crumbling toilet bowl as the contents of my stomach splatter onto the old porcelain.

How old was she? I try to visualize her height. I want to go back in to take some photos so I can review it all later when I'm calmer and can rationally understand what I saw. What I *heard*. My hand shakes as I press a finger to my lips. Why are they shaking like this? Leaning against the green-painted walls, I rest my hands on my knees in an attempt to stop it. The noise is fading in and out, the floor a blur of brown-and-blue mosaic tiles. Distant voices filter in from the hall, the clink and clatter of traders on the street outside the old Victorian window. Time slips away. I have no idea how long I stand like this, pulling my breath in and pushing it out, trying to keep standing, keep breathing, keep suppressing the nausea.

The little girl's face pops into my head unbidden and with such clarity that I lurch sideways over the toilet again, bringing up more of the chicken and jollof rice I ate for lunch. I wipe a sweaty hand over my face, yanking the ancient flush and fumbling over to the cracked sink to splash some water on my face, drying it on the bottom of my shirt. As I lift my head, a woman with a pasty face appears in the decaying mirror over the sink and stares at me.

What just happened?

CHAPTER 29

Liss

Saturday, February 26, 2022

Outside of the plane window, the sky is an inky black—is it nothing or something? A reflection of seats and lights and people engrossed on phones and screens. A strange lethargy has taken over my body. I have no memory of getting back to the hotel after I left the talk, but suddenly I was in my room, stripping out of sweaty clothes, standing in the shower and then lying on the bed in my underwear. I don't remember sleeping. The night outside turned black, the room went dark, and I lay on the covers as the moon tracked across the ceiling: me and ten brown marks on the plaster.

At some point, I got up and drank neat gin from the minibar. Guzzled it like water and lay back down. In the morning, all the spirit bottles were empty. As the room became lighter, I must have dozed. The blare of my alarm woke me up at 7 a.m., and I got up and came to the airport, checked in and sat watching the people come and go—kids, families, grandparents.

My eyes droop and my limbs are heavy like I'm swimming in molasses. *I don't want to think about it*. But it keeps popping into my head like a fly stuck inside a mosquito net.

"*When will Daddy be finished?*"

Twisting on the woman's hand, scuffing her shoes on the floor. How tall are children at certain ages? She seemed ... she seemed ... *big*? And my eyes have strayed to every child I've seen since. I can still see the blonde curls resting against the woman's waist. When did Dan have her? Before or after me? Who is the woman? Part of me wishes I'd stayed and faced whatever there was to face, but it felt impossible, my body just not capable of ... A long sigh seeps through my clenched teeth. If I'd known how much I was going to torture myself, I would've waited. *Maybe*. And there's no doubt some questions have been answered now. Leaving me was deliberate, and he had a small child, and therefore, presumably, another relationship.

The little boy in front of me peers at me over the top of this seat, eyes huge like a frog, and I smile at him.

"Hello," I say, and he instantly ducks down, but seconds later a small face appears in the gap between the seats. I wink and he vanishes again, and the lady beside me chuckles and I share a smile with her. It's rusty, like my fun mechanism is broken. I stare out into the sky again, but the little guy in front is determined to be curious. He peeks around the seat again, right next to the window.

"Hello," I say again, and this time he giggles.

The woman in the seat next to him moves and leans over to say something to him, and he disappears, permanently this time. I close my eyes and must fall into a deep sleep because, before I know it, an announcement starts in the speaker overhead and the woman beside me shifts, putting her bag under the seat in front and heading out of her seat, presumably to the toilet.

I sigh, check my seatbelt and flick through my phone, which is useless without Wi-Fi or a mobile signal. In no time at all, the tarmac and lights are rushing closer and the plane jolts as we squeal onto the runway and people stand as soon as we stop taxiing, pulling their luggage from overhead bins. As we're standing waiting to exit, the lady from the seat in front turns.

"I'm sorry if he was bothering you," she says.

I give her my rusty smile.

"Not at all." I look at the dark curls and big, solemn brown eyes of the little boy.

She rumples his hair. "You're a nuisance," she laughs, and my heart aches for him a bit.

"It was fine," I say. "He was no trouble."

I'm oversensitive to these kinds of parental comments, an echo of the malicious remarks my dad subjected me to, although there's no real animosity in her tone.

"You always worry that they're bothering other people," she mutters with genuine concern in her eyes, hand on his head as he gazes up at me.

"How old is he?"

"Four," she says, and I nod.

That seems to finish the conversation. The random few words you have with strangers when you're waiting for something to happen. People close to us start to move forward, and she grabs the boy's hand and heads up the aisle. As I follow her, all I can think of is how his dark curls reach up to her waist.

CHAPTER 30

Liss

Friday, March 4, 2022

A shadow crosses the open doorway, and Brian looms in the gap.

"Brian, this is a pleasant surprise," I say.

"I'm glad you think so," he says, with a slow smile that doesn't quite reach his eyes. "You got time to grab something to eat?" His gaze skims over the piles of paperwork on my desk.

I rub my face. I want to sweep all this onto the floor. I've been here until 10 p.m. every night since I got back a week ago. Maybe a bowl of comfort food and a chat would shore me up for the afternoon. I stand and gesture to the door, and, as we walk toward the nearby café, Brian updates me on Nkamira camp in Rwanda, and what's happening with James, his produce shipments, and the local government officials who stick their noses into everything we do because money is involved. I briefed Brian when I got back from South Africa, although I'm sure there were huge gaps in what I told him, and then I buried that visit in a vault somewhere deep in my body.

When we roll into Mimi's, I stand and stare at the menu on the wall. Could I eat something? I'm not sure. Brian touches my arm.

"Liss?"

Akaras—bean fritters—are simmering away in the pan behind the counter, and I point at them and the lady nods, scooping six out of the hot oil onto greaseproof paper. She hands it over to me as Brian asks for the same in Swahili.

"A stew and coffee," I say automatically. It's always safer here when the water has been boiled.

"Make that two," Brian adds.

We slide ourselves in around a table, and Brian studies me steadily. "Are you okay?"

I nod. "Just a lot to do."

My briefing to Brian avoided any mention of Dan. *Should I tell him?* I eye his peppered beard and kind eyes. *It might be good to talk to someone.* But as if he can read my mind, he says suddenly, "I'm here because Dan contacted me this morning. I thought I should come and tell you straightaway." He looks down at his food, chewing his cheek. "I've also got a confession to make. I knew Dan was going to be there. When I got the email about the meeting, there were several pictures. He looked completely different, but after a while I realized it was him."

I'm halfway through a bite in my sandwich, and I choke, my throat dry like dead summer grass. My stomach goes into freefall.

Brian reaches out and squeezes my fingers. "I'm so sorry I didn't tell you. I thought I could engineer a meeting. I thought you might be relieved to discover he's alive, that it would answer some questions." He winces and a notch appears between his eyebrows. "I'm sorry if I did the wrong thing."

"He was on the platform," I say, rubbing at the dry skin on my hands. The lump in my throat swells. My eyes fix on his left shoulder.

Brian clears his throat. "He said he saw my name on the list of organizations that were invited to the conference, and wanted to reach out to me. He said he'd seen you at the meeting and was contacting me on the off chance I might know where you were."

Oh, shit. I try and swallow past the golf ball that seems to have lodged itself in my throat.

"He asked me if I'd had any contact with you, if I knew where you were, what you were doing," Brian adds.

"Did you tell him I was here?"

Brian spreads his palms flat on the bench, and my gaze jumps to his face. "I didn't want to lie when he asked me if I'd seen you." He sucks on his lower lip. "That was probably the wrong thing to do, I'm guessing."

I shake my head, sucking air into my lungs to stop myself gasping. What a catalog of disasters. But Brian's always been so good to me; I'm sure he was trying to help.

"You didn't mention that you'd seen him." There's a question mark in his tone. "After what you said about trying to track him down, I …"

I trail patterns on the battered table in front of me. "I'm sorry. I wasn't … I didn't feel …" I take a long breath. Brian doesn't say a word, face sympathetic. Embarrassment flushes through my body. I'm like some cliché, shocked at finding out about the other woman, an idiot about men.

"I didn't want to talk about seeing him," I whisper, then shake my head. That's not right. "I *couldn't* talk about it."

"What happened, Liss?" He takes my hand and rubs it between his two bearlike paws. "Talk to me."

"His wife was there," I murmur, picking at the side of my nail.

"His *wife*?" His eyebrows shoot up.

"And his child."

The word sticks in my throat like sandpaper, the girl's blonde curls dancing in front of my face. So cute.

"God, Liss. He's *married*?" His nostrils flare.

"Yeah. I didn't … I couldn't … That was difficult to process. It was a shock."

"I'll bet it was. *Jesus*, Liss."

"I think I was waiting until I could have a calm conversation about it," I whisper.

Brian nods and leans back against his chair, still holding my hand in his. It's strangely good, like a lifeforce is seeping from his big, rough hands into mine. Words start to tumble out.

"Of all the scenarios I considered when I couldn't find him, I told myself finding him alive would be the best thing. And I had a complete failure of imagination because I never pictured a wife and a child. I mean that's crazy, right? He was older than me, so why wouldn't he be married by now? I'm stupid."

"Jesus, Liss, you're not stupid. I don't think anyone would expect that. After all you told me, how he came to the US and what he said … I'm surprised. *Really* surprised. God, I should have said something before you went … what was I thinking? I'm an interfering old fool."

I squeeze my fingers around Brian's as if doing that will give me more strength to say what I need to say. To say the words out loud, to admit my darkest fears to someone else.

"The thing is … the little girl looked about four, maybe older?"

Brian frowns and a dull red starts at the base of his throat. "*What?* I don't understand." His brows crease further. "Are you thinking he had her before … before you and he …"

"I think? I mean …"

"Oh my *God*!" Brian runs his free hand through his hair, jaw tightening as he stares out the window before his enraged eyes swing back to mine. "Jesus Christ, I should *never* have told him I'd seen you. I thought I was helping! I didn't think he was a cheating asshole. *Fuck!*" He groans.

I shake my head. Somehow, I can't reconcile the Dan I knew with the words "cheating asshole." He's achieved such a status in my head over the last three years with how lovely he was after all my man disasters, how smitten he seemed to be, and the fact he came after me. I can only erode my view of him bit by bit.

"Tell me what he said," I say.

"He asked me what I was up to and if I knew what you were doing. Specifically, if I had a way of getting in touch with you."

"Getting in touch with me?" I squeak. *This was obvious from the start, you chump.* "What did you say?"

"I wasn't sure what to say. I'm so sorry, Liss." He buries his head in his hands. "I said I could probably contact you."

"Oh God." I put my cup down too abruptly and coffee slops over the side. But this is at least partly my fault, I should have told him what happened as soon as I came back.

He mops at the coffee distractedly as I poke my stew. "I'm so sorry," he mumbles.

"It's fine, Brian. I mean, he saw me there. It was only a matter of time before he tried …" I swallow. "I guess I don't really understand. Why would he want to see me? Does he want to explain? If he had a wife, why wouldn't he just be embarrassed? Wouldn't he want to avoid any sort of confrontation?" I chew my lip. "He cut off all communication, disappeared, and has never tried to reach out to me." Who am I asking these questions of? Myself? I'm not sure I've got any answers.

Brian shakes his head and purses his lips. *Always so patient.* I study his kind face, the grooves worn by years of helping people.

"I don't know what happened at the meeting …" I start and then it all streams out. Seeing Dan on the platform, him raising his hand, realizing his wife and child were standing there, and how I left. Sickness roils in my stomach again, along with a clawing sense of alarm, and it makes my mind up.

"I don't want to see him."

How could I see him, happy, with someone else? Not having the right to touch him, to be friends. Nausea fills my mouth. Another woman holding his hand … I slam the shutters down.

Brian stares off into the distance, then waves his hand. "Of course, of course you don't. I'll make up some excuse, some story."

"I'm not sure I would deal well with seeing him face to face, have him tell me about his family. Ugh. I wouldn't be able to be cool at all."

Brian nods, opens his mouth, and closes it again, then says, "If Helen hadn't died …"

He's never talked in detail about his wife, and I stare at him. He coughs like he's trying to build up courage. "If Helen hadn't died, but had gone off with someone else …" He fiddles with his fork. "I understand, Liss. I'd murder him with my bare hands."

I smile sadly at him.

"I still miss her every day." His eyes glass over.

I put my hand over his on the table. "I'm sorry, Brian." A simple sorry could never cover what happened to him. He shakes his head, eyes watery.

"I decided I needed to move on. There's a lady here who I see sometimes …" He pauses as he chews his cheek. "For sex." I gape at him. It seems like my torrent of detail and emotion has unleashed something in him, and my toes curl, heat climbing up my neck.

He drops his head, hands clasping the back of his neck. "It's torture."

"*What?* Why?"

"Every time we"—he coughs—"go to bed together I can't get Helen out of my head; it's like she's all around me. I feel terrible. I'm forcing myself through something, and I wonder whether it's just making it all worse."

And oh my God, I understand this, so well. I forced myself through everything. He wipes his hands across his eyes, closes them, and tears leak out from under his lashes. *Oh shit.* This is so much bigger than any of my disasters.

I grip his hand tighter, and he squeezes back.

"Thank you, Liss. Jesus, I'm sorry. I don't know where all this is coming from."

"Perhaps you needed to talk."

He nods. "You're a good listener."

"Glad I'm good at something."

He half laughs at this, wiping his eyes again.

"You're amazing at a lot of things, Liss." He pauses. "I feel so guilty, like I'm using her," he whispers.

"You could try talking to her?"

"Her English is not so hot."

I nod—I appreciate what he's saying. It's not that kind of relationship.

He shakes himself and straightens.

"If I can do anything …" I say.

He offers a weak smile. "This has been very helpful."

"Okay," I say.

"I could say you've moved on from here?" Brian says, circling us back to Dan, and I blink at him. I'd almost forgotten my own problems in the depths of his.

"That sounds sensible."

He inclines his head. "When you said you don't understand … you're right, none of it adds up. Why was he doing a PhD in Harare? Why would he come to see you in New York if he had a wife and kid in South Africa?"

"None of it makes any sense. The fact he disappeared makes no sense. Well, maybe it does make more sense now, seeing as he had a wife and child. I was a fling, and then he cut off all contact. But you'd think he'd be happy he dodged a bullet." I roll my lips together. "But I am glad he's alive. In my darkest moments I was convinced he'd been killed." I sweep my hand around. "Like some random mugging. Or the fighting. It's not like it's uncommon."

"Yeah."

"I appreciate you doing all this," I say.

He gapes at me. "I think it's a problem I created, Liss. God, I'm sorry."

"Stop apologizing. I'm glad I've seen him in some ways; it's answered some questions that have tormented me these past few years."

He squeezes my hand where he's still holding it over the table.

"We've known and helped each other for a long time, Liss. You drew me out of myself when I first came out here and I was struggling to cope with my new life and Helen being gone. I'll try and put him off the scent and make it right that I told him I'd seen you. I'm not comfortable with what his motives might be. Let me see what I can concoct."

I have the best friends. *Here. Everywhere.*

CHAPTER 31

Liss

Saturday, March 12, 2022

My phone buzzes as I'm wading through emails on patchy Wi-Fi, and I frown at the number. *Why is the hotel calling me from downstairs?* I lift it to my ear, and the lady who mans the reception informs me that I have a visitor. Someone called Daniel Falinsburg is here to see me.

Falinsburg?

I roll the unfamiliar surname over my tongue. *Wow.* I should have picked that up from the meeting in South Africa, but I'm not sure I registered much of anything that day. All that effort looking for Dan Andrews—he used that false name at the university too. *How many lies did he tell?* I spent money, money I couldn't afford, with a private investigator.

But fuck, he's here.

After Brian talked to him again, he told me he got the impression that Dan wouldn't let it go.

And that name is familiar, itching away at the back of my memory. I stand up and head to the bathroom and splash water over my face. A woman with wild hair stares back at me in the mirror and I wrinkle my nose. I'd like to appear cool and sleek, but when have I ever managed that in front of Dan? I collapse back down on the bed and suck in a deep breath. Why are you scared, Liss? He's the asshole here—this is your chance to tell him face to face how long it took you to pull yourself back together.

My stomach follows the descent of each painted floor number in the stairwell. When I reach the lobby, he's sitting, so casually, on a sofa near the entrance. His hair is shorter, tousled, and his beard trimmed: He looks more like the man I knew, but the old confident swagger and the way he held his body are gone. His eyes catch mine as I walk over the shiny linoleum floor to the red-fringed couch, and it's like falling from a great height. *He's alive. Okay.* The pain in my chest takes over my whole being. Goddammit, Liss. *He has a child, a wife.* Guys like this … you've been there before.

His eyes follow me, sparks on my skin everywhere his gaze lands, and as he rises to meet me, I paste a smile on my face. *Get this over and done with.* I want to ask what the fuck he thought he was doing disappearing on me with no explanation, but starting this conversation at confrontational and angry doesn't feel right.

"Dan," I say, fixing my lips in an upward curve. "It's great to see you after such a long time!" My voice is full of warmth and surprise, and fuck, I can do convincing well when I want to.

He nods, fiddling with the sleeve of his shirt. "And you." Tightness creeps around his eyes. "It was a shock to see you in Johannesburg," he says slowly. *He's treading cautiously.* He sinks back down onto the sofa, and I perch on the edge of the seat opposite him like a bird about to take flight.

"Yes!" I nod. *Too much, Liss, not so manic.* His tan skin is glowing in the afternoon sun, light catching the blond in his hair. Did he always look so indecently handsome? I try not to bare my teeth at him.

"I was surprised to see you too," I say, pushing forward. I don't want him to think that my visit to South Africa was to chase after him when he tried so hard to hide. "I came down there in an attempt to sort out our supply issues. I had no idea how big a problem the strike was across South Africa."

If I talk about work, my racing heart will slow down, and I can deal with the fact he is standing right here, talking.

"I think you were waiting afterward to say hello," he says, tipping his head sideways in a familiar gesture.

Say hello? Like we're two casual friends who are always bumping into each other. And I can't say I ran because I worked out that he had a kid and couldn't face him.

"Yes. I'm sorry I dashed off. You were clearly tied up, and I didn't want to disturb you. It would have been nice to say hello, but you didn't need to come all the way up here. We could have caught up another time. I'm sure I'll be back in South Africa." I laugh, and even to my ears it sounds false. "Certainly, if these transportation problems continue."

His face pinches. "No, we couldn't do that, Liss. I couldn't wait."

Oh, shit. "Oh! Okay."

"I've been wanting to talk to you for three years."

My eyebrows rise into my hairline. *He's* been wanting? He disappeared on *me*. And what the fuck? He could have got in touch with me—he knew my details. I'm on social media for God's sake. My heart sinks. I think I'm about to be fed some explanation and excuses I don't want to hear. After all my work to find him, after *three years*, it tears at something deep inside. *I let it go*. It feels wrong to bring it back up, like reliving a bad dream over and over. Either he was already married, or he went straight into another relationship and had a child. Both options make me nauseous.

I wave my hand. "You don't owe me an explanation. It doesn't matter now."

He frowns. A muscle ticks in his jaw, as if he's fighting something. If I didn't know better, I'd say it was anger. What's he got to be angry about?

"Do you really think that, Liss? It matters to me."

I stand up. The desire to flee is strong.

"It was a long time ago. It's way too late for this conversation now. It's not going to change anything." I almost roll my eyes at how dramatic this sounds.

"Do you really think that?" His tone is rough as he stares up at me, not moving.

"Of course, Dan! You have a family and a farm and …"

"You know about my family?" he says, and hearing that admission come out of his mouth, just like that, punches all the air out of me, and I collapse back down with a whoosh into my seat. He tilts his head and scans my face.

"I … well … I just … when I saw you, they were there …" I wave my hand. "After you came to New York and disappeared"—I swallow past the tightness in my throat—"I didn't understand what had happened. I looked for you."

When I think back to that New York visit, I'm light-headed at his duplicity.

"You looked for me?" He sounds stunned. But why is he surprised? Of course I looked for him! Then his mind seems to jump on. "What do you mean, *they* were there?"

But I want some answers of my own. "Why did you come to see me in New York?"

He runs a shaky hand through his hair. "It was special, Liss." His voice is tight, with a slight wobble in it that tells me he's as affected by this conversation as I am, or else he's one hell of an actor. "I wanted you to come back to Africa. I was worried that you wouldn't."

What on earth is he saying? Maybe he wanted a mistress? Oh. My. God. *That's* what he thought this was? Is he thinking I would be *flattered*? Is this why he's here *now*? *Holy shit.*

"I don't think that would have happened."

"You wouldn't have come back?" His face goes white. "You promised me you would."

My lips thin. "I think I would have realized about your family sooner or later. Were you planning on keeping it a secret?"

"No, no. Of course not. I would have told you eventually."

Something white hot flashes through me. *He was expecting me to just fall into that?* Is he crazy? God, I don't know him at all. And he certainly doesn't know me. "I'm not okay with being lied to."

His face creases like he's in pain. "I'm so sorry, Liss. I couldn't use my real name in Congo. It would have made things very difficult. I thought …" He pauses and lets out a long sigh. "My father was too well known."

His *father*? "What?"

"He was Minister for Finance in South Africa. He owned a lot of land and business interests there and was well known across the continent. He was shot and killed a week after I came back from New York. That's why I left Zimbabwe: Life got pretty complicated for a while. I had to go back to South Africa immediately."

My mouth falls open. His father was *shot*? And there's so many things in what he's said—where do I start?

"I came to the address you gave me in Zimbabwe," I whisper. I'm not sure why I say this—it's far too revealing.

"*What?*" His voice is loud and cracking. People in the reception area turn around, and the lady at the next table peers at me over her cup, then at him as he lets out a long groan.

She's still looking at us when I lean forward, lowering my tone. "After I didn't hear from you, after I couldn't raise a response by email or text, I went to the address you gave me. They'd never heard of you."

"You came back for me?" His whole face changes, his voice eager, hurried. "I gave up the house when I went back to South Africa. I had to leave immediately. There were some threats, credible threats, and the Secret Service put us in a safehouse. But my father has an estate, a big farm, and with the overthrow of the government recently, there's … well, it's safer now, and we've been able to go back there."

Hearing the word "us" and "we" makes my skin crawl. Did he live in the safehouse with his wife and child?

He laughs harshly. "The farm. It's a mess. Such a lot of work. I've … I'm … it's been a tough and unhappy three years."

"But your family are there with you? On the farm?" Ugh. The fact he's unhappy lights up something inside. And it shouldn't. It really shouldn't. But I'm only human.

He sighs. "Yes. It's been my family home for generations."

Well, that explains that. Perhaps he wanted a mistress, some kind of fling, and then got overtaken by events. It's all moot now, a strange accident of fate. I put on a polite smile.

"It's been a relief to clear this up, Dan. I worried for a long time that something had happened to you."

I put my shaking hand on the arm of the chair in preparation to stand. My skin crawls with what we did together, how I was so in love with him, when he was somewhere else entirely.

"Wait." His hand shoots out to my arm. "You're going? We still have so much to say."

I'm not sure I want to find out any more about his family, his little girl. I shake my head.

"Can I see you again?"

"I don't think that would be a great idea, do you?"

"What? Why? Is it so hard to forgive?"

I gape at him. "The fact you didn't tell me you had a wife and child?" My voice is incredulous.

"What? What do you mean, a wife and child? What are you talking about?"

I swallow. "Your family? I saw them waiting for you after the meeting."

"What family?" He stares at me frowning. "Wait … you mean Nisha and Benny?"

God, they have names. Of course they do. I close my eyes. All I can see is her blonde curly hair, so like his. Someone is sawing a knife through my abdomen.

"You mean my half-sister. My father's child, Benny. Now my ward. And her nanny, Nisha." His voice is urgent, soft.

Someone has doused me in icy water. My eyes pop open, and his face swims for a second, and when I focus on him again, tightness hovers around his eyes. The conversation twists and bends in front of me.

"I don't understand. They were at the meeting …"

"Nisha and Benny," he says, more firmly now. "When my father was shot, we all had to go into hiding. My mother died a long time ago …" He hesitates. "My father had a lot of affairs. And I mean a *lot* … Benny is his child from one of those relationships and was living with him when he died. A woman he got pregnant who left her with my father." His face goes dark. "He didn't care about anybody, me, my mother, but least of all Benny. But she had a wonderful nanny, Nisha, who's been a kind of surrogate mother to her. She's always lived on the farm, but we had to take them someplace safe."

He peters out, blinking. "You thought I had a *wife*?"

Shock is pouring through my body like ice in my veins. I can hardly process what he's saying.

"You thought I'd done all these things with you … and I had a *wife*?" He laughs incredulously. "*What?* How long have you thought that? All this time? Three years?"

I shake my head, gulping. "Only since I saw you in South Africa."

"But Benny is four …"

Oh God, I was right about her age. I close my eyes, but they pop open again when he exclaims.

"Oh my God! You thought I had a wife and child when I met you in Congo? *Liss! No!* What must you have thought of me! No wonder you didn't want to meet up when I contacted Brian. My God, it's all making sense now."

His eyes are wide and panicked. "I've been with no one since." The words tumble out of his mouth, eyes tighter now, pleading.

"What? No way." A flash of hot and cold runs through me. All my failed relationships. *Ramesh.* I've been with other people since Dan. Of course I have—I thought he was gone. The woman at the nearby table shifts in my peripheral vision.

He glances off to the side, jaw clenched. "What we shared, Liss, nothing else …" He shakes his head. "I told you I'd wait for you. I made you a *promise*. You went to the Philippines, I think? I thought that perhaps you never came back?"

He followed what I was *doing*? A small incoherent noise creeps out of my mouth.

He frowns again, chewing his lip. "Wait. Have I misunderstood this whole conversation? You thought I was asking you to … to … like some arrangement?"

"Yes." I croak out.

He laughs, collapses back in his chair, and laughs manically, causing more people to turn around. I'm not sure I care.

"But the email, the texts I sent you. I tried so hard to contact you. Why didn't you respond?" I say. I can't believe this is true. It can't *be* true.

"My father was the number two in the South African government, and I've always had to protect my identity. For a long time, I've used a different surname. I was never in the public eye, but it just kept any questions and the consequences of that at bay. When he was assassinated, the security services took over everything. Turned out the rebels who killed my father were tracking his communications, and knew who I was, where I was. The security services had evidence, credible evidence, that they were planning to come after my brother and me. They wiped my email account, any record of me being in Zimbabwe, and destroyed my phone, and then flew me straight back to South Africa to a twenty-four-hour security detail and a safehouse. They were worried whoever had killed him had inside information, that it was someone on his team. The whole thing was a mess."

He has a *brother*? But I'll have to come back to that. He never got any of my messages. Over the years I've convinced myself he ignored or deleted them, or that he was dead. But just a minute, he still knew where I was.

"Why didn't you come to find me, explain?"

He runs his hands through his hair. "God, Liss. I wanted to. You don't know … I was terrified of putting you in danger. I wasn't allowed to go anywhere or contact anyone for ages, nothing that would identify who I was, where I was. I didn't know who to trust. For over a year, I had no online accounts, no phone." He leans forward and puts his head in his hands. "They knew I went to New York. I was beside myself. What if they held you hostage, or something worse? What if they were still somehow tracking me and I reached out to you? I couldn't take that risk."

He raises his head. "But now the rebels have achieved their objective, which was to get my father's party out of government, and who knows where that will lead. The Secret Service has told us that the threat is now minimal, and we've been back on the farm for five months. I've been so desperate to speak to you, to see you. But I …" He blinks up at the ceiling. "I'm still terrified of who I am, who my father was. We moved around different safehouses for two and a half years. I think I've got a little paranoid, but also I'd never forgive myself if something happened to you … and I thought there was no chance that you would've waited for me. But then you were there at the meeting, and seeing you there … after so long. I just couldn't leave it."

"Two and a half years!"

"It's been like a prison."

"I was worried you'd died. You disappeared and everything ended with no warning, no explanation. I came to Zimbabwe, dug around at the university and employed a private investigator, but every trail we followed was cold."

His eyes go wide. "A private investigator?"

I nod, and his eyes close with a pained expression. He reaches out to touch my hand, and grabs my fingers, squeezing tight. "I'm sorry," he says. "To be honest, I'm relieved you're still talking to me, that you're not married."

"I am actually," I tease, and his eyes snap wide, zooming in on my finger.

I grin at him, but it dies when I see something in his expression. "I saw a picture on Facebook when you were in the Philippines," he says, raising an eyebrow, and I nod. "There was a picture of you." He swallows like it's painful. "With a guy, a boyfriend."

Oh my God, Ramesh. The guy who got me through the worst time in my life, who got me over Dan. Who understood my whole story, how in love with another guy I was. Who listened and listened and looked after me anyway. Who picked me up from my lowest ebb and restored my confidence. Who made me think decent guys existed in the world, and I could find one. I remember the picture Dan's talking about, we're wrapped around each other. Ramesh took it when he kissed me and tagged me in it.

I look away, swallowing.

"You're not … you're not still with him?" Dan croaks.

"No."

"You looked so happy." He presses the tips of his fingers against his lips. "I … I started to think that maybe what happened was for the best, that you had moved on and you would be safe with him." His eyes fill with tears. "I thought maybe this was something you do, Liss. You go abroad and have relationships with guys. You were reluctant to commit, in New York. I … I …" He looks away and whispers, "Despite everything we had, I think I lost my mind a little."

My throat seizes up. The need for him to understand forces the words out of my mouth:

"After I came back from trying to find you, I lost my mind. My friends realized I was burying myself in Manhattan, and they persuaded me to go away somewhere different, somewhere with no memories. And I came across a voluntary organization that worked in the Philippines, and Ramesh was my guide. The last thing I wanted was any kind of relationship, believe me. But he was the best kind of friend to me, he looked after me in my misery, and I ended up staying for eighteen months. I thought perhaps I could move on with him. I thought you were dead, after all. But it wasn't right. He pulled me through, restored me to myself, and he was a lovely, lovely guy, but I was never in love with him."

I reach out and touch his hand. "I'm sorry," I say.

Dan lifts my fingers to his lips, kisses them, eyes closing with a pained expression. "The thought of you with someone else …" My heart lurches. "… But really, Liss, after all that's happened, I feel like the luckiest guy in the world."

I laugh, and he tugs my hand, trying to pull me forward, into him. I shake my head. We still need to talk.

I want to confess. "I feel like I used him. I'm so ashamed of that relationship, but so grateful to him too."

"Who? Ramesh?"

I nod.

"He listened to me go on and on about you and looked after me anyway. I owe him a debt I can never repay."

He squeezes my hand.

"He sounds like a good guy. I hate him."

I laugh.

"Can you forgive me for not telling you about my father? I don't know how to make this right."

"There's nothing to make right. Seeing you here …" I press my hand to my chest. "God, it's so much better than where my imagination took me. And I get it, Dan. I have an asshole father, not as bad as yours I think, but he tried to straitjacket me. It's not the same but …"

"No, no. I understand." He wraps his fingers around mine. "Come *here*, Liss," he says.

I stand, and he pulls me forward onto his lap. As I sink down, he hardens under my leg, and a smile curves over my lips.

"Stop laughing at me, woman. I've just told you how long it's been for me," he growls.

My whole body is hot. I want to take him upstairs and strip him naked, but we're rushing things here. He buries his face in my neck, letting out a long groan. His broad back is thinner than it used to be, but he's still so big, solid and *real*, oh so *real*. My eyes drift over the lobby. Half the people are staring at us out of the corners of their eyes.

"Tell me this is not a dream right now," he mumbles.

I pinch his bicep.

"I think the pinching thing is an old wives' tale." He draws in a sharp breath. "Can I come upstairs with you?"

Oh God, I want it. But I'm hollowed out, wobbly. What would sex with him do to me?

"It's too soon, isn't it?" he says into my neck, and I hug him closer as he groans. "I'm sorry, I'm just … you're here and it's been so long."

"I can't believe you won't disappear in a puff of smoke again." I drag up my deepest fears. "I still can't believe you're here."

He pulls back and squints at me. "I can't say I'm not still worried, but at least you know now. I won't disappear again. I promise."

I nod, but how can he say this, given what's happened? "Okay, but you're going back, right?"

He nods and sighs. "Yes, I have to."

"So, what are we talking about here, trying to do something long-distance?"

Suddenly, I want *everything* to be clear. I know he had his reasons, but now that I know what happened, I want to make up for all the direct questions I didn't ask last time.

He narrows his eyes at me. "Maybe to start with? Until we can find a way to be in the same place together. Does that sound okay?"

It sounds like a dream.

"I'll come up as often as I can," he says.

"Or I can come to you," I say, watching his face.

He grins. "That sounds amazing. I can show you the farm."

"You're running it?"

He nods. "With my brother."

"I can't believe you have a brother. How big is the farm?"

"Twenty thousand hectares."

"Oh my God, Dan."

He chuckles. "It's in the Western Cape. We've only been back there for five months. For me it's a big learning curve, but the workforce is committed." He runs his hands through his hair. "It's been badly managed for years. My father was never interested. We've started working on a way of improving the crops and the profit and sharing it out. My brother, Jed, has a degree in agricultural management."

"What happened to your father's business interests?"

His face darkens. "When he died, the government sequestered his assets, and we've only been able to start a legal process in the last five months. The farm was in Jed's name, and there were some other company holdings in Jed's name that we've been able to sell and we're using the money from that to pay lawyers. It's not good, Liss. I'll take you through it all some time."

"I'd welcome that." I take in the deep lines around his mouth and eyes and cup his jaw. "Are you okay?"

"I am now," he says, with a lopsided grin, squeezing my hip.

"I'm sorry about your dad."

"Don't be—he was an asshole. I'll fill you in sometime, but not now." His hand slides down to my knee. "I just want to enjoy this. Will you have dinner with me tonight?"

I nod.

"Are *you* okay, Liss?"

"I am. Seeing you here … it's amazing."

"God, I'm sorry I put you through that."

"How long are you here for?"

"Twenty-four hours."

My jaw drops as he gives me another squeeze. "That's all the security services were happy with. We don't have a security detail anymore, but we still have to let them know when we travel. Next time I'll come for longer."

CHAPTER 32

Dan

Friday, April 1, 2022

The darkness of an early morning presses in around me, and I heave a deep sigh as I pass from dirt to the asphalt of the main highway away from the farm. A huge weight eases off my shoulders. Over the last three weeks, I've had a life outside of here, a life beyond the mess here. I've been more measured in my interactions, and calmer in my decision-making. This whole mountain we've got to climb sorting out my father's estate, his shadow hanging over us, is receding like a wave: Someone has given me a future, and my heart is light with it.

I lean over to connect my phone to the car speaker system, and the cool voice of my audiobook fills the car. This should distract me through the five-hour drive down to Cape Town. I grin to myself: Listening to books about renewable agriculture and feeding my ideas into the farm is seriously pissing Jed off.

When I arrive in Cape Town, I text Liss to let her know I'm here and how much I'm looking forward to seeing her tomorrow. Then I spend four hours in meetings with lawyers, teeth grinding as it becomes clearer and clearer that almost no progress has been made since we started this process. *Fuck. That.*

The other side is stalling, no doubt with the aim of racking up our legal costs. The head lawyer on our team presents me with a bill that makes my hair stand on end. The pile of cash we made from the sale of the assets in Jed's name is dwindling fast. What do I have to do to hurry this process along? They're all smiles and apologies, but at the end of the meeting, I pull the head guy to one side.

"It can't go on like this," I say quietly. "We'll run out of money very quickly."

He nods. "I know, you said at the beginning how much you might be able to afford."

"I'm so frustrated."

"Rest assured, we are too. The other side wants to make this difficult for you. They want a fight, and it's no secret you and your brother are struggling for money. They're trying to force you into a corner, and unfortunately it's a legal strategy that works. I'm sorry to say that, after how your father was in government, they're determined to make you suffer."

"Can we avoid going to court?"

"We can try and negotiate a settlement, but it's likely you'd get nowhere near the real value of your father's holdings."

I nod at this. The alternative is to put the farm up as collateral to pay for lawyers' fees. I don't want to do that, and I certainly can't do it without talking to Jed first.

"I need to talk to my brother about our next steps," I say. "I'll let you know."

I step outside into the warm sunshine and pull my phone out of my pocket. I don't want this sitting on my mind all weekend with Liss. The phone rings once, twice.

"Yo!" Jed's loud shout reverberates over the clattering of what sounds like the thresher.

"Where are you?" I can't help shouting back.

"In the old barn. Hang on."

The insistent rattle rattle of the thresher fills the line, a radio blaring heavy rock in the background. If he heard his phone, he wasn't wearing ear defenders again. *Fuck.* I've nagged him about this. The machine grinds to a halt with a clatter and a sigh while Van Halen keeps exhorting me to "Jump!" I can envisage him standing in his sweat-damp shirt and hair stuck to his head, just like when we worked together when we were younger.

"Were you wearing ear defenders?"

"Calm down, Mom, my phone was in my pocket on vibrate. I had the goddamn things on. Make my head sweaty as hell."

I grin into the phone.

"What is it?" he grouses.

"They're stalling. We're going to run out of money, Jed."

He lets out a snort. "Tell me something new."

I ignore him. "I worked through the funds we have left for the legal dispute this morning and we have enough to do one fight in court, *maybe*. But that's a big maybe. If they drag it out or countersue, then we're screwed. I talked to the lawyers today about trying to negotiate a deal."

"We'd get very little in a negotiation, wouldn't we?"

"Yeah. The only other option is to put the farm up as collateral."

"To pay for lawyers' fees? Fuck, I hate that."

"Yeah, me too."

"And the outcome is completely uncertain."

"Yeah. I think the chances of us winning are low. We could get a better settlement than what they'd offer us in a negotiation, but whether we'd ever see any of that money with them dragging their feet and appealing or ..."

"God, I hate this shit. Can't we find someone to lean on them or take it on for a cut of the settlement or do it ourselves? Could we learn enough?"

At this point, I already know far too much about company law and shareholders and director contracts. The last thing I want to do is spend the next five years of my life fighting a legal case in South Africa.

"One of us needs to date a lawyer," Jed mumbles, and it makes me laugh, because it's a good fucking idea.

"Gonna have to be you, buddy, you're the charmer out of two of us."

"Used to be, not so good with the ladies now. Anyway, there's not exactly a load of them on a twenty-thousand-hectare farm in the Western Cape." He pauses for a beat. "You don't want to do this, do you? You don't want to fight a legal case."

I blow out a long breath. "No. No, I don't."

"We can't put the farm up, Dan. It would be good money after bad."

"Yeah." I sigh. I knew he'd say that, and actually, I agree with him.

"What about the 'no win, no fee' option?"

"Those guys are sharks."

"Yeah, but it's better than agreeing to be fleeced. We could at least talk to them."

I glance at my watch. Liss is coming in tomorrow, and it's already getting late. "Leave it with me. I'll see who I can talk to now, find out what the score is, and see if anyone is prepared to take us on, what offers they might be able to put on the table."

"Sounds good. Have fun."

"Yeah. Yeah. Asshole." I say, but he's already hung up.

CHAPTER 33

Liss

Saturday, April 2, 2022

When I arrive at the airport in Cape Town, my nerves are electric eels twisting through my body. *Four days.* Brian and James offered to babysit my project in Kiwanja while I came here for four days. I could hardly sit still on the flight. Am I destined to always be experiencing a nervous breakdown on a plane?

Turns out, there wasn't a next time Dan could come and see me. With all the strikes, commercial flights into our part of the DRC from South Africa have been few and far between. I'm on the first plane out for three weeks. I'm worried I might not be able to get back, but Brian was having none of it, said he'd arrange some help if needed. He told me he was secretly hoping I'd be stuck in South Africa with Dan, and I punched him in the arm.

As soon as I'm through passport control, I scan the crowd and, when I spot Dan's tousled hair, my heart leaps as my throat tightens. The simple joy of seeing him across a teeming space and knowing it's *him*. My eyes scratch and pinch as his gaze tracks over the hordes of passengers and he suddenly stops on me, his face breaking into an irrepressible grin. As he fights his way toward me, I register that he's shaved and wearing a suit, and I press my hand to my chest. He's so gorgeous, why aren't all the women here falling at his feet? Tears start leaking out the corners of my eyes, and he frowns, but, as if answering the call of mine, his eyes redden and by the time he gets to me, they're damp. He pulls me close, kissing my head.

"What's up, Liss?" he mumbles.

"You look so good in a suit, and you've shaved," I say nonsensically.

He leans back to look at me, and I shake my head, pressing my face into the fresh white cotton of his shirt.

"I didn't know what had happened to you," I garble into his chest. "I dreamed of this."

He squeezes me tighter.

"I feel like I'm dreaming now."

He shudders. "Liss. *My God.* I should have reached out to you sooner. I've been going over and over this." His breath gusts over my neck.

"You did the right thing, Dan. I understand." I hiccup. "I keep wishing that I'd looked harder, that I hadn't stopped the private investigator I hired."

"I still can't believe you hired one at all." He lets out a long sigh, and when I look up at him his gaze is far away, as if fixed on something over my head. "When my father was shot, there was a lot of panic in the government about who might be next." Then he sighs and peers down at me. "Come on. We are not starting these four days with a conversation like this. I want to talk about it, but not now." He gives me a squeeze. "I'm so pleased to see you—I feel like it's been weeks."

I laugh at this. "It has been weeks."

"Oh yeah," he says, grinning.

Tentatively, he puts his hands on either side of my face.

"Can I kiss you?"

I smile at him. "You're asking?"

He closes his eyes, licks his lips. "Ever since I saw you in Kiwanja, I've been thinking about it." His eyes pop open. "I swore to myself I'd kiss you at the airport." He smirks.

"Be my guest," I say, licking my lips as his eyes drop down toward my mouth.

His head comes down, and his touch is tentative, soft, a sharing of breath. His lips press into mine unmoving. I remember his heat over me, his mouth wide and desperate, the demand of it, and without warning pain yawns like a hole in my chest as the memories flood in. The laughter, the incredible sex. Then his lips brush against mine, slow and gentle. I push my tongue forward and touch the tip to his lips and he opens his mouth, hesitant. It's like no kiss he's ever given me: apologetic, unsure. I run my tongue along his top lip and our tongues tangle, his hands tightening on either side of my face. Then he pulls back, resting his forehead against mine, eyes closed. I kiss him again, and his lips curl up.

"That was good," he says.

"That was amazing," I say, and he opens his eyes, blinking as he lifts his hand and rubs a warm thumb across my cheek. He drops his hand to wind his fingers through mine. It's unreal.

"You alright with that?" He gestures at my backpack, and I nod.

"How long is the journey?" I ask as we head over the patterned marble to the nearest exit.

He makes a face. "Around five hours, I'm afraid."

"I've never seen you suited and booted." I track down at his body. "I like it."

He holds his hand out to his side, laughing. "Well, don't get too used to it—it's not a look I wear on the farm at all."

"How did your meetings go?"

He walks over to a beaten-up old Land Rover, and I smile as I take in the state of it.

"Ugh, lawyers. A lot of stalling and very little progress," he says.

*

Five hours later, after travelling east through rich farmland, Dan turns through rusting wrought-iron gates onto a dust-covered road. Trees point their branches to the sky on both sides of the pale-cream track, rust-colored earth butting up on either side. The road rises up before us, ridges of hills in the distance, and as we rumble over the uneven surface, the view starts to open up. I wind down the window and inhale the warm air and earthy smell of the soil, cicadas chirping and stones pinging off the underside of the truck. I glance over at Dan, and he grins, lifting my hand up and giving it a squeeze before placing it on his thigh.

"Tired?" he asks.

I'm sticking to the seat with my sweat, but nothing could be better than sitting next to him in this vehicle.

"A little. This is beautiful."

"It certainly is."

As the ground rises in front of us, the land transitions into vines on either side of the road.

"Wine?"

"Among other things. The grapes have been giving us the biggest problems." He laughs, shaking his head. "The amount of work I've had to do learning about wine production. What was I thinking wasting my time on a PhD, when I could have been here gaining knowledge about something useful?" He pulls a face, eyes rolling toward me. "You can try some later."

"Sounds good." I smile, turning my head to gaze out the window. "You grew up here?"

"Yeah." Something about his tone makes me study his profile.

"My mom left when I was young, and we only had sporadic contact with her before she died. My father was away a lot, but a ruthless bastard when he was here." His hands tighten round the steering wheel, eyes fixed ahead. "One of the reasons I went to Zimbabwe was to escape him, escape this legacy." He sweeps his hand out in front of the window. "It's a bit ironic I've ended up with the legacy anyway."

"Your mother left?"

He shifts in his seat. "Problems with her family in Joburg. She went back to take care of her parents." He shakes his head. "It was a mess."

God, what a life he's had. "And your brother? He lives here too?"

"Yes."

"Oh my God, I'm going to meet your brother."

Dan laughs. "Well, you won't meet him just yet—he's out today seeing to the sale of some grain. He'll be back tonight."

It's like opening a door to a different Dan, and my chest warms. We could have talked about all this on the journey down, but instead we've been talking about my work, about aid, about problems in Africa. *He's asked all the questions.* But deflecting is probably a habit he's developed over the years. I open my mouth, determined to ask more, but we suddenly top a rise, and a white house appears at the summit of a hill in the distance. The land is green and golden, the vines stretching as far as the eye can see on either side and in front of us, melting into yellow-headed sunflowers.

"You're quite the farmer. I'm impressed."

"Don't be." He glances over at me. "Trust me the house looks great from here, but you'll see what a state it's in when we get closer. The amount of stuff we've got to sort out." He gestures to the fields, blowing out a long breath. "You wouldn't believe."

"You said you weren't happy here," I say, "when you came to see me."

He sighs. "Sometimes I love it here; other times I hate it. All my bad memories of my father are rooted in this place. When I was younger, I was desperate to escape." He chews his cheek. "Zimbabwe was that escape, and having to come back here has been … it's felt like quitting on the life I wanted." He glances over. "I had a different future mapped out for myself."

I nod, swallowing down the tightness in my throat. "Me too."

He squeezes my hand. "I'm wondering if I'll feel differently about it with you here, seeing it through your eyes. The winter, though …" He shudders.

"No one to snuggle under warm blankets with." It's out of my mouth before I can stop it.

He swallows thickly, and the car rumbles to a halt in a cloud of dust. When he turns toward me, his eyes are bright and glassy. "You said you had dreams …" he starts. "You have no idea how much I wanted that."

He puts his hand out across the seat, and I scoot closer to him. The pain is carved in the deep grooves of his face, the thin rigidity of his back. *It's been worse for him than it has for me.* My heart aches for him.

"I'm here now." It's all I can think of to say.

"Thank you for coming here—you've no idea how much I needed it." He closes his eyes.

I shift into him, and his arms come around me. He isn't bitter and twisted yet, but I can see how losing all his opportunities and doing something he doesn't want to do has ground him down, leaching his confidence and slowly destroying him. I ache with the desire to give him his life back.

"Come on," he mumbles into my hair before pulling away. He puts the car into drive again and moves forward. I squeeze his thigh, and he clamps his hand over mine, keeping me there.

As we pull farther up the driveway, the house and the buildings beyond come into view. It's pretty, but I can see that the white walls are peeling, the window frames practically devoid of paint. Everything is dusty, and what was clearly once a lawn opposite the house sits bare and parched. The outbuildings past the house aren't in much better shape.

"We've had no time to do anything other than work on the farm and collapse back into bed each night," he says, with a grimace, looking at the house through the dust-covered windscreen. "It's not going to be luxurious I'm afraid. We might not have hot water."

"Such a comedown from what I'm used to," I murmur, and he grins. "I remember you and that nice cold shower …" I start with a smile as we pull to a halt.

His eyes fix on my lips, and he leans toward me, just as the door of the house bursts open.

"Danny! Danny!"

Her feet scuff the gravel as she races toward the car, and Dan gives me a rueful smile before swinging the door open. How like "Daddy" her words sound almost stops my heart. Why haven't I thought about this part of the visit more? Everything that happened at the supplier meeting has faded to a distant haze in the relief of finding him. The woman I saw there with Benny is standing smiling in the doorway.

"How are you doing, poppet?" He bends down, and she wraps her arms around his neck as he scoops her up. "Come meet a friend of mine." He walks to my side of the car with her as I open my door and jump out. She buries her face in his collar.

"This is Liss," Dan whispers into her ear, nodding in my direction.

She still doesn't raise her head, and I smile at Dan. He looks so happy with her, and I revise my earlier opinion of him having nothing to pull him through: Perhaps he had Benny and his family.

"You're not going shy on me now, are you?" he says, his smile widening, and her little head pops up with a ferocious scowl. She swivels around to examine me, giving me a proper look at her face. She's the spitting image of Dan, and it makes my heart bump in my chest.

I grin at her. "Hi, Benny," I say.

"Hello," she mumbles, not meeting my eyes, leg swinging against Dan's thighs. "We made cupcakes!" she exclaims out of the blue and starts to wriggle, landing on the dust and grabbing Dan's hand. She glances shyly at me before pulling him toward the house.

*

After some hot tea and cupcakes that we both compliment profusely, Dan decides he needs to ditch the suit and drags me upstairs to a light-filled bedroom.

"Is this the bedroom you grew up in?"

He smiles. "Yes, and you're in here with me. Is that okay?"

I smile back at him. "More than okay."

I look around in wonder at the old wardrobe and the bed with the crocheted blanket before wandering over to an old desk. There's a dusty Airfix Land Rover, a pile of books and a photograph of two curly-haired boys and a fair-haired woman with her arms around them.

Dan comes to stand next to me. "My mom," he says, and I step forward into him sliding my hands around his waist as I rest my head on his chest. This tiny view into his past after everything tightens my throat.

He groans and bends his head and I lift my face to his as he brushes his lips across mine, curling my fists into his shirt. I step backward, and he smiles against my mouth as we tumble down onto his bed and he trails his mouth down my neck, lighting my skin on fire.

"It's so fucking good to see you, Liss."

"Can we do this now?"

"Five minutes tops before Benny charges up here."

"Better make it a good five minutes then," I whisper.

Growling, he brings his hand up to cup my face as he kisses me, more demanding now, and I wrap my arms around his shoulders, trailing a hand down to squeeze his butt. It feels glorious, and as soon as I do this, he shifts over, notching himself between my legs. I widen them to let him press against me just where I want it.

"Liss, God, I …" he groans into my mouth.

"I know. I know," I gulp, nodding as his forehead stills against mine.

He laughs. "I'll probably come in two seconds flat."

"That actually sounds nice."

He starts to laugh and props himself on his arms, looking down at me. "We got used to doing it fast, didn't we?"

And now I've got playful Dan, and my heart thuds in my chest. How easily have we dropped into this again, despite everything that's happened?

"We did." I nod and nod as my eyes wander over his face. *This lovely smiling face. I never thought I'd see it again.* And just like that, my eyes fill with tears.

"Oh, fuck, Liss, I'm sorry." He buries his head in my neck. "We don't have to …"

I squeeze his ass again, and he looks up.

"I'm just reminded sometimes that I never thought I'd see you again."

His eyes tighten, but then his lips curl up. "Well, you're never going to get rid of me now."

I laugh as he pushes back off the bed and stands, grabbing my hand and pulling me up too. "Come on, we'd better go and …"

"Danny!" A little voice drifts up the stairs followed by thudding footsteps.

He smiles ruefully at me.

As he turns, I slap him on the ass.

"Just you wait until tonight," I whisper, as a small body barrels into the room.

Later, after a huge pot roast dinner and a walk through the vines in the fading light, we wind our way back up the steep stairs to his room, collapsing down on the bed and groaning about our full stomachs. He rolls, kissing my neck before moving over me, and I push my hips up into him, the heat of earlier returning with a vengeance as he groans into my mouth. The zipper on his jeans gets stuck under my fumbling fingers, but then suddenly my hand is in his boxers, wrapped around a hard length, and as I stroke up he immediately bats my hand away.

"Nope. Nope. Nope," he mutters and sucks in a deep breath. "God, I'm not going to last."

"Then get inside me already."

"Hush woman, let me savor this body a bit." His hand runs down my front and over one breast, hardening my nipple. And then he tugs at the bottom of my T-shirt, so I half sit as he whips it over my head and throws it onto the floor, attacking my jeans with shaking hands. I examine the freckles on his face and the blond lashes sweeping his cheeks and break into a big smile.

"Hey, Dan?"

He looks up from where he's undoing my top button.

I smile at him, and he grins back.

"Whatever happens tonight will be amazing," I say.

He closes his eyes. "Sorry, I'm a bit wound up," he whispers. "It's been a while."

He pulls my zipper down, and I lift my hips as he pushes my jeans down my legs. I examine him as he rises to stand at the bottom of the bed to drag them off. I can't take my eyes off his perfect cock, sticking out between the fabric of his pants, and he shucks those off too, along with his boxers, so I lift my butt and drag my boxers off as well.

"I always loved the boxers you wore," he says.

"Really? They're not very sexy."

He grins as he comes down on top of me. "They are with you in them, Liss."

And he kisses down my body, nuzzling my stomach before breathing hot air over my mound.

"God, I've been dreaming of this ..." He doesn't finish, but instead widens my legs and parts my folds and licks me all over like he's starving for it and—oh!—tremors run right down to my feet and make my toes curl. It's soooo gooood.

And I must have said that out loud because he laughs against me, making my hips jerk up into his face. But he just pins me down and nuzzles into my heat, sucking and licking like he can't get enough. And I'm getting there embarrassingly fast.

"Dan. I'm close," I gasp.

He reaches over to the bedside table and pulls a condom out of the drawer.

"We don't need one," I say. "I'm covered."

He shakes his head. "That sounds amazing, but I'll be one thrust and done if I don't wear a condom right now."

And I watch him roll it down, his rough hands somehow so sexy while he's doing it. Then he's back over me and pushing inside, and he makes an unreal noise like an animal in pain, and I know I want to hear that noise again but I don't think I ever will.

He stills for a few seconds. Goddammit, Dan, I want it hard and fast. I want to *feel* him everywhere, so I grab his ass and squeeze, locking my legs around his hips and lifting up into him.

He groans again and grinds against me, and my breath stalls.

"Dan, I ..."

His mouth locks onto mine as he begins to move, and in seconds I'm tightening around him.

"Fuck, fuck, you're there. So fast. *Jesus, Liss.*"

He props up on his hands and looks down at where he's moving in me, his eyes closing as if he's in pain. "Oh God, I didn't need to see how good that looks, " he says. "Oh God, Liss. I can't hold back. I'm just …"

And I'm looking into his eyes as my orgasm barrels through me, muscles locking up, and I feel him pulsing as he shudders and fights to keep his eyes open.

"Oh, fuck," he says, collapsing onto me, hot breath gusting and loud in my ear. The whole house feels like it's groaning, pipes creaking happily. Dan suddenly lifts his head, curls a sweaty mess as he grins down at me.

"Glad to see we haven't lost the knack of good sex at speed," he says.

CHAPTER 34

Liss

Sunday, April 3, 2022

The house is full of old dark furniture, rattling pipes and scuffed floors, but I've stayed in places without any electricity or running water, so it's all luxury to me. When we went all around the farm yesterday evening with Benny, it became clear to me that Dan's commitment to her is a huge deal. How are we going to compromise and have some kind of long-distance relationship?

As I come slowly down the wooden stairs the following morning, a rumble of voices reaches me from the kitchen. His brother didn't turn up last night, and I'm curious to meet the only member of his immediate family that's left, but my steps slow as I approach the room and hear the tenor of their voices.

"We've got three calves that are sick so far."

"Do we know what it is yet?" Dan's voice.

"No clue. Hammond is coming out today to inspect them."

"God, I hope it's not serious."

This produces a grunt of agreement.

"We can't afford to have anything else go wrong. We're short enough of money as it is."

"I know that, Dan. Fuck, I know that. Any progress with lawyers yesterday?"

"I talked to a few 'no-win, no-fee' guys. They didn't give me an immediate no. I'm setting up some meetings."

"Well, at least that's something. Do we both need to go?"

"We probably should." There's quiet for several seconds until Dan says, "You remember Liss came down yesterday?"

"Yeah. Sorry I didn't get back until three in the morning. Too many things to deal with."

"Where were you?"

"The usual place."

A strange silence descends when Dan's brother says this, and I'm about to move forward when his brother clears his throat.

"Is this the woman you told me about from Congo? What's she doing now?"

"An aid project."

"Wasn't she doing that when you first met her?"

A note of hostility threads through his voice, and I press my hand to my chest, grimacing as my focus on the wooden floorboards under my feet blurs.

"Yeah, she used to volunteer in the DRC then go home to earn enough money to come back out to help more."

"She still do that?"

Dishes clink as someone runs the water.

"She's getting paid on a permanent project now." Dan's reply is clipped.

"She's a charity worker then?"

I'm shocked to hear the thick disgust in his brother's tone, and the hairs on the back of my neck lift up. He has a problem with aid work?

"What's your point?"

"Well, she's not well paid or independent."

"She earns her own money, Jed. When she's in the US she teaches at NYU. She's an independent woman."

Jed makes an odd harrumphing noise to this.

"She didn't know who I was when I met her, Jed. I was using the surname we always used. Jesus, what's with the questioning?"

"I'm just worried, Dan, after what happened with Linda."

My heart beats hard in my chest. *Linda?* Who's Linda? An ex of Dan's?

"She's not Linda."

"She better not be."

"Don't you think I'd be a smarter judge of character than that?"

"I wasn't."

I'm confused now—was Linda with Dan or Jed?

Then silence, and the clink of plates and cups again.

"Sorry." Dan's voice again.

"It's okay, I love being reminded what a fuck up I am where women are concerned."

"You're not that, Jed. You know it. You got conned once. Stop extrapolating one bad event to every relationship you have."

The tight bands around my chest ease. The mysterious Linda appears to belong to Jed and not Dan.

"Do you think it's wise to introduce her to Benny?"

"Come on, Jed, are you going to be like this all weekend? I'm not sure I want to introduce her to *you* now."

"Not many women, Dan, want to take on a kid."

"Will you let up?"

"We're Benny's only family. She's never known anyone else."

"Okay, Okay. I get it."

"Does she know about Dad, about the money?"

I step back against the wall as footsteps cross the kitchen. I can see someone moving through the crack in the door. I glance back up the stairs. Could I pretend to come down again, and make more noise this time? Chewing my lip, I press farther into the wall. I don't want whoever is at the sink to catch any movement, even out of the corner of their eye. The tap squeaks as it's turned on.

"I didn't tell her anything when we met, and she knows about the court case, but not the specifics. Honestly, do you think I'd do that?"

Money? What money? I study the cracked ceilings and sagging walls. Are they having to pay off huge bills on this place? And what liabilities do you take on when somebody dies? I chew my lip. I don't even understand how that works.

"Just remember what happened with Linda. She was a money-grabbing ..."

"Will you give it a rest!"

"Sometimes you can think things are great, but when push comes to shove, it's something different."

There's silence, and Dan sighs heavily.

"Let's talk about the vineyard."

I lean against the wall while they chat about yields, crop disease, and last year's harvest. If I wait it out, they'll think I came down later than I did. Eventually, I creep back up six stairs, making some noise as I come back down again. Wandering into the kitchen, two pairs of matching blue eyes turn toward me, and my God—Jed and Dan could almost be twins, with the same shock of curling blond hair.

Jed's face tightens slightly as his blue eyes lock onto me, but I smile at him, holding out my hand.

"Hi, I'm Liss."

As he rises from his seat, I realize the similarity ends at the hair and eyes. He's much shorter than Dan, built like someone who body builds, probably from the day-in, day-out nature of physical work. He's a good-looking guy. What a gene pool. The facade of a smile graces his lips as he sinks back into his chair.

"Liss, it's great to meet you. Sorry I didn't manage to do that last night."

I shake my head at him. "No, no, you guys have a big farm to run, don't apologize to me." I turn to Dan. "Did you two start early? You should have woken me, I would've helped."

Jed lets out a snort, and my eyes dart to his face, but he's looking at Dan, who's wearing a sharp frown. Dan turns to me and tags my hand.

"I know how much you like building toilet blocks and the like, Liss, but I thought I'd let you rest."

"Well, don't. It'd be fun to help."

He grins. "Noted."

Jed rises from his seat again. "Apologies, Liss. I've got to talk to our manager this morning, and I've already spent too long jawing with this guy." He jerks his thumb at Dan. "I'd better leave you guys to it."

"We'll all go," Dan says, and Jed's jaw tightens again. Wow, he doesn't like this at all.

"Nah, you make Liss some breakfast and come out and meet me at the barns. We can check out some of the vehicle repairs." He turns to me. "Are you any good with engines?"

I make a face at him. "I've been known to get the odd engine working again, but I would say my experience is more ad hoc than any specific expertise."

"Yeah, I remember that," Dan says, and I know what he's going to say before it's out of his mouth. "I used to think you were amazing at fixing engines until you blew up the tractor on that old guy's farm."

I laugh. I worked all day on that thing. I thought we'd got it sorted out, and then the guy turned the ignition and the whole thing went up in smoke.

Jed's shoulders ease a little as he listens. "I'll make sure not to let you loose on the tractors then," he says with a wink, and then he's out the door in a swirl of grumpiness.

"Jed's a bit tense?" I say, after some thought, as Dan beavers around making me eggs and toast. Even without hearing the earlier conversation, Jed was brusque with me. It'd be odd not to mention it.

Dan sighs. "Yeah, the farm is one huge headache for the pair of us, so neither of us is sunshine and roses most of the time. It's been on the edge for years, not helped by the fact we weren't here for two years. Alongside that, he doesn't like women much. I should have warned you."

"Any particular reason?"

"He got badly burned by one. I'll give you the whole story sometime."

CHAPTER 35

Liss

Monday, April 4, 2022

Despite my attempts to be useful, Dan is having none of it. He didn't wake me yesterday, and when I get up on the second day, he's disappeared again. So I fling myself out of bed and pull on some old clothes, heading down into the quiet downstairs. I stand by the back door, scuffing my shoes on and peering out at the rolling hills. Is there a problem I could help with?

"There's not going to be a lot of money, you know."

I whirl around, hand against my throat when Jed speaks behind me, eyeing me like I'm an unexploded bomb.

"A lot of money ...?"

He waves an arm. "With Dan, the farm."

Is this some kind of warning? That Linda woman really did a number on him, didn't she? But hey, I empathize with having a faulty radar with the opposite sex.

"I'm not good at picking men," I say, tilting my head at him.

He folds his arms on his chest, expression surly. "So, you just go for the ones with money?"

What? I shake my head. "No, I'm saying I get why you mistrust women. I'm like that with guys: I haven't had a bunch of great experiences."

"Perhaps that's because they see beyond the exterior to the real person beneath."

"Excuse me?"

"Why do I feel like we're having two different conversations here?" he says.

"Maybe because we are?" I try for a bit of light-heartedness and a smile, which usually works, but, if anything, his scowl deepens.

"A lot of women like you use how attractive they are and their personality"—he waves a hand at me—"to get what they want. What I'm telling you is that Dan isn't going to come into a ton of money."

I let out a long breath. "I appreciate what you're saying, Jed."

He frowns. I don't think he likes the fact that I'm not rising to the bait.

"I understand what women like you are like."

This time I do take the bait. "Do enlighten me."

"Men fancy you, so you think if you flirt and smile you can persuade them to do what you want. I see straight through that."

I fold my arms over my chest. "And what do you see straight through to?" Wow. How cynical is he?

"I see a very attractive woman who's using my brother."

"You don't think I like him because he's a nice guy?"

He tilts his head. "I'm sure that's a bonus."

"Wow. You really hate women, don't you?"

"No, not at all. I just don't think you have a sincere bone in your body, and you know how to use men. What you've mentioned about your past history confirms it."

Oh my God! Is he ever a guy to jump to conclusions. I thought maybe he'd been stuck out on a farm in the sticks for too long, but this is way beyond that.

"Look, Jed, Dan told me what happened with you and Linda ..."

His eyes widen as the skin reddens at the base of his throat, and his voice comes out flat and sarcastic. "That's good because you're a carbon copy of her. But I don't think you should presume to get what's gone on in my life, Liss. I've seen a lot of women like you."

"I'm glad you understand me so well after two days."

His mouth curls at one corner. "And now we see the real person coming out."

"Oh, for God's sake! You're character assassinating me based on nothing at all, and you expect me to not defend myself?"

He folds his arms across his chest. "You need to stop chasing around after Dan."

"Chasing around? … You do know he came to find *me*, right?"

"I'm sure you left a trail of breadcrumbs … He said you turned up at a meeting in Joburg." He leans close into me. "How did you eventually find him, Liss? Did you use someone to track him down?"

My mouth gapes. Does he know about the private investigator? Did Dan tell him? But he's gotten completely the wrong end of the stick.

"Yeah, like three years ago," I say, with a frown. "Dan and I met in Congo. Then he disappeared … I mean …" How much has Dan told him? "He came to see me in New York after I left, and then he went back to Zimbabwe, and all contact abruptly stopped. I was worried about him."

This is an odd conversation to be having with Jed. Does he really know so little about Dan and my relationship? I believe the story Dan told me about his father's assassination and what they had to do, but is something else going on here? Maybe I should have checked his story? But God, I don't want to doubt him.

"Did Dan tell you I used a private investigator?"

Jed folds his arms over his chest.

"It was a guess. A good one as it turns out. We knew someone was trying to track him down; the security services told us. But we didn't know who it was. They looked into everyone Dan had contact with."

My breath halts. They looked into me? And the other volunteers too?

"An extreme reaction for a 'friend' to use a private investigator, yeah?"

Jed pulls me back into the conversation.

I almost laugh at this comment. On the one hand, he's right, but on the other hand …

"Look, Jed, why don't you talk to Dan about this?"

"I want to hear from you why you've gone to such great lengths to find him."

"Oh, for God's sake. We were close in Kiwanja. He came out to see me in New York."

I grimace. Is he going to use this to distort what we had to fit his cynical view of the world?

"We texted and emailed every day, and then the texts stopped without warning. I was concerned. I came out to Zimbabwe to try and find him." And how strange was that visit to Harare? "As I searched for him, I thought at first he'd cut off contact and didn't want to see me anymore, and I wanted an explanation. But when I got to Harare, I was increasingly concerned that he'd disappeared and left no trace. It was odd. I was worried he was lying in a ditch somewhere, and no one was missing him. He didn't tell me anything about his family, you, or Benny. I felt like the only person who cared."

Jed's lip curls at me. "So, you were close, but he didn't tell you about his family? Must have cost you a bit. Flights, fees. Dan tells me you don't have any money."

"I don't. My friends in New York helped me out, and I paid them back."

It's important that I'm honest with him. Will he use this information against me somehow? Maybe. But I don't want to be caught out in a lie. "You need to speak to Dan about his and my relationship. I don't think I should be the one to fill you in. Suffice to say, I'm not the one doing the chasing."

Jed shrugs. "It doesn't sound like it to me."

He's determined to judge me, so I shake my head at him.

"Talk to your brother."

*

Eventually, I find the keys to the jeep, the anger still fizzing inside me. Jed is an asshole. I just need to find Dan and stop letting whatever is up with Jed ruin what little time we have together. As I drive across rutted tracks through the fields, I stop and ask some people working in the fields where I can find Dan and they direct me to a barn sitting just before the vineyards merge into the corn and the wheat. And when I walk into the darker interior of the barn, Dan is next to an old machine that's making the most unholy racket. He has ear defenders on, and sweat is sticking the cotton of his T-shirt to his broad shoulders, tools scattered over the floor at his feet.

I move to catch his eye, and he sees me suddenly, his eyes widening, and he grins before stepping up to slap his hand against a huge button. The machine grinds to a shuddering halt with a loud clacking noise. The silence is deafening. He wrenches off his ear protectors and moves closer, pulling me into a kiss and running his fingers through my curls, as he watches his hands.

"You're a welcome sight. How did you find me?"

I grin up at him. "People seemed to know where you'd be."

He laughs and gestures behind him. "Yeah. Unfortunately. We're desperate to keep this old thresher running. We can't afford a new one."

"I wish you'd let me help."

He steps back and shakes his head with a smile. "Jed just asked me to sort this out this morning. It's been running slow and stopping for weeks. We need it out in the fields today …" He chews his lip. "I thought it'd be an easy fix, but it's going to take me a while. I wanted to take you and Benny out riding today."

"Benny can ride?"

He laughs. "She's a demon on a horse. It's Nisha's day off today, and Benny needs an adult with her when she rides. Nathanial is good but …"

"Nathanial?"

"He looks after the horses."

"I'm not a great horsewoman, but I've done some riding. I can go out with her while you fix this."

"We can go this afternoon."

"No seriously, I'd love to take her out."

"I feel like …"

"This is normal life, Dan—things get busy and we have to help each other out. I reach out and squeeze his hand. "You have no idea how glad I am to get this kind of normality back. I'd love to spend some time with her, and then when you're finished, come and join us or we can have a picnic or something."

He groans and pulls me back in for a warm hug. "A picnic sounds good. Thanks for being amazing," he says, kissing my cheek, and I laugh, patting his face.

I leave Dan trying to weld something together and head back to the house to make myself some breakfast. Jed's in the lounge at a desk, and I brace myself as I tell him the plan, but he just narrows his eyes and looks at me for long minutes before grunting and waving his hand. When I find Benny in the kitchen with the old housekeeper and suggest riding, she squeals and races around.

So I steal the jeep again, and Benny directs me to the stables as she chatters away about her pony, Skedaddle—Skye for short—and how she rides her every day. She's bouncing on her seat as we get close to a low building that looks beautifully cared for: better looked after than the house.

An old man with gray hair and a limp comes out of a stall, and I jump down from the jeep.

"Nathanial?"

"Aye, that's me."

"The animals get all the luxury around here, hunh?" I say, gesturing at the pristine building, and he guffaws showing rows of broken teeth. Then he moves over to open the car door, and Benny flings herself at him.

"This is Liss, my girlfriend," she says. "We need something nice and easy for her to ride."

I laugh as my heart flutters at the description.

A half hour later, Nathanial and I are sitting on two of the most placid horses I think I've ever come across as we watch Benny race her little pony across the open field, hanging on for dear life.

"Oh my God!" I gasp. "Should we …?"

"My heart's in my chest every time I watch 'er," he says. "But she's been on the back of a horse since she was a baby. She'll be okay."

I turn to him, laughing. "Seriously? I can't believe she's only four! Did you teach her?"

"Yeah, I did. Wonderful it was putting 'er on a horse. A natural talent just like her ma. Beautiful woman she was." He smiles.

"I haven't talked to Dan much about her mom," I murmur. And now I'm curious. One of his dad's women, he said. How could we have missed out on that little detail?

"There's always been bad blood between Dan and his dad. But Samuel—that's the old Mr. Falinsburg—driving Linda away was the icing on the cake," Nathaniel says.

"Linda?"

"Benny's mom."

I can only hope that the shock isn't showing in my face. Ice drips down my spine. Benny is *Linda's* daughter? Jed's Linda? *Holy crap.*

"Linda lived on the farm over there for years." He waves his hand toward the hill behind the house. "She used to come over regularly to ride, 'er family didn't keep horses, see? She was a good horsewoman—used to travel all over to ride; And the old man liked her, 'e paid for all the trips, and she took his horses. He went to see her jump sometimes: I think he liked the glamour of it." He leans forward and lowers his voice. "I think she was after his money."

Their dad had money? My God, Nathanial's a total gossip.

He sucks on his teeth. "... Terrible business losing your mom. I heard Samuel chucked her out." He eyes me sidewise, like he's hoping I might confirm or deny this. *He thinks I know anything?* "Too fond of his fists Samuel was. Benny still had Dan, though. Made all the difference in the world."

Dan's dad sounds like such an asshole. "Yes, and Jed too, I guess."

Nathanial chuckles. "Jed had a bit of a thing for Linda I have to say. He's a charmer like the old man, but 'e was never going to get a look in with Dan around."

What? Nathanial is looking out across the field. A smile splits his face as Benny wheels the pony through the long grass. The heat shimmers off the brown fur of my horse's ears in front of me as he flicks flies off them, and I swallow, head swimming. What is he saying? That Linda and Dan …

"He's been a great dad to 'er. Came back from that fancy university of his for all the appointments when Linda was expectin'."

He came back … Why would he do that? … A great *dad*? Now it's my turn to look at the side of Nathanial's weathered face. My mind plays over the soft look on Dan's face when he held Benny in his arms and my heart skitters.

"That's good." I swallow.

I'm confused. Really confused. Dan had a thing with Linda? Is Nathanial saying he's her *real* dad? *Jesus Christ.*

Nathanial lets out a long whistle, and the pony pricks his ears and turns, racing back toward us. He chuckles. "It's my special signal. All the horses know it."

*

My heart thumps as I stand panicked and hot in the dust motes swirling through the late-morning air. Dan is whistling in the distance in the kitchen as he preps some food for our picnic. The old lounge furnishings gleam in the warm sun, faded brown fabrics on the chairs blending into the dark wood floor and a rug with long stripes where it's been bleached of color. Jed's desk in the window is piled high with papers, and his comments about money drift through my head. It wouldn't surprise me if they were struggling, and my heart aches for them. I wander over to the desk and skim over the piles of invoices and lists of feed and spreadsheets, and as I peer closer, some have eye-watering sums on them. One bad season and it must be so easy for the bottom line to be negative in a business like this. I sink down into the chair at the desk, stomach warming: It's a huge credit to the pair of them that they're managing to keep it going at all.

'E was never going to get a look in with Dan around. Fuck. I pull out the central drawer. I don't even know what I'm looking for, but goddamn it, I need some answers. The drawer is stuffed with pencils, erasers, and a stapler piled on top of several notebooks. Another side drawer is full of brown cardboard folders with "FEED," "LIVESTOCK," and "MORTGAGE,"

written on the top right corner in a red felt-tip pen. They have a mortgage on the farm? I open it up, but it's some other property in Cape Town—another family house? How much debt are they in? Dan did say he'd explain all this to me sometime.

In the next drawer down, there's more folders. One for Benny contains papers to do with her school, and two horse-riding certificates. At the bottom of the pile, a pink folder has the word "DOCUMENTS," scrawled over it, and I flick it open. Two passports tumble onto the floor, and I bend down and open them, finding a picture of Dan and one of Jed, both staring back at me looking ridiculously young and cute. My heart flutters in my chest as I take in Dan's casual grin and blond curls: He looks so like the man I met at Adebe and Gloria's house.

There's divorce papers for Samuel and Elizabeth Falinsburg. *Wow.* Dan didn't tell me they were divorced, just that she'd died. The next set of papers are clipped together, and it's a clutch of birth certificates: A old one with elaborate script I can hardly read, then Dan's, Jed's, and the last one is newer, folded over. Maybe it's Benny's? I unfold it with shaking hands and examine the ink of the registrar giving the date and place of birth. The name of the mother is Linda De Bruyn, and I can't believe the name of the father that's written in the registrar's slanted handwriting:

Dan Falinsburg.

The paper flutters as my hand shakes, and I stare down a document on my lap, swallowing. Someone has blown a missile straight through the place where my heart used to be.

Dan?

Dan is Benny's father?

Nathanial was *right*?

How could that be? Dan told me Benny wasn't his. He lied to me?

Oh, Jesus.

Benny was born a year before he met me.

I close my eyes as the room swims. Nothing has been how he made it out to be. He disappeared in Zimbabwe, and I've only his word, and maybe Jed's, for what happened. Now this. It couldn't be more black-and-white than this. I'm so fucking *trusting*.

Dan's whistling in the kitchen at the other side of the house reaches my ears again as I blink at the piece of paper in my hand. I pull my phone out of my pocket and snap a quick picture, putting the certificate back in the folder and placing the whole pile back in the drawer.

How can I ask Dan now? I'd have to tell him what Nathanial told me. And I've just gone snooping through his brother's desk. *I wasn't really snooping*. I was just interested in their business and looking at all the farm stuff and feeling sympathy for them and … *Holy shit*. Okay, I was snooping, but … Would it all get Nathanial into trouble or even fired? I guess it's quite likely Jed would find out, and I don't trust Jed as far as I can throw him. He's clearly got a temper on him.

I look at the sun bleaching the world to white and straighten my spine. If I think about it logically, *like Kate*, everything Dan told me *is* ridiculous. *Who disappears because their father is shot?* And for *two years*? It's like some Cold War thriller.

And not being with anyone else? Do I believe that? I've met a lot of charming, convincing men. I don't know what I'm going to do, but whatever it is, I need to go back to Congo and think without him persuading me into believing some other fairytale he might want to spin me.

CHAPTER 36

Liss

Wednesday, April 6, 2022

Staring out of the window of my office two days later, my phone vibrates on the desk. I've been avoiding Dan's calls and messages ever since I got back to the DRC. I thought it would be better away from him, but of course it isn't. What do I *say*? My anger is getting worse, not better. Denying you have a *child*? I run a sweaty hand down my pants. Ugh. That's a huge red flag, never mind all the other lying. I should have talked to him there, but I didn't trust myself not to lose it. Or embarrass myself. Or even give in. I groan. *Is every prince destined to be a frog?*

I pick up my phone to look at the message, and a photo of a hand sporting a huge diamond ring is sitting in my WhatsApp. Followed by a picture of my sister in tears being hugged into a broad chest. *Shit.* I press the call button.

"Oh my God, Lauren!"

David laughs in the background as my sister hiccups in my ear.

"Oh, Liss …" she garbles.

"He proposed? Oh, congratulations, honey!"

A shaky breath whispers across my ear, and David murmurs, "You okay?" before his chuckling fades away.

"He left clues all over the house!" she chokes out, snuffling.

I lean back in my chair. "He did?"

I grin up at the ceiling. *David, you star.* And I love having this to think about: I want a blow-by-blow account.

"Oh, Liss! I love him so much."

"I know you do, you sap. Now fill me in already."

She sighs. "There was a bit of paper attached to the front door when I got home and it said, 'Follow the clues.' When I opened the door, the little rabbit he gave me on our first date was sitting at the bottom of the stairs with a note."

God, I love these guys. Who brings a toy rabbit to their first date? David, that's who. I knew David was a keeper from day one. And he's only gotten kinder and more protective of my sister since then.

"How did he find the rabbit? I haven't seen it in years." She hiccups quietly. "Although I do have a system for organizing all my souvenirs."

Of course she does. "What was next?"

"A ticket from the first basketball game of his I went to at college. Oh my God, Liss. He was so handsome and so determined when he played! I think I lost my heart then."

"Has he worked out that you fell for him then?"

"No! He put the ticket in because it was the first time he kissed me."

"David!" I shout. "She's been holding out on you!"

"Oh, shut up, you!" She laughs. "I had a pass, so I went down to the locker room after it finished. He was in the corridor all sweaty and triumphant because he scored the winning basket. He'd been more like a friend before then, you know? We'd shared lecture notes because we had some science classes together, and we'd studied in the library, and he was cool with me, so I didn't think he was particularly interested. But when I went back there after the game, he had this huge smile on his face, and as soon as he saw me, he grabbed me and kissed me while his teammates whooped! I was so embarrassed!"

He grabbed her and kissed her? *David?* Very interesting. This is the longest speech I've ever heard about their relationship. "And breathless I hope too."

She hums in my ear. "It was a good kiss."

Because she's well aware of my propensity to ask personal questions, she switches track. "All the clues were in chronological order."

I start to laugh. *Of course they were*. David would so do that and my sister would so appreciate it. God, they're going to be perfect together.

"What was next?"

"Oh! There was a load of other things … A letter I wrote him, a photograph, a song on his phone I had to play." She lets out a long sigh.

"And?"

"Well, it all led to the bedroom, and he was lying on the bed with no shirt and a big red ribbon tied around his waist and I thought …" She sniffles and lowers her voice. "I thought he'd gone to all this trouble because I've been busy and tired and we haven't … you know … and I got all flustered and started apologizing but he shook his head and beckoned me over, so I sat on his lap and untied the ribbon and underneath the bow there was a box …"

She begins crying again and, goddamn it, I'm tearing up now too.

"So, he opened it"—she gulps—"and said, 'Will you do me the honor of becoming my wife.'"

"Oh Lauren, oh my God!" Definitely damp eyes now.

"Of course, I said yes, and that's when he told me."

"Told you what?"

"That Dad said no."

"*What?*" A strange roaring noise starts in my ears.

"Dad said no, Liss! David decided the decent thing to do was to talk to him first, and he said no! Said right to his face he didn't want him as his son-in-law."

Holy shit. Red mist creeps around the edges of my vision. Since David mentioned my dad's bullshit comments last time we talked about a proposal, I'm thinking he hasn't filled Lauren in.

"You. Are. Fucking. Kidding. Me."

"Don't swear, Liss. And no, I'm not kidding. Imagine if David had listened to him! He might not have proposed. Dad could have killed this whole thing dead. He's such as asshole."

And I start to laugh. She's swearing, and in all these years she's never said anything bad about Dad; she's always been calm and understanding. "I've been telling you this forever," I say.

"I know that, Liss," she says primly, "but he's also our father."

I want to punch through walls. *Fucking hell.* Moving on. "So, what's happened?"

And then she starts to cry.

And my chest hollows out. *Oh God.* When she got upset when we were younger, it was like a big cavern opening up inside me—if my big sister lost it, then the entire world was caving in. And they don't deserve this—they are the sweetest couple on earth.

"It's such a mess, Liss. Everyone's taking sides and falling out with each other."

And I stand up, sweat trickling down my spine. Out of all of us, I'm best placed to take on my dad. If I could sort this out for her … deal with that asshole once and for all. *I've got a bit of money now.* I could go back. And it would give me breathing space from this whole thing with Dan and get my head on straight. Solve someone else's problems for a while. I know I need to talk to Dan, but seeing Kate and Jo and Lauren and David, if only for a week or so, to figure out how I feel suddenly feels like the greatest idea in the world.

CHAPTER 37

Dan

Friday, April 8, 2022

Jed peers at me over the paper, bleary-eyed, and I'm sure I look the same. I still can't believe you can do a half day's work by 9 a.m. There's usually some satisfaction when the morning chores are done and we're finally getting breakfast, but today I'm not feeling it.

"Okay," he says, eyes fixed on me. "What's happened?"

I grunt and scowl at my phone, pulling up the weather forecast for the week. He snaps the paper shut and puts it down, then reaches over and knocks the phone out of my hand. I turn quickly, fists balled. I know I've been grumpy, and this morning was particularly hard: too many problems piling in all at once, followed by a calf ripping its skin to pieces struggling to break free from a wire fence. An unholy mess.

"If you don't stop snapping at everyone, I'm chucking you off the farm. What's going on?". His eyes narrow on me. "Is this something to do with Liss?"

I scowl at him. I'm not fucking going there with him.

His eyes scan over me. "Okay, so this is clearly to do with her, given your face." He draws a circle around my head. *Nope. I'm done.* I rise from my chair, and he slaps his hand down on the table with a sharp crack.

"Sit down!" he barks, sounding so like our father that my eyebrows shoot through my hairline.

He grimaces and sighs. "Come on, Dan, talk to me. You play your cards close to your chest most of the time, but I'm not going to put up with you behaving like someone's stolen your puppy. This farm's tough enough without that."

I sink back into my seat, lifting the half-cold cup of coffee to my lips. "I fucked it up again," I mumble.

"Fucked what up? Liss? How did you fuck it up? She seemed into you when she was here."

"Honestly? I've no idea. I haven't heard from her since she went back." I run my nail down a groove in the old, battered table. "I think I've lost her again. Something happened while she was here, I don't know what. She's had other relationships while she's been abroad. What if I'm just one in a long line?"

"Then she's probably choosy and doesn't put up with any crap."

Is that what this is? She was quiet on the way back to the airport in Cape Town. Maybe she saw the situation here—the struggle of the farm and the money—and thought twice about it. Maybe she's looking for a way to let me down gently. The golden fields dance in the light beyond the window. It's like the most perfect view in the world and the beauty of it is in complete contrast to the turmoil in my stomach. All the work on the farm is pointless. I'd started to hope, but losing her again … Why isn't she responding to my texts?

Jed purses his lips and stares at the floor. I don't like the look on his face. "I gave her some shit about you and the money."

"You did *what*?" I jerk to my feet. *Oh fuck.* I lean over the table and get in his face. "What the hell did you say to her?"

Jed bats his hand at me. "Only that there wouldn't be any money. Calm down."

"You did *what*? If you've fucked this up …"

He narrows his eyes at me. "Then she doesn't care enough if your grumpy brother could scare her off." He laughs. "She didn't take any shit from me."

"You *asshole*. What the fuck did you say?" I slump back into my seat. "Maybe she saw how much trouble the farm was in and decided I wasn't worth it."

"Are you serious? She really doesn't come across as the kind of girl that'd be concerned about the state of a *farm*."

"And yet you felt it necessary to give her, and me I might add, a load of shit." Fucking Jed and his interfering ass.

"When have I not looked out for you?" He adds, eyes narrowed. "That's what we do. I was just feeling her out. My overall conclusion was that she doesn't spook easily. I don't get the feeling she's interested in money at all. I'm sorry if I did something, okay?"

His words burn through me. "No, she isn't." She wouldn't live off me, and she could have had a much easier life if she hadn't resisted the route her dad wanted her to take. Liss comes across as so confident, but maybe Jed's wrong and she is jumpy about men. She mentioned a terrible history with guys, but didn't tell me anything more. *Oh! The irony*. I rest my head on my arms on the table, and Jed squeezes my shoulder.

"What's this about?"

I lift my head to look at him.

"It's fucking terrifying. She's it for me. I knew from the first moment I saw her. What if I'm not her it?"

If I was expecting sympathy from Jed, I don't get it.

"What crap is this? I don't know what being someone's 'it' even means. After all we've been through, our whole lives torpedoed and fucking living through two years of safehouses and the legal nonsense with Dad's money, I can't believe you're mooning around here." He lets out a long, controlled breath. "You really like her, hunh?"

"She's the most amazing woman I've ever met."

"Then go after her, goddammit! She's only a flight away."

"A flight to New York, yeah."

"*What?* She's gone back to New York?"

"Yeah. Seems like it."

"It can't be because of what I said to her, Dan. Honestly, I think she thought I was an ass."

I look down at my phone. "I've been texting her since she left and heard nothing back, but I think she's forgotten that this time around we shared our locations on Google Maps so we can both see where the other one is and it's showing her in New York. Perhaps she's got some guy in Manhattan."

"She didn't tell you she was going home?"

"No. I mean she told me her job in Kiwanja was a six-month contract, but I don't know when it started and when it was due to end. Suddenly, Google Maps is saying she's in the US: no warning, no explanation."

"Look, just go and fucking sort it out. Stay there if you have to. I need you to deal with the legal stuff, but I can do the farm on my own."

He's offering this? "Go where? Manhattan?"

"Yeah, you idiot." He gets up and starts clearing plates, taking them over to the sink, every line of his body tight.

"We can't afford it."

"We can't afford new fencing, or a threshing machine or help in the house." He grumbles. "It's a question of priorities, isn't it? If you need to go, you need to go. We'll weather it."

I look at him, heart lifting for the first time in days. "I didn't take you for the romantic sort, jetting halfway across the world for a woman." Maybe he's feeling guilty.

He scowls at me. "You're an idiot, you know that?"

I grin at him. "Yeah."

"It's only because I can't stand looking at your miserable face for one more day. You've been like a bear with a sore head."

"Can bears even get sore heads?"

"Who the fuck knows? If you don't shut up, I'll give you a sore head with my fist. Just make sure you get the cheapest fucking flight out there you can find." He growls and stomps out of the room.

CHAPTER 38

Liss

Saturday, April 9, 2022

I haven't told my parents I'm back when I ring the polished doorbell on their suburban New Jersey home. I don't want to give my dad any time to marshal his usual bullshit or manipulate anyone into providing him with reinforcements.

When my mom answers the door, her face breaks into a huge smile and my chest warms. She won't stand up to my father, but all the kind, caring parts of my family come from her. My dad lucked out, although the arrogant bastard has no idea how lucky he is.

"Liss, sweetheart. What are you doing here! Oh, my goodness!" She presses her hands to her face, and I step forward as she stretches out and pulls me into a Chanel-scented hug. Her cheek is soft against my face.

"I'm back for a short visit. I thought I'd surprise you."

"Oh, it's so lovely to see you!" She steps away. "Your father is out back. How's the new job going?"

"Good." I smile at her. "Lots of problems to solve."

I don't tell my mom about the trouble in Congo: the fighting, the everyday trauma of displaced people's lives or the depth of their poverty. I don't want her to worry.

My father comes in through the patio doors at the rear of the house as we enter the open-plan kitchen diner, the old pine table and oak cabinets gleaming in the spring sunshine.

He's wiping his hands on a rag, the mower sitting on the grass outside. "Alicia. To what do we owe this pleasure?" He raises an eyebrow.

I've told him before to his face that I avoid coming when he's here, so he's no doubt guessed something's up.

"We need to have a conversation about Lauren and David."

My mom exhales sharply behind me.

My dad shakes his head. "It's nothing to do with you."

"She's my sister. He'll be my brother-in-law. You know, my family."

He narrows his eyes. "I seem to remember you opted out of this family."

It's not the first time he's said crap like this, and mostly I ignore it. *Mostly.* "You do realize I have all my own relationships with my brother and sister, and we meet up and everything? Mom too."

His gaze flickers over my mom, and he purses his lips. "Well then, I'll have to put more effort into stopping that happening, won't I?" he says softly.

My mother moves behind me, and when I swing to look at her, her hand is pressed to her chest.

He glances at her and harrumphs, waving his hand out. "David's weak. Always has been. Always will be. Backs down from an argument. She's not marrying him."

I stare at him. How is he going to stop it from happening? How's he going to prevent me from seeing or talking to my siblings? This is why we've always done things behind his back—because he's an asshole. An asshole who likes to threaten people.

"Exactly how are you planning to stop her from getting married?"

"I'll cut her off. She might have got some money from me, but not if this goes ahead. She's always been easy to break, too ready to keep the peace. I keep telling you, Alicia, you've got to find people's weak spots and exploit them."

It's like a line from an action movie. What a strange man he is. And exploiting people? He's talking about his family, the idiot. My sister doesn't care about some inheritance she might receive from our dad. And he's way underestimated how much she loves David.

"Like you tried to cut me off when I didn't do what you wanted. What a stunning success that was. You realize we're not living in the nineteenth century, don't you? Cutting your children off these days makes no difference to their lives, and they'll be quite glad to get rid of you. I know I am. The relief of not having to hear your bullshit has improved my life immeasurably."

Who cares if I sound childish?

His hands ball into fists. "I think you underestimate the pull of money. And I don't care to be insulted in my own home. Get out and don't come back."

I laugh. "What are you going to do, old man? Throw me out? Do you know how strong I am? You just have to sit and listen and do as I say."

It was a phrase he threw at me all through childhood, but I'm enjoying this too damn much. He takes a step toward me, and I crook my fingers to beckon him forward. "There would be no greater pleasure than to take you down."

"If it wasn't for your mother, you wouldn't be allowed in this house."

I turn and look at my mom who's moved to the window and is staring out at the grass.

"It's fine, Mom, we may all end up not talking to him, but we'll always talk to you."

My father puffs up his chest and opens his mouth as if to say something. I glance at my mom, but she's still looking out into the yard.

"I'm not missing my daughter's wedding," she says suddenly, swinging around to look at my father. And oh, she's never said anything like that in my presence before!

A flush is building on his throat, and suddenly I realize he's going to be a sad, lonely old man. Despite my siblings placating him, they hate him too. They just won't verbalize it.

My dad studies her. "We'll talk about this later."

"No, we won't," my mom says firmly. "I'm not missing David and Lauren's wedding. I'm not missing going and choosing dresses with her and helping her decide on flowers. I'm not missing one darn thing about it."

Holy shit. I think that's the longest speech my mom's ever given.

My dad's lip curls.

"And if you try and stop me from going, then I'm walking out the door."

So this is why Lauren told me that it's all kicking off. She'll be devastated if her marrying David forces my parents apart. And I'm not the secret weapon; *Mom* is. Is she *his* weak spot? Ha, fucking, ha.

I look at my dad. "I think you need to think carefully about what you're doing. Carry on like this, and they won't have you there. Are you really going to miss the opportunity to give your only remaining daughter away? Because you won't *be* at my wedding, let alone walking me down the aisle."

I've never articulated this, and my mom looks at me, something working behind her eyes. Sometimes when you get the showdown you've been waiting for all your life, it's something different than what you expected. Maybe it's someone else's showdown. And they had your back all along and you didn't realize it.

I smile at her. "You can give me away," I say with a wink. "Well, this has been enlightening, but I think it's time I got back on the road." I spin on my heel and head down the hallway, and I can hear my mom's hurried footsteps behind me.

When I reach the door, I turn around and her eyes are sad. I pull her into a hug, kissing her cheek. "Lovely to see you, Mom."

She pats my back. "I miss seeing you, hearing your news," she says, and I lean back to look at her.

Have I neglected her because of falling out with him? Of course, of course I have.

"I'll reach out more often, Mom. I've missed seeing you too."

Her expression eases. "Good. Send me updates."

"I met a man," I blurt out. "A good one I think." I don't know why I'm telling her this—I haven't talked to her about men in years.

"Really?" Her whole face lights up. "If he's a good one, make sure you hang on to him. They're few and far between."

I roll my lips together. "He lied to me."

She tilts her head. "What about?"

"Fathering a child. A little girl."

Her eyebrows raise. "Oh dear, does he not have anything to do with her anymore?"

"No just the opposite actually. She lives with him, and he's wonderful with her. But he told me she wasn't his child, and then I found her birth certificate with his name on it. I don't really understand why he'd lie to me."

My mom hums. "Did you talk to him about it?"

I look down and scuff my foot on the mat by the front door. "No."

She chuckles, and my eyes snap to see a broad smile on her face. She reaches out and ruffles my hair. "You were always such a passionate, spontaneous child. Always moving in such a hurry, never stopping to think for too long. And I loved that in you: By God, you can take too little action in life." She glances over her shoulder down the hall before looking back at me. "But it got you into such trouble."

I gawk at her. Was I really like that?

She leans forward and kisses my cheek. "Sounds like it's worthy of a conversation at the very least."

I nod. "I've probably messed it up already."

"I'm sure you haven't. You've always been good with people. If he likes you and you like him, all the rest is window dressing. You'll get through the hiccups."

Will we? The need to go back and talk to him seethes under my skin.

"I'm sorry about Dad," I say.

She laughs. "He'll come round—he's just a stubborn old man."

I stare back toward the kitchen, and I must make some face because she pats my arm.

"Leave it with me."

A secret weapon for sure. I think I've misjudged her all my life, misjudged all the quiet negotiators who play their cards close to their chest but are loyal and unwavering.

CHAPTER 39

Dan

Monday, April 11, 2022

When I arrive in Manhattan, I head straight for Liss's apartment, dozing on the bus heading into the city. It's taken me two days to organize my flights and get here, and I rub a sweaty palm down my shorts. The security services were relaxed about me coming here, reassured me that the threat has pretty much gone, but it would be good if neither Jed nor I stepped into politics. I told them there was no way that was ever fucking happening.

Liss's old US number is dead, and her DRC phone number is going straight to voicemail. Her Google Maps location has also stopped updating … Ice slides through my veins. *Nausea too.* Liss must have felt like this when she got no response from me, and God, I wish I hadn't put her through that. She's probably thoroughly fed up with me. There's no answer when I press on her buzzer, and I examine my watch: 1 p.m. local time. Where would she be at this time? *Shit.* She could have moved. My knowledge of her life here is three years out of date. *What am I doing?* I lean against the wall, the silence of the apartment pressing down from above.

What went wrong on the farm? I pinned Jed down and made him go through the conversation he had with her word for word. He was fucking awful, but was it bad enough to cut off all contact like this? What Liss said back to him doesn't chime with her flying halfway around the world and not responding. More like her stomping into a room and telling me what an asshole my brother is.

Does she feel for me what I feel for her? I tip my head back, the cold brick like a hard dead end. What if I can't put it right?

A couple of people walk past on their way up 22nd Street, clutching books and wearing backpacks. *The university*. Maybe I could track her down there? They funded the project she was working on in Kiwanja. I blow out a long breath: It's a starting point at least. I push off the wall and head off up the sidewalk, examining the route on my phone as I pass a man on an extended conversation on his headset. God, I like the optimism and ambition of New York. Too many places are ground down by a lack of opportunity. I understand why Liss keeps coming back here, why she can't quite leave and cut all ties. I don't think she looks at it like this, but she has an amazing life. Rich, fulfilling, doing good. It seems pretty damn perfect to me.

Once I've mapped out my route, I rattle around the subway, eyeing my fellow travelers. A young hipster couple, professionals with polished shoes. When I dreamed about a life away from the farm, this is what I saw. Sharing a space with ambitious young people, wearing a suit, purposefully traveling, seeing everything life had to offer, and going into an air-conditioned building with a coffee in my hand. *A coffee, Dan?* I huff out a laugh. I know about growing the plants, not share dealing or whatever these people do. There's nothing more earthy than the farm. I've thought about moving to Cape Town, but how could I leave Jed to the mess and sheer grind of it? I loved my life at university, the research, the thinking—and no doubt the escape from my father played a huge part in that—but I also met people like the ones swaying on a train with me now.

Before long, I'm out of 8th Street—New York University Station and on the sidewalk again. Some guys are yelling on some building site over the road, almost drowned out by the incessant noise of drills. I breathe it all in. The desire to be working on a career yawns like a sinkhole inside me.

When I arrive at Washington Square, so many university buildings line the sun-dappled streets. Where do I start? Would Liss work here in the central university location? On impulse, I head to the library. The girl on the desk is kind, but spectacularly unhelpful. I realize I don't even know what department Liss teaches in. But she hands me a map with a smile, and I unfold it to try and figure out what's most likely.

A half hour later, I've been into the Politics and Humanities faculties to find blank faces, and a man has directed me to the School of Social and Cultural Analysis. It's a real eye-opener the kinds of departments and studies that exist here. I stand in the street people-watching for a couple of minutes, breathing in slowly, filling my lungs with the buildings and lecture halls. *I've missed it.* Something bone-deep takes hold of me. I need to leave the farm, and I need to talk to Jed about it. After two years in safehouses, I can't do this to myself anymore.

I head over to the redbrick building down the street, hoping against hope this isn't another fruitless quest. The young woman at the front desk eyes me dubiously. Do I look like a stalker? After several minutes, an older guy appears behind her, eyes flicking down to her screen, and back up to me.

"I'm a friend of hers," I say. At least they appear to know who Liss is, thank God. "We met in Kiwanja three years ago, and spent some time working together while I was gathering information for my thesis. I saw her again when she was over recently."

The older man leans forward to look at the screen and squints up at me. "Why are you over here?" he asks.

My eyes flick to him. "I came to see her," I say.

And his expression morphs into wariness. Dammit, but I don't want to elaborate. The desire I have to always play my cards close to my chest is letting me down here.

"Do you have her number?" he says.

Damn. "Her African one, yeah." I look down at my phone. "But she's not using that one here."

The idea she might be in this building, but they're not going to cooperate causes desperation to slide up my throat.

"Sir, we can't really …" the receptionist starts.

"We can't inform strangers of our staff's whereabouts or details," the older man interrupts. "You appreciate that."

Fuck, they're closing this down. But the phrase *our staff* makes me want to pump my fist.

"I have her email and her address. She wouldn't have given me those if I was a stalker," I say, fingers tightening around my phone as my words come out in a sharp burst.

"Yes, but she still might not want to see you," the woman mutters.

"We certainly can't …" the guy starts.

"I'm … I'm … I'm in a relationship with her," I blurt out. God that sounds worse. "She left suddenly, and I want to put it right. Look."

I pull out my phone and show him my home screen: a picture of Liss and me on the farm.

Whoever this man is, his expression totally shuts down now. He must think she's avoiding me, and he's probably right. He shakes his head. Ugh.

"I think you need to communicate with her directly, check whether she wants to see you," he says.

I sigh at this and look down at my phone. How am I supposed to do that? Fuck.

"Could I leave a note?"

"Of course."

He didn't say it was pointless leaving a note, did he? She's here or she's been here and is coming back. I'm sure of it.

"Okay. Thanks." I take the pen and paper the receptionist offers me and scribble down that I'm here and I want to talk to her.

"My name's Dan Falinsburg," I say.

"I'm sorry," the guy says quietly.

I study his face, but he's giving nothing away, so I head out of the door into the cool afternoon, and stare up at the building.

Are you in there, Liss?

I should hang out and wait for her here. I turn my phone over in my hand. The door next to me flies open and I'm nearly knocked off my feet by a group of students who are messing about as they come through the doors and spill out onto the sidewalk.

"Sorry, man!" One of them waves at me as the others start laughing and a girl shrieks, "Oh my God, Dean!"

I smile and wave my hand as they mill around goofing about. They begin to split up from each other, and I catch the word "café" and suddenly a decent coffee while I'm waiting sounds like the best idea in the world. I need to regroup, think a little, and decide my next steps. Maybe buy her a cookie as a peace offering. I trail after them, head down on my phone, so they don't think I'm following them.

When we get to the café, I hesitate as they head through a set of glass doors. Will I require a security or a student card of some kind? I stare off down the sidewalk and then back through the window of the café, eyes roaming the queue and the tables.

A dark-haired woman is seated at a table next to the window and my heart starts beating out of my chest. *My God, is that …? It's Liss.* I start forward at the same time that I realize that she's not alone. A gorgeous dark-haired man is sitting opposite her. He's so good-looking, it's almost painful. Tousled hair, trendy clothes. I couldn't look as good as him in a million years.

He leans toward her, talking and focused on her in a way that makes my heart light on fire. All the concerns I had about other guys, about her life being a series of flings, about whether she had someone back here, come roaring back. And here I am in New York having come after her. *Again. I'm a fucking idiot.*

Do I go in? Do I walk away? I can't tear my eyes away. His hand covers hers on the table, and she shakes her head and bites her lip. She looks away from him straight toward the window, toward me. *Fuck.* Her eyes snag mine and widen incredulously. *Oh shit.* My limbs lock up as her mouth drops open, and she half rises out of her chair. The guy says something urgent and stares at the window too, eyes finding me before leaning over again to say something. Her hand flaps at him. *Oh shit, oh shit.* I whirl around—*fuck, fuck*—then my feet are moving up the street. I do not want to confront him and her together. *No way.* A shout echoes behind me, and I speed up, half jogging along the sidewalk.

I hear my name. And again, closer this time. But I don't clock the running footsteps until someone grabs my arm and the noise of pounding feet fades back in.

"Dan?"

I swing back to find the guy from the café, and I step away from him, mouth open. He's even better-looking close to. A heat, hot and sharp, makes me recoil, but his hand on my bicep presses insistently. How does he know my name? He tilts his head, eyes roaming over my face.

"Who are you?" I bark at him and watch his face melt in relief, and then something else, *amusement*? The burning inside starts to take over my whole body.

"Dan!" My eyes swing over his shoulder when I hear her voice. She's running up the sidewalk a few yards behind Mr.-Tousled-Hair. This gorgeous lover of hers. Her curls are a wild disarray around her head, and it's so like how it is in the morning that my eyes tighten uncontrollably.

"Where are you going? What are you doing here?" she stutters out on a breathless exhale.

I shake the good-looking bastard off my arm. My skin prickles like someone took wire wool to me, sharp and raw, and I hunch over as I crumple inward.

"Is he another one of your lovers or the permanent one you have at home?" I lean into her and hiss, unable to keep a hold of myself, of the anguish and panic of this day, of the fire inside, and stop it from pouring out all over her.

She reaches out and touches my arm, and I flinch. She flinches too when I do it, but she gestures to Mr.-Good-Looking.

"This is Janus. He's married to my friend Jo." Her voice is level, the weight of her gaze like a soft but insistent pressure. She's holding herself still, as if waiting for a signal, some cue from me.

Oh fuck. Oh fuck. What do I do now? Is this true? What the hell have I said? He examines me steadily.

"I'm Janus Phillips. I run a software company here. Liss is best friends with my wife. Look me up if you don't trust her." He gives me a half smile and pats Liss's arm. "You're a very lucky man to have her. Don't fuck it up."

I turn away, running my hands through my hair, and he murmurs something to Liss. When I spin around again, he's gone. His tousled head is farther down the sidewalk, weaving through the crowds.

"Dan," Liss says, and my gaze swings down to find her wide eyes, a flicker of pain shining through, a vulnerability that makes my stomach churn.

"Fuck, I'm sorry," I groan, looking up at the sky but I'm damn sure I'm not going to discover the answer up there. "He's married to your friend? *God.* You looked … you looked … he took your hand in his!" My fists clench tightly as it bursts out of me. What am I? Sixteen?

A smile curls over her mouth as she murmurs, "I'm certain I would have reacted the same if I'd seen you sitting with some gorgeous woman."

I rub my chest trying to dispel the bruised feeling that's making so many exposed words tumble out. "No doubt." I take a few deep breaths. "You think he's gorgeous?"

She grins at me. "Of course he is, I'd have to be half-dead not to realize that." She gives a typical Liss grin. "He's not you, though."

I look down the sidewalk at where he disappeared. "Yeah, I don't look anywhere near as polished or as trendy as he does."

"No, you're so much more interesting than that."

She can't mean that. I scan her face, but her expression is soft. She takes a step toward me and I get a whiff of the warm scent of Liss: earth and sweat and some sweet perfume. It reminds me of the best sex of my life, of lying under the stars, of cicadas loud in the night air. She smells like heaven. I groan and put my hand out, and she shifts right into me, wrapping her arms around my waist. The feeling of her slight body pressed into mine makes me heady, like a cocktail of drugs is washing through my system.

"I missed you," I say, pulling her into me, my voice vibrating against her hair, and she sighs into my chest.

"I missed you too."

"Why did you go?" My throat tightens as the words stumble out, raw and wounded, and I'd give anything to reel them back in. It's like I've been rubbed across a cheese grater, abraded and badly scraped.

"I never expected you to come after me," she sighs.

I pull back and take her face in my hands. "I love you, Liss."

Her lips part, eyes filling with tears. "I love you too," she says, and my eyes widen, a wildness galloping through my chest.

"You do?" It's a raw croak.

She laughs, tears spilling down her cheeks. "Of course, you idiot, from the moment we met. You were so goddamn cute. I don't know what woman could have resisted you."

I crush her into me. "Why did you go?" I repeat.

She shakes her head. "I don't want to talk here. Let's go back to the apartment."

I growl at her. "Are you still in the place that …"

"Yes."

"I have dreams about being in that bed. If we go back there …"

She smiles and squeezes my hand. "I know."

I stare at her for a beat. *I'm not going to press her now.* We're going back there, and I'm going to get her to give me some goddamn answers.

CHAPTER 40

Dan

Monday, April 11, 2022

The black outline of the entry door looks no different the second time around, and a reel of her enormous smile and the way she jumped on me the first time I came here flickers through my mind. I spent the whole journey over worrying about how she'd react. And, my God, the amazing sex we had afterward. I squeeze her hip and nuzzle into her neck as her fingers slip on the keys to the lobby door.

"I have very good memories of this place," I mumble, inhaling her skin like a dog sniffing a bone.

She laughs and turns her head, so I slide my hand along her chin. Her mouth opens, lips warm and seeking, and my cock hardens as the need to take and take and take burns through me. *She loves me?* I was expecting more hesitance: She *left*. But in the softness of her lips, my thoughts are whipped away, seeds in the wind.

She pulls back, the lock finally gives a satisfying click, and we fall through the door. Her hand slaps the elevator button as I pull her into me: impatient, demanding. I want to be over her and inside her, I want her begging. My hands are grabby as I latch on to any damn part of her I can reach, rubbing against her shamelessly, but she's right there with me, her hips moving so she can get my erection right where she wants it, gasping when I fit into the notch at the top of her thighs.

"Dan," she whispers.

A ping reaches through the haze, and I drag myself away from her warm skin, sucking in a deep breath as I shuffle us around and into the elevator. Her hands are up my shirt, down into my pants.

"Hold on, hold on … *Jesus*."

Cool fingers circle my cock as she moans, and a shudder runs through my body: *too fucking good. What are even we doing?*

Her thumb drifts over my tip and my eyes roll into the back of my head. I'm half hoping no one sees us, half hoping she finishes me off here. Her mouth is open and messy against mine, my hand in her hair tensing and releasing as she strokes me up and down. I pull my hips away with a groan, and she groans too.

"Shhh, shhh. I'll come too fast if you do that." I nuzzle her cheek, trying to slow this down, but it's a fruitless exercise.

The elevator shudders to a halt, and we stumble out into the dimly lit hallway. I herd her down the corridor, grinding against her ass, pinning her to the wall by the battered door to her apartment. *Here. Right now.*

"Key!" I bark out, voice hoarse, but her fingers scrabble at my ass with one hand as she latches on to the front of my jeans again, so I grit my teeth and I pull back, unsteady. She looks like some kind of water nymph, hair falling all over her face, in a halo from my fingers, mouth pink and wet and swollen. *The most important thing in my life, right here.* I sway on my feet, adrenaline still coursing through me from the guy in the café and running away, but it's fading now. Why am I so fucking hot? I shift my cock trying to make myself more comfortable, and her eyes pop open to fix hazily on mine as her hand fumbles in her pocket, pulling out the keys with a triumphant half smile. I snatch them, slot them into the battered lock and turn.

As soon as the door swings open, I crowd her into the wall in the hallway, kicking the door shut with my foot. We are fucking right here, right now. I push her coat off her shoulders, sinking my teeth into her collarbone as I pin both her hands on either side of her head and I grind my aching cock into her hip. Under her jacket, she's wearing a short skirt and a tight T-shirt which leave nothing to the imagination, and I want to stare and stare at the lace of her bra and the swell of her breasts.

"Dan," she gasps, winding a leg around my calf, pressing her heat into me. Then she nips my lip, and I lick the sting before licking along her lips, biting back. She shifts in tiny little movements, and my pelvis is on fire, making me rough and desperate. I pull my hips back and she groans, but I fist my hands in her skirt, and it gives easily as I shove it up to her waist, tugging at her underwear. Her hands take over from mine, wiggling to push her panties all the way off as I take her mouth again in a bruising kiss.

"Fuck. Liss. Get them off," I growl, lifting a foot to stamp on the panties halfway down her calves and kicking them across the floor. My cock throbs as I undo myself, fumbling my pants and boxers down my hips, her hands scrabbling alongside mine. Then she moans, wrapping her hand around my length and caressing me reverently, cupping my balls as her fingers stroke gently behind. *God, that's good.*

"Liss." Her name slips out raw and hoarse.

"Yes," she hisses, winding her leg around my hip as I grip my length, pushing forward, and totally lacking in finesse as I probe. The feel of her wet folds against the tip of my cock, *oh my God*. My eyes roll back in my head as I tip back and stare at the stark white ceiling. The clench of her sends tingles all the way down my legs. *So wet and warm.* Nothing is like this. For the life of me, I can't make any coordinated movement, and my head snaps back down, my lips an erratic trail across her cheek.

"You ready to be fucked hard?" I mumble, sinking my teeth into her earlobe, the desire to pin her down running sharp and hot.

She whimpers, so I ease forward, canting my hips to find the right place and the right angle, moving my fingers on her as I push: It's not the most sophisticated caress in the world, but her head thunks back against the wall. Glancing down, my eyes snag on her nipples, hard peaks through her top. *I need to …* I drag my hand up, pushing the soft fabric and her lace bra up around her collarbone, squeezing her breast. The solid weight of her is so good in my palm, and I bend my head and roll my tongue over her nipple, pulling back to look at the wetness from my mouth. *Mine. Mine. Mine.*

"Dan," she chokes out as I press on her clit, feeling it swell under my thumb. "Oh God. Oh God."

She's close? *So fast.* It's in her gasps, and how she's trembling against me, the wetness all over my fingers. I thrust forward, burying myself to the hilt, pinning her to the wall and thumping her tailbone into the plaster brutally. But before I can ask her if she's okay, she moans, hands fluttering like she doesn't know what to hold on to. *Fuck, yeah.* I pull back and slam in hard.

"Oh, oh, oh."

It's so easy, it's *always* so easy, so I let loose. I've never been this rough, but I'm wound up and feeling as territorial as fuck: a potent brew roiling through me. Another guy holding her hand? *Fuck. That.* Her breath catches in her throat in anticipation of each thrust, and her fingers dig into me, leg gripping my hip and thigh like a vice. Is this good for her? I dance all over her clit applying just the right amount of pressure.

"You going to come for me here, hard against this wall, all over my fingers?" I whisper, licking her mouth as her exhale gusts short and sharp across my face. I flick her clit a couple of times and she strains against me, trying to arch. *No way.* I nuzzle her cheek. *Take it, Liss.* I want in deeper. I slide my free hand under her ass and lift her and she winds her other leg around my hip giving me her weight as I push and grind all over her, sliding in farther. *Oh, Jesus. Hot. Wet.* Everything is a red haze. The tightening, telltale tingles run down my cock into the base of my spine and my crotch.

I groan into her mouth.

"Yes, Dan, yes I …" I pull out and thrust back in, and a strange noise which sounds like nothing I've ever heard before leaks out of her throat.

"You like being pinned and fucked, don't you?" I mumble, lungs constricting my chest. I'm trying desperately to hold off, to let her come, but I'm riding a dangerous edge. I rub her clit again, and she lets out a long wail right in my ear as her walls clamp down.

"Oh, Dan, I'm … please … no … more … Oh yes. Oh yes."

Suddenly she's shuddering against my body, contracting around my length like a vice. *Fuck. Fuck. Fuck.* I can't … I just can't … I tip into oblivion, thrusting deep as my cock jerks and I empty myself into her, breath coming out in a wheeze over her cheek.

Sounds come back slowly. The distant rumble of traffic on a nearby street, vague footsteps from the apartment next door. Can I move? *I need to get us both to a bed.* I shift both hands under her butt to find a better hold, and she collapses into my shoulder, winding tightly around me, soft curls tickling my chin as I head down the corridor and shoulder into her bedroom. I tip forward and fall with her onto the covers, still hard inside her as my mouth smears across her face and she tenses her muscles around my cock, making shivers run down my legs.

"Stop that," I say, as she licks my neck, giggling. Fucking giggling. I need the bathroom and I want to get her sorted out. I pull out and shift up onto my knees as I examine her face, eyes still closed as she pouts, so I lean in and kiss the tip of her nose.

"You okay?" I say.

She nods.

"Not too rough?"

Her lips curl up, and her eyes open to fix softly on mine. She shakes her head.

"Not talking?"

She closes her eyes, her smile widening, and I grin at her. Maybe she can't talk. Putting the weight on my heels, I straighten, tremors still rolling through me. She puts an arm behind her head and watches me with eyes half-mast. Smiling, I shake my head before heading off down the corridor to find a warm cloth. When I come back, she closes her eyes on a long sigh as I wipe carefully between her legs, then throw the cloth on the floor and pull the white cotton duvet over us both, curling around her.

The silence of the apartment shifts through me, and I close my eyes inhaling the scent of her hair, her warmth and softness, her skin against my forearm where it's resting on her stomach. I'm bone tired. Losing her and the panic of the last few days, the physical labor of the farm, has wiped me out.

"I couldn't get hold of you. Your location stopped updating. I knew you were here, but not where. Your DRC phone died and your old US number doesn't work anymore," I mumble.

She sighs. "Yeah. I changed my US number. After you went missing, it tortured me for a long time. I kept hoping that one day I'd get a text from you."

God. I kiss her temple. "I'm so sorry. For all of it." And Jesus, I understand. The panic. The powerlessness. "Don't fucking leave me again," I mutter into her hair. After what I put her through, is that even fair? I'm behaving like a caveman.

She shifts around and I open my eyes to look at her. Her gaze is wide, and a small frown sits between her eyebrows. *Fuck.* She licks her lips.

"I know Benny is your child," she says.

CHAPTER 41

Liss

Monday, April 11, 2022

I don't like the look on Dan's face when I say this. My stomach drops.

"What makes you think she's mine?" he asks.

Ugh. This is the problem with poking around: You eventually have to admit to it.

"Nathanial implied you were her dad when I took Benny down to the stables."

Dan opens his mouth, and I rush on.

"But then I … I looked at some papers on Jed's desk. I wasn't really snooping; it was more sympathy for you with all the work on the farm and how difficult it all was … but I did look through stuff and I discovered her birth certificate." She rolls her lips together. "I'm sorry. I shouldn't have gone looking, and once I had, I didn't know what to do with what I'd found."

"That's why you ran away?"

I screw my face up. "Sort of. I actually came back to confront my dad."

"Your dad?" Then he shakes his head. "Let's discuss this first and come back to your dad." His eyes narrow. "Would it matter if Benny was my child?"

Is he saying she's his? "It would matter that you'd lied to me," I say as steadily as I can, rolling back flat on the bed, shifting away from him. I stare at the ceiling. I want to be clear about what I say here. "After everything that's happened, the way you vanished … maybe you don't trust me because you think I keep leaving, but you disappeared and appeared again with a daughter. I want to be on a firm footing with you, not half-truths. My dad did things behind my back all the time, and I need someone who'll give me honesty."

Dan props up on one arm immediately, looking down into my face. He looks serious. Concerned. And my heart sinks.

"Linda used my father's horses to ride for years, but then she and Jed got together and while he was trying to extricate himself, Linda slept with my dad and got pregnant: deliberately. Jed overheard her scheming one night out in the barn when she was talking on her phone. Her plan was to take us for as much money as she could, and you've probably realized by now my dad was a wealthy man. The problem was that Linda had form. She married an older guy when she was young and then divorced him, netting herself a tidy sum. So my dad, Jed, and I had a meeting: We couldn't let her go after the farm. My father was a devious asshole, but Jed and I went along with it because there was no way we wanted Linda to get her hands on everything. She was already threatening Dad with paternity lawsuits and media exposure. We agreed I'd be the fall guy. Dad took me out of his will and left everything to Jed. I got friendly with Linda and made her think that I'd look after her. Even though she slept with my dad, he was never interested in her, and she knew he was a womanizer and that he'd fight her tooth and nail. I persuaded her to put my name on the birth certificate.

Of course, it gave her very little claim on anything. She was furious when she found out, and she walked out, leaving Benny with my dad. Legally, I'm on the birth certificate and we'll have to sort that out at some point, but it's way down the agenda. Neither Jed nor I have felt like getting into more legal issues. Timing-wise, there was, and still is, a question of whether Jed or my dad is

Benny's father. Jed's always said it doesn't matter to him, that he sees Benny as his whatever."

But my heart is expanding like it's going to explode with relief. He didn't lie to me, that he just didn't tell me the whole story. And God do I know about scheming people and the constant rearguard action you have to take to stop yourself from getting sucked into their bullshit.

Dan rolls onto his back and looks at the ceiling. "I didn't tell you this because I'd just got you back in my life and it didn't seem that important." He runs his hand through his hair. "That probably sounds terrible, but compared to what we've been through over the last three years, Benny's birth certificate seemed like a nonissue." He winces. "Obviously it isn't. I'm so sorry, Liss."

"No, I get it."

"I don't like what I did with Linda, but it felt really necessary at the time. Now … I don't know. On the one hand I feel terrible, like I'd do anything to protect my family's money. And maybe I would. But on the other hand, the farm was in real trouble then; it was burning through cash and we didn't have a lot of options. My dad was furious about Linda, Jed too, with himself more than anything. Jed's a difficult guy, but he's been there for me and I wanted to be there for him." He runs a hand down his face. "In theory, the farm is worth a lot of money, but as you probably realized if you looked through the desk, it's only valuable if you can make it into a profitable business."

"And she abandoned her only child? My God, I just can't imagine …"

"Benny was just a means to an end for Linda. She was an awful woman. In the short relationship I had with her, it became abundantly clear how devious she was." He turns his head on the pillow. "I asked whether it matters with Benny because she's important to me. Even though she's not my child, in some ways I love her like she is. She's a sister, maybe a niece, but she feels like more than that."

Guys have lied to me so often that I've wondered if I have a radar transmitting that I'm a gullible fool. How do my friends end up with trustworthy guys who care about them while I keep picking manipulative bastards? But I've seen nothing in Dan to suggest he's manipulative at all. I turn over, curling into his warmth, my hand coming up to run through his blond chest hair. He closes his eyes and kisses my head.

"I've got no way of proving any of this to you, Liss. You can talk to Jed, but Linda is long gone." He draws back, eyes fixed on mine. "You're going to have to trust in what I tell you."

I nod. I know I am.

"That's why I asked if it matters." He rolls into me. "You can't keep bolting each time someone says something. We're going to meet a lot of bumps in the road. You can't doubt me at every turn."

Silence settles over us while I think about what to say. "I didn't really come back here because I was running away." This is a half lie, I know—it *was* part of it.

He sighs and rolls onto his back. "What am I saying? That was too harsh. I'm sorry. Shit, I understand, Liss. I had an asshole father too. Not the same as yours I think, but he was terrifying. I learned at an early age to stay quiet, to say anything he didn't like would result in a beating. So, my instinct in a lot of cases is to dodge questions or say as little as possible. We've both got our own crosses to bear. All I can say is I'll try. I'll try and tell you more about everything."

I nod at this. "And I'll try not to take off every time I get panicked." I smile at him, and he laughs. "So … Jed will inherit all of it?"

Dan snorts. "The farm has been in Jed's name for a while. The one reason we've still got it is that my father transferred it to Jed two years before he died, partly because of Linda, but also because he knew Jed would look after it. If we realize any assets after all the legal shenanigans, then yes, he will inherit everything. But despite his surliness, I trust him. It was always him and me against the world."

I think about my siblings. Jed's as grumpy as hell, but I can see he has a good relationship with his brother.

"He encouraged me to come here," Dan adds.

"He did?"

"He's not a bad guy, just cynical, and he's good reason to be." Dan chews his lip. "There's a lot of money tied up in Dad's business interests: Shares in companies, land, you name it. At the moment, it's likely we'll lose all of it in lawyers' fees." He lets out a long sigh. "Dad was a public figure and had so many hangers-on in his life. As we got older, it affected us too. Jed was always more prepared to be involved in my father's life than I was. My father was a very controlling man, and I fought it and Jed decided it was easier to go with the flow, to do what my father wanted him to do. There was an endless round of women, drugs, and booze. The only good to come out of it was that Jed learned about the farm. My father liked to play the big chief, but he didn't treat the staff well and couldn't run a business. Jed worked out how to run it. I'm grateful now—we would have been lost without his knowledge.

"I should be living in Cape Town. In theory, the lawyers have started sorting my dad's will out, but they're fleecing us. I can already see how it's going to go: We're five months in and they are still talking about the scope of the dispute. It's in their interests to drag it out."

He rolls over and curls into me, pressing up tight, arms coming around and pulling me into him.

"It's one of the things I really liked about you when I met you. I mean you're so bright and beautiful, Liss." He leans back and strokes the hair away from my face when he says this. "But you don't care about money—you're always giving so much to help other people. Your drive and fire were inspiring then, and still are. How you do all this, work here, make money, go back?" He shakes his head.

I sigh. "Sometimes I think it's stupid. Like I've spent my whole life trying to prove my father wrong."

Dan laughs and moves, hardening between us as I shift my hips against him, forcing a groan from his throat. "I can't lie in bed with you naked and not get a hard-on. Stay still, woman."

I grin at him.

"Anyway." He frowns. "What were we talking about? Oh, yeah. Proving your dad wrong. I've attempted to do that all my life too, and now he's dead. You know he'll never say sorry, right? He'll always be an asshole."

"Yeah, I guess. It's significantly depressing. I want an apology; he makes everyone's life a misery."

"What's happened with him?"

"My sister Lauren's long-term boyfriend, David, finally proposed to her. They've been together for years. David asked my father's permission—old fashioned, I know, but that's the guy he is. My dad said no. Lauren doesn't fight my dad normally, and she and David are both amenable, keep-the-peace-type people, but she's mad and my family are in uproar about it. So I decided I needed to come here and have her back."

"Against your dad?"

"Yeah."

He grins at me. "Are you going to sort it out like you sort everything, Liss?"

I can't believe the way he sees me sometimes. "Lauren told him where to stuff it. I'm just encouraging her not to invite him to the wedding." I grin back at him. "And my mom is digging her heels in with my dad, which is radical for her."

"Like mother like daughter?"

"Not at all. She never crosses him. I think that's why everyone's so jumpy."

He hums at his. "My dad was such as bastard: If anything didn't go his way, he dealt with it with his fists. I was under his thumb all my life. Going to Harare was the best thing that ever happened to me. I still can't quite believe he agreed to it."

"He paid for it?"

"Yeah, fees anyway. I had to support myself otherwise."

"And he left you alone?"

"Once or twice he dragged me into stuff, but being out of his sight he mostly forgot about me. He was lazy and I was in another country, hard to get hold of. But life was harder for Jed after I left. He went to an agricultural college in Cape Town, so he came back more often than I did and took the brunt of my father's bad moods and womanizing."

There's silence for a long time. I can hear the reassuring buzz of the fridge in the kitchen. Someone shouts from far away, from the street or a nearby apartment I can't tell. The sweet scent of him mixed with musk and sweat seeps under my skin, his arm resting heavily on my waist like an anchor. Despite how exposing this conversation has been, the honesty of it settles in my bones. I let my fingers curl through the hair on his chest and gradually it all fades away.

I open my eyes to darkness, halfway between sleep and wakefulness, and blink at the clock. Three a.m. It all comes flooding back, Janus turning up, concerned, seeing Dan. *Dan.* But as soon as I think it, I know he's not in the bed with me. *Has he left?* Given up on me and my country hopping and running away? I pull on a robe and slip out the bedroom door, padding quietly down the corridor and a weight lifts off my chest when I find him sitting in jeans and with no top on the sofa in the dark.

"Are you okay?" I whisper. I don't want to wake Matt.

He beckons me over. "Yeah, yeah. Just awake, thinking. Probably jet lag. I didn't want to wake you." His quiet tone matches mine. When he pats the cushion next to him, I collapse onto it.

He glances at the other bedroom door. "Does Kate still live here?"

"Kate moved out to live with her boyfriend, Fabian. A friend of ours, Matt, took over the apartment when I went to the Philippines, and I moved back in when I came back. He found someone to take my room when I got this contract in Kiwanja, but he said I could stay here this week as the guy who rented my room is away on a work placement."

I watch in curiosity as he closes his eyes. "Please tell me Matt is a woman with a strange guy-type-sounding name."

"Nope."

"You're living with a *guy*?"

His eyes grow dark and heated, fixed on me as a frown slashes across his forehead. I grin at him and rub the crease between his eyebrows, but he lunges at me, pushing me horizontal and lying on top of me as a little shriek spills out. He grabs my hands and nuzzles my throat.

"I'm going to fuck you here noisily, so there's no doubt about who you're with."

Goddamn caveman. “Nothing is going on with Matt and me,” I say, squeezing his fingers.

He pulls his head up, eyes calmer now, but some edge to him that makes me feel all wiggly inside.

“You only think that. There’s no way a guy is sharing an apartment with a woman as beautiful as you and doesn’t want to get in her pants, Liss, unless he’s gay. Is he gay?”

“No! And I don’t care what guys think, Dan! Matt’s a good friend. He took on the lease for this place and is happy to find short-term lodgers so I can move back in whenever I’m back,” I whisper shout at him.

He lets out a groan. “God, it’s worse than I thought, he does all that shit for you too?”

“Stop,” I say. “What were you doing sitting staring into the darkness anyway?”

“Good change of subject.”

“And?”

Dan pulls back and sits up, pulling me into him. “I was actually thinking you have the perfect life.”

“The perfect life.” I gape at him. “You’re kidding me, right?”

“No. New York is great. Going to Africa, helping people ... that’s great too.”

“No money. Desperately trying to make ends meet. Living in the same cramped, sketchy apartment I’ve lived in since I was a student …”

“Hey, this apartment and that bed are my happy place. Anytime I want to escape the drudgery of the farm, I imagine myself here.”

“You wouldn’t think that if you lived here. Noisy neighbors, 24/7 traffic, parties at all hours …”

“I was thinking I should live here for a bit, live your life with you, maybe travel back and forth.” The words come out carefully, and he eyes me sideways.

My heart is going to burst out of my chest. “Are you *serious*? What about the farm? Benny?”

“That’s what I’ve been going over in my head, but it’s all doable. Any problem is solvable, ultimately. She could spend some time here, or she could stay there with Jed. It could be a wonderful experience for her, a mix of culture and places—there's nothing wrong with moving around. Jed says he'll look after the farm. All he wants me to do is the legal stuff. He doesn't hate the farm like I do, and we could get more help."

A long, controlled explosion detonates inside. I've spent my whole life battling an idealized version of what my father dictated my life should be. To have someone come along and admire the crazy life *I've* chosen is so at odds with my family's views I almost can't make sense of it. I press my hand to my chest: *I love my life. I do.* I love doing both things. Teaching here, helping out there. All this time I've been trying to prove my dad wrong, I've been creating the life I want.

My voice catches in my throat. "I … I can come out to the farm. I can do good in South Africa. Plenty of problems to sort out there, right? The country doesn't matter."

He nods. "I want you to do what motivates you, Liss. I don't want you to compromise because of me."

I frown. "You're compromising for me."

He shakes his head. "Not really. I've been treading water for three years, Liss. I can't stay on the farm. I don't know where I'm headed, but I'm hoping with you I can discover myself again, find something that uses what I can do. I loved the research I did into rural communities affected by conflict and poverty: I loved living in Harare. That was what I wanted my life to look like three years ago. I've still got to sort out my father's estate, but I need to move on. I want to do that with you."

I close my eyes for a beat and open them again as I lean in and kiss his perfect mouth, trying to put all of the electricity that's coursing through me into one small kiss.

"I never thought I'd find this," I say softly, against his lips.

His mouth follows mine. "Find what?"

"Someone who let me be me. Someone who thinks I have a good life, who would want what I want. I can't quite believe …"

"Believe it," he growls. He pulls me up and over his knee, parting my robe and looking down at my breasts and sleep shorts. "Fuck, Liss, I can't sit and talk about important life decisions when you're half-naked under this thing." His fist tightens on the fabric.

I laugh and slide forward, resting my sex against where he's hard, grinding down a little as he lets out a groan. I press my hand over his lips, giggling. "Shhh."

He licks my fingers. "I want to be so loud we wake up that asshole you're sharing with."

I clamp my hand over his mouth, eyes going wide. "*Dan*. Shut up. He's a nice guy."

His lips cover mine, and I'm not sure about the abrupt end to such an important conversation, but what more is there to say? He squeezes my hip before invading my sleep shorts and pulling my hips right into him. His whole body is tight, muscles bulging, erection pressing hard and insistently between my thighs. An answering ache spreads up the center of my body.

His hands dig in, and he rises from the sofa. *How can he lift my weight like that?* My legs wrap around his waist, and I wind my fingers through the softness of his hair. I lean in and kiss his eyelids as his eyes flutter closed, the blond of his lashes faint against his tanned cheeks as he carries me down the corridor to my bedroom. As we tumble onto the bed, his lips trail messily down my chin and across my collarbone as he scrabbles at the elastic waistband of my shorts.

"I'm sorry I'm so insatiable," he mumbles into my breast before following the shorts down my body with his mouth, kissing my stomach and down, down, down. He groans loudly, pushing them off my feet and parting my folds, his hot breath and the wetness of his mouth sliding all over me. And Christ-alive, he's wild. Using the pads of his fingers and slipping haphazardly, alternating with his tongue, nibbling down my thighs. He's as messy between my legs as he was over my face, and it's a sign of how overwhelming this whole thing is. The idea we might be together somehow, that we're both going to change our lives to make it happen. We've talked about it before, of course, but never has it felt like such a reality. My throat is tight with the impossibility of it, that after everything I might have found something good, *my one good guy*.

I widen my legs, giving him more space as his fingers press more insistently, sliding down through my slick wetness to my entrance, wandering all over the soft skin as I tighten up and shake. He twists his hand and slides a finger inside, hooking it around and pushing, making me arch, muscles clamping down, but it's nowhere near enough.

"I want you in me," I choke out, but he ignores me.

"Oh my God, Liss, you're so wet still. How is that ...?" The rest of his words disappear in his mouth on my clit, his thumb rubbing as he licks over everything. Tingles radiate out across my stomach, my breath gusting short and sharp. His hips shift against the bedcovers, and how turned on he is is clear from his shaking, uncoordinated wildness.

"Come up here," I gasp.

I only know he shakes his head because my fingers are still lodged in his hair. My calves cramp up and I move, trying to stretch, to get wider somehow, as I push myself into his mouth, down onto his fingers.

"If you don't stop, I'm going to come, and I want to come with you inside me," I choke out.

He groans, rising and kissing up my body, breathless and sweaty, chest heaving when he reaches me. I wind my legs around his hips, and sneak my hand down fumbling to get a purchase on his cock and get him where I want him. He shifts forward into the wet at my entrance with a loud groan as his eyes close. I study the long silk of his lashes, the small mole on his forehead, where the crow's feet around his eyes are white from screwing his face up against the sun. The stretch as he pushes, filling me, moving in an inch at a time, is unreal. He stills for a beat, mouth against mine, a smirk playing over his lips. I raise my hand to rub my thumb over the hair on his chin, and his eyes open as he nibbles my finger. I'm not sure if he sees something on my face.

"You okay?" he murmurs.

I nod, smiling. "More than okay."

I move my hips, and he holds me down with his hand, tilting his pelvis, so slow he's hardly moving. But I can feel the pressure of it. So different from the frenzy of earlier, controlling all my movements as well as his. I try and wiggle, but his hand clamps harder. There's something so hot about the way he pins me down, every time. He's not using me to get off; he just knows exactly what will make me burn bright, and he's got better and better at it. *He pays so much attention.* And the thought brings tears to my eyes as he stills, watching my face.

"Liss," he groans. "You're …"

He starts to pull out. *Fuck no.* My hand shoots out to grab his tight backside, and the muscles are so amazing I dig my fingers right in. He takes in a shaky breath as he stops moving—cock half in, half out.

"Don't stop, don't you dare stop."

A shuddering exhale. A hip thrust. Then he collapses on one arm and buries his face in my neck.

"Tell me you're okay," he mumbles, nibbling my ear and I kiss his temple.

He lifts his head and I stretch forward, biting his ear. "I'm fine, Dan. I'm just emotional watching you."

His hips snap back as soon as I say this, thrusting back into me with a long groan, hand in my hair shaking, eyes losing focus.

"Fucking hell, always so good. You feel amazing, woman. Hot. Tight." He punctuates each thrust with a word. "*Oh God.*" And my orgasm is suddenly back with a vengeance. I tighten my legs around him, hand scrabbling over his wide back to get some purchase. He props himself up on his hands and looks down at where he's moving in me.

"Ohhh … that's too good," he says.

"Jesus."

"I'm …"

"Liss …"

"Look …"

"Just fucking look."

Propping up on my elbows, I look down, before sliding my hand down my stomach to touch myself, missing his friction. With a growl, he pushes my hand away, holding himself on one arm and brushing my clit, starting and stopping and making my toes curl. *Such a tease.* His bicep bulges as he holds his weight on one hand, the golden hair on his chest curling down to that sexy trail in the middle of his six-pack I saw the first morning I caught him asleep in the hammock, shirt awry. The hair on his stomach is dark with sweat.

My God, he's gorgeous. Pink on his cheeks, his mouth all shiny, a faint sheen of sweat on his face and body, pooling at his temples, creating dark wet curls. How is it possible this man is in my bed? This man who wants to live my crazy goddamn life with me. Tears fill my eyes, and I flick back to look at him, worried he'll notice. But he's been watching me looking at him this whole time, and my stomach clenches when his eyes tighten at the corners.

"Liss," he croaks, leaning down to kiss me.

"I love you, Dan."

His eyes flutter closed as he groans. "Ever since I met you, Liss. Fuck. You knocked me right on my ass. You were like holding a live wire. You still are."

The movement of his hips stutters as emotion overtakes him, and I raise my hips into his.

"You're so fucking wet, woman—it's all over me."

I laugh, tears spilling down my cheeks as I try and pull the moment back.

He shifts down, lips sealing on my parted ones, tongue invading my mouth. "Fuck, but I love you too."

His eyes are watery as he pulls back, breath gusting out over my chest, kissing my nose, eyes red and watery. Rubbing against me, he doesn't look away.

"Oh. Oh."

"Yeah, Liss. Oh yeah. You going to come all over my cock?"

His dirty words drag me right back into my body. I collapse back, and he moves to rest on his elbows as he winds his hands through my hair. He looks and looks, thrusting lazily, grinding as he watches. It's too good with him filling me and watching me so closely, and my body arches and my legs start to shake as my thighs grip his hips, resting my feet on the back of his calves. I shift my knees upward, and it opens me up and he makes one more rotation against me, and, fuck, I'm going to explode.

"Oh, oh, oh."

He rubs his nose with mine.

"Yeah, Liss, come on."

"More," I gasp.

"More what?"

"Pressure. Anything. Oh God, more." I grab his ass, rubbing myself shamelessly over him.

"Get yourself off on me. Oh, fuck."

Everything frays at the edges. He pulls back onto his knees, pinning both my thighs outward as he fucks into me hard and fast, watching his cock disappear into me over and over. With the lack of friction right where I need it, my orgasm starts to back off, but he grinds into me, not letting up on the pressure and I explode around him, body arching off the bed as he rubs wantonly against me, my orgasm shuddering on and on with his cock all the way in.

"Yes, Liss ... Jesus." He keeps the pressure up until I subside and grips my knees hard and starts moving. I tighten my muscles and he lets out a sound like I've never heard before. One more thrust, two, and he buries deep as he jerks above me. The pain and pleasure on his screwed-up face make tears track down my cheeks again. I am not a crier for fuck's sake—what is wrong with me?

He collapses down, and the ticking silence of the apartment fades back in against the loudness of our breaths. He rolls to the side, eyes closed, and I follow him.

His chest is rising and falling, sweat running down his temple and I grin at his profile.

"Let's make a plan," I say.

SEVEN MONTHS LATER

EPILOGUE

Dan

Monday, November 7, 2022

Water is streaming down the pane of the window. How can there be so much water in one place and so little in another? I know why this is, but it still astonishes me that you can fly from one country to another in sixteen hours and go from baking heat to this.

The café door opens in a gust, and the people at the table next to me flinch from the cold and damp swirl that accompanies it. Liss's dark curls are in a crazy halo around her head, and I can't help the smile that breaks free: Her hair looks like it does when we're sweaty and spent in bed and I harden in my jeans. *Every damn time.* Will this intensity slack off? When we have several kids under our belt and we're tired and fed up and sniping at each other after a long day of work? My heart swells as she heads toward me. *I have this now.* Losing my mother and in all the trouble that was my father, I never thought I would.

She plonks herself opposite me at the table, droplets of water bouncing off her shoulders onto the Formica as she starts unwrapping layer after layer of clothing.

"Warm enough?" I say.

"How can it be so cold here?" Her thoughts echo mine so perfectly it makes me laugh.

"I could definitely do with the nice balmy warmth of Cape Town right now."

She looks out at the students scurrying across the intersection, dodging the dancing raindrops. Then she turns to me and grins. "I could eat a horse. How did it go today?"

"Good. I think."

My first day of teaching Economics in a temporary post at the university. It's taking me months of networking and volunteering to secure it. It only happened because someone had to go on maternity leave, and NYU was happy to get a working visa for me. But it's a solid six months, and having a job has lifted a load off my shoulders.

"We'll end up staying here a while." I chew my lip.

After I came to see Liss seven months ago, I went back to talk to Jed about the farm and what I wanted to do. We decided that Benny would stay with him for the time being, until Liss and I could work everything out. Benny has always been used to me coming and going, and Liss and I Skype with her almost every night.

Liss squeezes my hand.

"It's not simple or easy to lead this life. The university is good to me because I've been with them a long time, plus John is so flexible. If he left, that could all change. We've just got to be adaptable. We can head back to South Africa when your six months are up. It might work out better for us to be there longer term."

I nod at this. And as Benny gets older, who knows? Maybe having family in the US could open up all sorts of options for her.

"I want to give you everything, Liss, everything your asshole dad never did." She hasn't let me meet her dad yet, but I've been living the furor of Lauren's wedding prep secondhand for a while.

Her eyes soften on me. "I'm so happy," she says simply.

"What, really? Despite all this …" I wave my hand around.

"Yeah. I know I've got worries, but being with you …"

This woman. I reach over the table and squeeze her hand. The last few months with Liss have transformed me, even with all my employment anxieties. I've got to know her friends: Matt her housemate, Janus and Jo, Kate and Fabian. Meeting all these ambitious, good people has put a rocket under me. Janus is the most protective guy I've ever met of anyone who's in his circle, and he insisted I use his international lawyers. They've waded into my father's mess in South Africa and got things moving in a way I didn't think would be possible. They've filed motions and been so aggressive that he's got them all running scared.

"I like being here. I like your friends." I grin. "And I love you."

She props her hand on her chin, eyes warm as they scan my face. "When are we babysitting again?"

"Saturday night."

"What made you think babysitting for Janus and Jo was a good idea?

I wink at her. "Good practice. And storing up favors for later."

She chews her lip. "So … you want children?"

I reach for her hand. "Of course, but not for a while. I missed three years with you, Liss I want to enjoy this. Enjoy what we have now."

"Me too."

I shake my head. "There's no rush. We can check out all the mistakes your friends make and do an awesome job."

She laughs. "I reached out to one of the universities in Cape Town."

I gape at her. "What? Why?"

"I wanted to explore our options. I got worried when you were having trouble finding something."

"You don't need to worry about me." I squeeze her cold fingers. "This is a great city, with so many opportunities. I'm so much happier here. I want to teach but, to be honest, I've got a PhD, I'm good at analysis, and have lots of experience of working in tough conditions. I understand food production and transportation as well. There are other jobs I could do here."

"I know, but I want to be flexible for you. I don't want to keep you away from your brother, from Benny."

I nod when she says this, but honestly? We've got our whole lives ahead of us to decide how we're going to shape this life we're mapping out. There's going to be a ton of traveling, that much is clear.

"How did the university respond?"

"I had a positive conversation with the head of International Studies. She might be interested in working with NYU." She shrugs. "Could be an interesting partnership?"

A buzz runs through me. We have so many opportunities unfolding before us: Maybe we could link several universities into local communities and aid in Africa. What might Liss and I be able to do together?

"Wow." I grin at her. "That could be amazing."

She laughs. "I know right?"

"You're an incredible woman."

She shakes her head and stares out the window, a small smile on her face. "What are you after?"

I lean over the table and take her chin in my hand, brushing a soft kiss over her lips.

"You," I say.

THE END.

THE TECHBOYS SERIES

THE REFUSAL

THE OUTCAST

THE SECRET

All books available now, in paperback and for Kindle, from Amazon.

REVIEWS AND MORE

I really hope you've enjoyed *The Secret*, the third book in my *Techboys* series!

If you have, please consider leaving a review on either the book's Amazon page or any review sites that you frequent. Your feedback and support is greatly appreciated.

There are more books to come in the *Techboys* series and I'd be super-excited to share them with you. If you'd like to be the first to hear about the new releases, pre-orders, bonus chapters and special freebies, please join my VIP mailing list:

evemriley.com/signup

Thanks so much!

ACKNOWLEDGMENTS

If my first year was a whirlwind with the success of *The Refusal*, releasing *The Outcast* stepped things up to a whole new level. Readers' enthusiasm for this series has surpassed all my expectations, and all the lovely messages have put a solid floor under this slightly nervous newbie. I can't thank you enough.

Building on the thirty-one awards now awarded to *The Refusal*, Fabian has jostled up behind Janus with twenty-four awards for *The Outcast*. And we are now on Book 3, and I am so happy with where *The Techboys Series* has got to and very excited about the stories to come.

But these guys and gals are never as easy as I expect them to be, and Liss and Dan and their global locations gave me a whole new set of headaches in terms of language and location. So I couldn't be more grateful to all the people who helped me to get *The Secret* into shape. Dan disappearing for a chunk of the book caused a few problems, and the lovely Sam Boyce pulled everything apart to help me put it back together. Sam, I could not do this job without you. A big thank you to my very own Techboy, Rob, who now reads the books at each stage and tears into the story logic as well as encouraging me at every point along the way. To Robert Tuesley Anderson, without your attention to detail and constant questioning, none of it would add up. Your positive comments are always vastly appreciated!

Thank you so much to my amazing beta readers: Donna, Sarah, Kelsey, and Caroline. I am eternally grateful for your uplifting and thoughtful feedback. My apologies to you all if what I have written doesn't match up to all the brilliant advice you gave.

To the villages that are BookTok and Bookstagram—thank you for your patience and all your support. The kindness you've shown is more than I could ever hope for. To all the bloggers, influencers, and book fanatics who helped me spread the word about *The Refusal* and *The Outcast*—thank you. A lot of you have been with me for three books now, so a big thanks to Adrienne, Amanda, Amanda, Andrea, Anna, Ashlee, Ashley, Ashley, Azalea, Dana, D.L., Dem, Devon, Em, Emma, Erika, Fabi, Flirtyquill, G.H., Jessica, Kerri, Kristina, Lanie and Allison, Linda, Lisa, Mac, Natasa, Nicole, Nicole, Nikki, and Rudra. But I am also looking forward to getting to know *all* of you who read these stories, so thank you for signing up for The Techboys.

To my lovely writing class and Nicky Melville—thank you for always being positive and patient and making my Friday mornings a joy. I couldn't ask for a better group to hang out and share my always questionable first drafts with.

Mark Thomas, you have produced a wonderful design for this series. I love it, and I love even more how it stands out in romance. Thank you for all your hard work on the cover and the interiors of this book, and for always turning things around so fast and with such enthusiasm.

To my daughter Grace, without your help and input over lockdown with *The Refusal*, I don't think we'd be here with the series. I can't thank you enough.

To everyone who reads this book or recommends it to a friend—thank you from the bottom of my heart. It means so much to me that you've enjoyed reading these stories as much as I have enjoyed writing them. And there are so many exciting things to come!

And finally, to my son Joe, you might be third in line age-wise, but you're never third in my heart. This one's for you.

ABOUT THE AUTHOR

I have worked for many years in the tech startup scene writing screeds of notes* that have percolated through my brain for years and have now weaved their way into *The Techboys Series*. *The Secret* is the third novel in this series, and in total eight books are planned.

I love helping people escape their daily lives for a short while with the help of a steamy romance, some fun, strong women, and gorgeous fictional boyfriends. *The Techboys Series* revolves around the tech scene and the people that work for technology companies in New York City, something I became familiar with through my work and regular annual visits to close friends who live there.

I am a Scottish author based in Edinburgh with my husband, and I have two grown-up children. When I'm not reading or writing, I love running and can often be found tapping away on my laptop in local cafés or out enjoying the beautiful wild landscapes of Scotland.

Thanks so much for buying this book. It's a joy when people reach out to me, so please feel free to contact me as follows:

Thanks so much for buying this book. It's a joy when people reach out to me, so please feel free to contact me as follows:

Website: www.everiley.com

Instagram: @evemriley

* I'm not a techy by background, which explains why all the tech references in the books are suitable for people whose level of understanding is plugging a wire into their phone to charge it up.

Printed in Great Britain
by Amazon

34417765R00162